THE FOXHOLE COURT

Nora Sakavic

ALL FOR THE GAME
The Foxhole Court
The Raven King
The King's Men

CHAPTER ONE

Neil Josten let his cigarette burn to the filter without taking a drag. He didn't want the nicotine; he wanted the acrid smoke that reminded him of his mother. If he inhaled slowly enough, he could almost taste the ghost of gasoline and fire. It was at once revolting and comforting, and it sent a sick shudder down his spine. The jolt went all the way to his fingertips, dislodging a clump of ash. It fell to the bleachers between his shoes and was whisked away by the wind.

He glanced up at the sky, but the stars were washed out behind the glare of stadium lights. He wondered—not for the first time—if his mother was looking down at him. He hoped not. She'd beat him to hell and back if she saw him sitting around moping like this.

A door squealed open behind him, startling him from his thoughts. Neil pulled his duffel closer to his side and looked back. Coach Hernandez propped the locker room door open and sat beside Neil.

"I didn't see your parents at the game," Hernandez said.

"They're out of town," Neil said.

"Still or again?"

Neither, but Neil wouldn't say that. He knew his teachers and coach were tired of hearing the same excuse any time they asked after his parents, but it was as easy a lie as it was overused. It explained why no one would ever see the Jostens around town and why Neil had a predilection for sleeping on school grounds.

It wasn't that he didn't have a place to live. It was more that his living situation wasn't legal. Millport was a dying town, which meant there were dozens of houses on the market that would never sell. He'd appropriated one last summer in a quiet neighborhood populated mostly by senior citizens. His neighbors rarely left the comfort of their couches and daily soaps, but every time he came and went he risked getting spotted. If people realized he was squatting they'd start asking difficult questions. It was usually easier to break into the locker room and sleep there. Why Hernandez let him get away with it and didn't notify the authorities, Neil didn't know. He thought it best not to ask.

Hernandez held out his hand. Neil passed him the cigarette and watched as Hernandez ground it out on the concrete steps. The coach flicked the crumpled butt aside and turned to face Neil.

"I thought they'd make an exception tonight," he said.

"No one knew it'd be the last game," Neil said, looking back at the court.

Millport's loss tonight booted them from state championships two games from finals. So close, too far. The season was over just like that. A crew was already dismantling the court, unhinging the plexiglass walls and rolling Astroturf over the hard floor. When they were done it'd be a soccer field again; there'd be nothing left of Exy until fall. Neil felt sick watching it happen, but he couldn't look away.

Exy was a bastard sport, an evolved sort of lacrosse on a soccer-sized court with the violence of ice hockey, and Neil loved every part of it from its speed to its aggression. It was the one piece of his childhood he'd never been able to give up.

"I'll call them later with the score," he said, because Hernandez was still watching him. "They didn't miss much."

"Not yet, maybe," Hernandez said. "There's someone here to see you."

To someone who'd spent half his life outrunning his past they were words from a nightmare. Neil leaped to his feet and slung his bag over his shoulder, but the scuff of a shoe behind him warned he was too late to escape. Neil twisted to see a

[2]

large stranger standing in the locker room doorway. The wife beater the man wore showed off sleeves of tribal flame tattoos. One hand was stuffed into his jeans pocket. The other held a thick file. His stance was casual, but the look in his brown eyes was intent.

Neil didn't recognize him, which meant he wasn't local. Millport boasted fewer than nine hundred residents. This was a place where everyone knew everyone's business. That ingrained nosiness made things uncomfortable for Neil and all his secrets, but he'd hoped to use that small-town mentality as a shield. Gossip about an outsider should have reached him before this stranger did. Millport had failed him.

"I don't know you," Neil said.

"He's from a university," Hernandez said. "He came to see you play tonight."

"Bullshit," Neil said. "No one recruits from Millport. No one knows where it is."

"There's this thing called a map," the stranger said. "You might have heard of it."

Hernandez sent Neil a warning look and got to his feet. "He's here because I sent him your file. He put a note out saying he was short on his striker line, and I figured it was worth a shot. I didn't tell you because I didn't know if anything would come of it and I didn't want to get your hopes up."

Neil stared. "You did what?"

"I tried contacting your parents when he asked for a face-to-face tonight, but they haven't returned my messages. You said they'd try to make it."

"They did," Neil said. "They couldn't."

"I can't wait for them," the stranger said, coming down to stand beside Hernandez. "It's stupid late in the season for me to be here, I know, but I had some technical difficulties with my last recruit. Coach Hernandez said you still haven't chosen a school for fall. Works out perfectly, doesn't it? I need a striker sub, and you need a team. All you have to do is sign the dotted line and you're mine for five years."

It took Neil two tries to find his voice. "You can't be serious."

"Very serious, and very out of time," the man said.

He tossed his file onto the bleacher where Neil had been sitting. Neil's name was scrawled across the front in black marker. Neil thought about flipping the folder open, but what was the point? The man this coach had researched so carefully wasn't real and wouldn't exist much longer. In five weeks Neil would graduate and in six he'd be someone else somewhere very far away from here. It didn't matter how much he liked being Neil Josten. He'd stayed here too long as it was.

Neil should be used to this by now. He'd spent the last eight years on the run, spinning lie after lie to leave a twisted trail behind him. Twenty-two names stood between him and the truth, and he knew what would happen if anyone finally connected the dots. Signing with a college team meant more than standing still. It meant he'd be stepping into a spotlight. Prison couldn't stop his father for long, and Neil wouldn't survive a rematch with him.

The math was simple, but that didn't make this any easier. That contract was a one-way ticket to a future, something Neil could never have, and he wanted it so badly he ached. For a blinding moment he hated himself for ever trying out for Millport's team. He'd known better than to step on a court. His mother told him he'd never play again. She'd warned him to obsess from a distance, and he'd disobeyed her. But what else was he supposed to do? He'd run aground in Millport after her death because he didn't know how to go on without her. This was the only thing he had left that was real. Now that he'd had a taste of it again, he didn't know how to walk away from it.

"Please go away," he said.

"It's a bit sudden, but I really do need an answer tonight. The Committee's been hounding me since Janie got locked up."

[4]

Neil's stomach hit his shoes at that name. He snapped his gaze from the folder to the coach's face. "Foxes," he said. "Palmetto State University."

The man—who Neil now knew had to be Coach David Wymack—looked surprised at how quickly he put it together. "I guess you saw the news."

Technical difficulties, he'd said. It was a nice way of saying his last recruit Janie Smalls tried to kill herself. Her best friend found her bleeding out in a bathtub and got her to a hospital just in time. Last Neil heard, the girl was on suicide watch in a psychiatric ward. Typical of a Fox, the anchorman had said in crass aside, and he wasn't exaggerating.

The Palmetto State University Foxes were a team of talented rejects and junkies because Wymack only recruited athletes from broken homes. His decision to turn the Foxhole Court into a halfway house of sorts was nice in theory, but it meant his players were fractured isolationists who couldn't get along long enough to get through a game. They were notorious in the NCAA both for their tiny size and for getting ranked dead-last three years running. They'd done significantly better this past year thanks to the perseverance of their captain and the strength of their new defense line, but they were still considered a joke by critics. Even the ERC, the Exy Rules and Regulations Committee, was losing patience with their poor results.

Then former national champion Kevin Day joined the line. It was the greatest thing that could happen to the Foxes and it meant Neil could never accept Wymack's offer. Neil hadn't seen Kevin in almost eight years, and he'd never be ready to see him again. Some doors had to stay closed; Neil's life depended on it.

"You can't be here," Neil said.

"Yet here I stand," Wymack said. "Need a pen?"

"No," Neil said. "No. I'm not playing for you."

"I misheard you."

"You signed Kevin."

"And Kevin's signing you, so—"

[5]

Neil didn't stick around for the rest.

He bolted up the bleachers for the locker room. Metal clanged beneath his shoes, not quite loud enough to drown out Hernandez's startled query. Neil didn't look back to see if they were following. All he knew, all that mattered, was getting as far away from here as possible. Forget graduation. Forget "Neil Josten". He'd leave tonight and run until he forgot Wymack ever said those words to him.

Neil wasn't fast enough.

He was halfway through the locker room when he realized he wasn't alone. There was someone waiting for him in the lounge between him and the front door. Light glinted off a bright yellow racquet as the stranger took a swing, and Neil was going too fast to stop. Wood slammed into his gut hard enough to crush his lungs into his spine. He didn't remember falling, but suddenly he was on his hands and knees, scrabbling ineffectually at the floor as he tried to breathe. He'd puke if he could only manage that first gasp, but his body refused to cooperate.

The buzzing in his ears was Wymack's furious voice, but he sounded a thousand miles away. "God damn it, Minyard. This is why we can't have nice things."

"Oh, Coach," someone said over Neil's head. "If he was nice, he wouldn't be any use to us, would he?"

"He's no use to us if you break him."

"You'd rather I let him go? Put a band-aid on him and he'll be good as new."

The world crackled black, then came into too-sharp focus as air finally hit Neil's tortured lungs. Neil inhaled so sharply he choked, and every wracking cough threatened to shake him apart. He wrapped an arm around his middle to hold himself together and slanted a fierce look up at his assailant.

Wymack already said the man's name, but Neil didn't need it. He'd seen this face in too many newspaper clippings to not know him on sight. Andrew Minyard didn't look like much in person, blonde and five feet even, but Neil knew better. Andrew was the Foxes' freshman goalkeeper and their deadliest investment. Most of the Foxes were self-destructive, whereas Andrew seemed keen on collateral damage. He'd spent three years at a juvie facility and barely avoided a second term.

Andrew was also the only person to ever turn down the first-ranked Edgar Allan University. Kevin and Riko themselves set up a meet-and-greet to welcome him to the line, but Andrew refused and joined the dead-last Foxes instead. He never explained that choice, but everyone assumed it was because Wymack was willing to sign his family as well—Andrew's twin Aaron and their cousin Nicholas Hemmick joined the line the same year. Whatever the reason, Andrew was blamed for Kevin's recent transfer.

Kevin played for Edgar Allan's Ravens until he broke his dominant hand in a skiing accident this past December. An injury like that cost him his college contract, but he should have recuperated where he'd have his former team's support. Instead he moved to Palmetto to be Wymack's informal assistant coach. Three weeks ago he was officially signed to next year's starting line-up.

The only thing a dismal team like the Foxes could offer Kevin was the goalkeeper who'd once spurned him. Neil spent this spring digging up everything he could find on Andrew, wanting to understand the man who'd caught Kevin's eye. Meeting Andrew face to face was as disorienting as it was painful.

Andrew smiled down at Neil and tapped two fingers to his temple in salute. "Better luck next time."

"Fuck you," Neil said. "Whose racquet did you steal?"

"Borrow." Andrew tossed it at Neil. "Here you go."

"Neil," Hernandez said, catching Neil by his arm to help him up. "Jesus, are you all right?"

"Andrew's a bit raw on manners," Wymack said, coming around to stand between Neil and Andrew. Andrew had no problems reading that silent warning. He threw his hands up in an exaggerated shrug and retreated to give Neil more room. Wymack watched him go before looking Neil over. "He break anything?"

Neil pressed careful hands to his ribs and breathed, feeling the way his muscles screamed in protest. He'd fractured bones enough in the past to know he'd gotten lucky this time. "I'm fine. Coach, I'm leaving. Let me go."

"We're not done," Wymack said.

"Coach Wymack," Hernandez started.

Wymack didn't let him finish. "Give us a second?"

Hernandez looked from Wymack to Neil, then let go. "I'll be right out back."

Neil listened to his footsteps as he left. There was a rattle as he kicked the door prop out of its spot and the back door swung closed with an agonizing creak. Neil waited for it to click before speaking again.

"I already gave you my answer. I won't sign with you."

"You didn't listen to my whole offer," Wymack said. "If I paid to fly three people out here to see you the least you could do is give me five minutes, don't you think?"

The blood left Neil's face so fast the world tilted. He took a stumbling step back from Wymack, a desperate search for both balance and room to breathe. His duffel banged into his hip and he knotted a hand around its strap, needing something to hold onto. "You didn't bring him here."

Wymack stared hard at him. "Is that a problem?"

Neil couldn't tell him the truth, so he said, "I'm not good enough to play on the same court as a champion."

"True, but irrelevant," a new voice said, and Neil stopped breathing.

He knew better than to turn around, but he was already moving.

He should have guessed when he saw Andrew here, but he hadn't wanted to think it. There was no reason for a goalkeeper

[8]

to meet a potential striker. Andrew was only here because Kevin Day never went anywhere alone.

Kevin was sitting on top of the entertainment center along the back wall. He'd pushed the TV off to one side to give himself more room and covered the space around him with papers. He'd watched this entire spectacle and, judging by the cool look on his face, was unimpressed by Neil's reaction.

It'd been years since Neil stood in the same room as Kevin, years since they'd watched Neil's father cut a screaming man into a hundred bloody pieces. Neil knew Kevin's face as well as he knew his own, the consequence of watching Kevin grow up in the public eye from a thousand or more miles away. Everything about him was different. Everything was the same, from his dark hair and green eyes to the black number two tattooed onto his left cheekbone. Neil saw that number and wanted to retch.

Kevin had that number back then, too, but he'd been too young to have it done permanently. Instead he and his adopted brother Riko Moriyama wrote the numbers one and two on their faces with markers, tracing them over and over anytime they started to fade. Neil didn't understand it then, but Kevin and Riko were aiming for the stars. They were going to be famous, they promised him.

They were right. They had professional teams and played for the Ravens. Last year they were inducted to the national team, the US Court. They were champions, and Neil was a jumble of lies and dead-ends.

Neil knew Kevin couldn't recognize him. It'd been too long; they'd both grown up a world apart. Neil had further disguised his looks with dark hair dye and brown contacts. But why else would Kevin Day be here looking for him? No Class I school would stoop so low, not even the Foxes. Neil's records said he'd only been playing Exy for a year. He'd been very careful this year to act like a know-nothing, even loading up on and lugging around How-To books last fall. It was easy to

[9]

pretend at first, since he hadn't picked up a racquet in eight years. The fact he was playing a different position now than he'd played at little league helped, since he had to relearn the game from a new perspective. He'd had an enviable and unavoidable learning curve, but he'd still fought hard to not shine.

Had he slipped? Had it been too obvious that he had past experience he wasn't talking about? How had he caught Kevin's eye despite his best attempts to stay hidden? If it was that easy for Kevin, what sort of beacon was he sending to his father's people?

"What are you doing here?" he asked through numb lips.

"Why were you leaving?" Kevin asked.

"I asked you first."

"Coach already answered that question," Kevin said, a tad impatiently. "We are waiting for you to sign the contract. Stop wasting our time."

"No," Neil said. "There are a thousand strikers who'd jump at the chance to play with you. Why don't you bother them?"

"We saw their files," Wymack said. "We chose you."

"I won't play with Kevin."

"You will," Kevin said.

Wymack shrugged at Neil. "Maybe you haven't noticed, but we're not leaving here until you say yes. Kevin says we have to have you, and he's right."

"We should have thrown away your coach's letter the second we opened it," Kevin said. "Your file is deplorable and I don't want someone with your inexperience on our court. It goes against everything we're trying to do with the Foxes this year. Fortunately for you, your coach knew better than to send us your statistics. He sent us a tape so we could see you in action instead. You play like you have everything to lose."

His inexperience.

If Kevin remembered him, he'd know that file was a lie. He'd know about Neil's little league teams. He'd remember the scrimmage interrupted by that man's murder.

[10]

"That's why," Neil said quietly.

"That's the only kind of striker worth playing with."

Relief made Neil sick to his stomach. Kevin didn't recognize him and this was just a horrible coincidence. Maybe it was the world's way of showing him what could happen if he stayed in the same place for too long. Next time it might not be Kevin. Next time it might be his father.

"It actually works in our favor that you're all the way out here," Wymack said. "No one outside of our team and school board even knows we're here. We don't want your face all over the news this summer. We've got too much to deal with right now and we don't want to drag you into the mess until you're safe and settled at campus. There's a confidentiality clause in your contract, says you can't tell anyone you're ours until the season starts in August."

Neil looked at Kevin again, searching for his real name on Kevin's face. "It's not a good idea."

"Your opinion has been duly noted and dismissed," Wymack said. "Anything else, or are you going to start signing stuff?"

The smart thing to do was bail. Even if Kevin didn't know who he was, this was a terrible idea. The Foxes spent too much time in the news and it'd only get worse with Kevin on the line. Neil shouldn't submit himself to that sort of scrutiny. He should tear Wymack's contract into a thousand pieces and leave.

Leaving meant living, but Neil's way of living was survival, nothing more. It was new names and new places and never looking back. It was packing up and going as soon as he started to feel settled. This last year, without his mother at his side, it meant being completely alone and adrift. He didn't know if he was ready for that.

He didn't know if he was ready to give up Exy again, either. It was the only thing that made him feel real. Wymack's contract was permission to keep playing and a chance to pretend at being normal a little while longer. Wymack said it was for

[11]

five years, but Neil didn't have to stay that long. He could duck and run whenever he pleased, couldn't he?

He looked at Kevin again. Kevin didn't recognize him, but maybe some part of him remembered the boy he'd met so many years ago. Neil's past was locked in Kevin's memories. It was proof he existed, same as this game they both played. Kevin was proof Neil was real. Maybe Kevin was also the best chance Neil had at knowing when to leave again. If he lived, practiced, and played with Kevin, he'd know when Kevin started to get suspicious. The second Kevin started asking questions or looking at him funny, Neil would split.

"Well?" Wymack asked.

Survival instincts warred with need and twisted into an almost debilitating panic. "I have to talk to my mother," Neil said, because he didn't know what else to say.

"What for?" Wymack asked. "You're legal, aren't you? Your file says you're nineteen."

Neil was eighteen, but he wasn't going to contradict what his forged paperwork said. "I still need to ask."

"She'll be happy for you."

"Maybe," Neil agreed quietly, knowing it was a lie. If his mother knew he was even considering this, she'd be furious. It was probably a good thing she'd never know, but Neil didn't think "good" was supposed to feel like a knife in his chest. "I'll talk to her tonight."

"We can give you a lift home."

"I'm fine."

Wymack looked at his Foxes. "Go wait in the car."

Kevin gathered his files and slid off his perch. Andrew waited for Kevin to catch up and led him out of the locker room. Wymack waited until they were gone, then turned a serious look on Neil.

"You need one of us to talk to your parents?"

"I'm fine," Neil said again.

[12]

Wymack didn't even try for subtlety with his next question. "Are they the ones who hurt you?"

Neil stared at him at a complete loss. It was blunt enough to be rude on so many levels that there wasn't a good place to start answering it. Wymack seemed to realize that, because he pushed on before Neil could respond.

"Let's try that again. The reason I'm asking is because Coach Hernandez guesses you spend several nights a week here. He thinks there's something going on since you won't change out with the others or let anyone meet your parents. That's why he nominated you to me; he thinks you fit the line. You know what that means, right? You know the people I look for.

"I don't know if he's right," he said, "but something tells me he's not far off. Either way, the locker room's going to be shut down once the school year ends. You're not going to be able to come here during the summer. If your parents are a problem for you, we'll move you to South Carolina early."

"You'll do what?" Neil asked, surprised.

"Andrew's lot stays in town for summer break," Wymack said. "They crash with Abby, our team nurse. Her place is full, but you could stay with me until the dorm opens in June. My apartment's not made for two people but I've got a couch that's a little softer than a rock.

"We'll tell everyone you're there for conditional early practice. Chances are half of them will believe it. You won't be able to fool the rest, but that doesn't matter. Foxes are Foxes for a reason and they know we wouldn't sign you if you didn't qualify. That doesn't mean they know specifics. It's not my place to ask, and I'm sure as hell not going to tell them."

It took two tries to get the word out. "Why?"

Coach Wymack was quiet for a minute. "Did you think I made the team the way it is because I thought it would be a good publicity stunt? It's about second chances, Neil. Second, third, fourth, whatever, as long as you get at least one more than what anyone else wanted to give you."

[13]

Neil had heard Wymack referred to as an idealistic idiot by more than one person, but it was hard to listen to him and not believe that he was sincere. Neil was torn between incredulity and disdain. Why Wymack set himself up for disappointment time and time again, Neil didn't know. Neil would have given up on the Foxes years ago.

Wymack gave him a second to think before asking again, "Are your parents going to be a problem?"

It was too much to take a chance on, but too much to walk away from. It hurt when he nodded, but it hurt more to see that tired look settle in Wymack's eyes. It wasn't the pity he thought he could see in Hernandez from time to time, but something familiar that said Wymack understood what it cost to be Neil. He knew what it was like to have to fight to wake up and keep moving every day. Neil doubted the man could ever really understand, but even that tiny bit was more than he'd ever gotten in his life. Neil had to look away.

"Your graduation ceremony is May eleventh, according to your coach," Wymack said at length. "We'll have someone pick you up from Upstate Regional Airport Friday the twelfth."

Neil almost pointed out that he hadn't agreed to anything yet, but the words died in his throat as he realized he really was going.

"Keep the papers tonight," Wymack offered, pushing his folder at Neil again. This time Neil took it. "Your coach can fax the signed copies to me on Monday. Welcome to the line."

"Thank you" seemed appropriate, but Neil couldn't manage it. He kept his stare on the floor. Wymack didn't wait long for a response before going in search of Hernandez.

The back door banged shut behind him, and Neil's nerves broke. He ran for the bathroom and made it to a stall just in time to dry-heave into a toilet.

He could imagine his mother's rage if she knew what he was doing. He remembered too well the savage yank of her hands in his hair. All these years spent trying to keep moving

[14]

and hidden, and now he was going to destroy their hard work. She would never forgive him for this and he knew it, and that did nothing at all to help the clenching feeling in his gut.

"I'm sorry," he gasped out between wet coughs. "I'm sorry, I'm sorry."

He stumbled over to the sinks to rinse his mouth out and stared himself down in the mirrors that hung above them. With black hair and brown eyes, he looked plain and average: no one to notice in a crowd, no one to stick in one's memory. That was what he wanted, but he wondered if it could hold up against news cameras. He grimaced a little at his reflection and leaned closer to the mirror, tugging hard at chunks of hair to check his roots. They were dark enough that he relaxed and leaned back a bit.

"University," he said quietly. It sounded like a dream; it tasted like damnation.

He unzipped his duffel bag enough to put Wymack's paperwork away. When he returned to the main room, the two coaches were waiting on him. Neil said nothing to them but went past them to the door.

Andrew opened the back door of Hernandez's SUV when Neil passed and gave Neil a knowing, taunting smile. "Too good to play with us, too good to ride with us?"

Neil flicked him a cool look sped up to a jog. By the time he reached the far edge of the parking lot he was running. He left the stadium and the Foxes and their too-good promises behind him, but the unsigned contract in his bag felt like an anchor around his neck.

CHAPTER TWO

Neil long ago lost count of how many airports he'd seen. Whatever insane number it was, he'd never gotten comfortable with them. There were too many people to keep an eye on, and flying with falsified passports was always risky. He'd inherited his mother's connections after her death, so he knew the work was good, but his heart did double-time every time someone asked to see his papers.

He'd never been through Sky Harbor or Upstate Regional, but there was something familiar about their frenetic pace. He stood off to one side of his gate in Upstate for almost a minute after everyone else from his flight rushed off to Arrivals or their transfers. The crowd swirling around him seemed the usual mix: vacationers, businessmen, and students heading home at the end of the semester. He didn't expect to see anyone he recognized, as he'd never been to South Carolina before, but it never hurt to check.

Finally he followed signs down a hall and up a flight of stairs to Arrivals. Friday afternoon meant the small lobby was comfortably crowded, but spotting the ride Coach Wymack promised him was easier than Neil expected.

It was the weight of his teammate's stare that brought Neil's gaze almost right to him. It was one of the twins. Judging by the calm look on his face, Neil laid his bets on it not being Andrew. Aaron Minyard was oft-referred to as "the normal one" of the two, though that was usually followed by a debate over whether or not he could be sane when he shared genes with Andrew.

Neil crossed the room to meet him. Neil had been the shortest player on the Millport Dingo line, but he had three inches on Aaron. The all-black ensemble Aaron wore did nothing to make him look any taller, and Neil wondered how he could stand wearing long sleeves in May. Neil felt hot just looking at him.

"Neil," Aaron said in lieu of hello, and he pointed. "Baggage claim."

"Just this." Neil tapped the strap of the duffel bag hanging off his shoulder. The bag was small enough to be a carry-on and large enough to carry everything Neil owned.

Aaron accepted that without comment and started away. Neil followed him through sliding glass doors into a muggy summer afternoon. A small crowd was waiting at the crosswalk for the light, but Aaron pushed right through them into the street. Brakes screeched as a taxi slammed to a stop inches from Aaron's pint-sized body. Aaron didn't seem to notice, more interested in getting a cigarette lit and between his lips. He paid even less attention to the rude words the driver yelled at him. Neil made an apologetic gesture at the cabbie and jogged to catch up.

A sleek black car was parked six rows back in the short-term parking garage. Neil didn't know much about cars in general, but he knew expensive when he saw it. He thought for a moment there must be a smaller car out of sight behind it, but Aaron unlocked it with a button on his key chain.

"Bag in the trunk," he said, opening the driver's door and sitting sideways in the seat to smoke.

Neil obediently put his duffel in the back before climbing in the passenger seat. Aaron didn't go anywhere until his cigarette was half-gone. He flicked the butt onto the concrete at his feet and tugged the door closed. A twist of the key in the ignition got the engine humming, and Aaron glanced at Neil again. The ghost of a smile tugged at one corner of his mouth, but it was a decidedly unfriendly expression.

"Neil Josten," he said again, as if testing the way it sounded. "Here for the summer, hm?"

"Yes."

[17]

Aaron cranked the air conditioner up as high as it could go and put the car in reverse. "That makes five of us, but word is you're going to stay with Coach."

Coach Wymack warned Neil the cousins Andrew, Aaron, and Nicholas would be in town, but it still didn't add up. Neil knew who that fifth person had to be. He didn't want to believe it even as he knew he should have expected it. Kevin had been glued to Andrew's side since his transfer. Still, Neil had to be sure.

"Kevin stays on campus?" he asked.

"Where the court is, Kevin is. He can't exist without it," Aaron said derisively.

"I didn't think it was the court Kevin was staying for," Neil said.

Aaron didn't answer. It was a short drive to the parking lot exit and Aaron had cash ready for the lady at the booth. As soon as the bar lifted to let them out, he stepped down on the gas. A horn sounded at them in warning as they cut right into traffic and Neil discreetly tightened his buckle. Aaron either didn't notice or didn't care. When they were on the road, he flicked Neil a sideways look.

"I hear you didn't hit it off with Kevin last month."

"No one warned me he was going to be there," Neil answered, watching the scenery rush by outside the window. "Maybe you'll forgive me for not reacting well."

"Maybe I won't. I don't believe in forgiveness, and it wasn't me you offended. That's the second time a recruit has told him to fuck off. If it was possible to dent that arrogance of his, his pride would have shreds through it. Instead he's losing faith in the intelligence of high school athletes."

"I'm sure Andrew had his reasons for refusing, same as me."

"You said you weren't good enough, but here you are anyway. You think a summer of practices will make that much a difference?"

[18]

"No," Neil said. "It was just too hard to say no."

"Coach always knows what to say, hm? It makes it harder on the rest of us, though. Not even Millport should have taken a chance on you."

Neil shrugged. "Millport's too small to care about experience. I had nothing to lose by trying out and they had nothing to gain by refusing me. It was a matter of being in the right place at the right time, I guess."

"Do you believe in fate?"

Neil heard the faint scorn in the other man's voice. "No. Do you?"

"Luck, then," Aaron said, ignoring that return question.

"Only the bad sort."

"We're flattered by your high opinion of us, of course."

Aaron pulled at the wheel, sliding the car from one lane to the other without bothering to check the traffic around him. Horns blared behind them. Neil watched in the rearview mirror as cars swerved to avoid hitting them.

"It's too nice of a car to wreck," he said pointedly.

"Don't be so afraid to die," Aaron said as the car kept gliding across the four-lane road to an exit ramp. "If you are, you have no place on our court."

"We're talking about a sport, not a death match."

"Same difference," Aaron said. "You're playing for a Class I team with Kevin on your line. People are always willing to bleed for him. You've seen the news, I assume."

"I've seen it," Neil said.

Aaron flicked his fingers as if that proved his point. Neil would be hard-pressed to say he was wrong, so he let it slide.

Kevin Day and his adoptive brother Riko Moriyama were hailed as the sons of Exy. Kevin's mother Kayleigh Day and Riko's uncle Tetsuji Moriyama created the sport roughly thirty years ago while Kayleigh was studying abroad in Fukui, Japan. What started as an experiment spread from their campus to local street teams, then across the ocean to the rest of the world.

[19]

Kayleigh brought it home with her to Ireland after completing her degree and the United States picked it up soon after.

Kevin and Riko were raised on Exy. When Edgar Allan's massive stadium Castle Evermore, the first NCAA Exy stadium in the United States, was little more than blueprints, Kevin and Riko had custom racquets. After Kayleigh's fatal car accident, Tetsuji took Kevin in, but the Ravens' new coach had no time to raise children. Riko and Kevin spent their formative years at Evermore with the Ravens instead and were considered the team's unofficial mascots. When they weren't being coached by Tetsuji, they were coached by the team, and tutors were brought on-site so they wouldn't have to leave the stadium for school.

Kevin and Riko grew up in front of cameras, but always with Exy as a backdrop and always together. Until Kevin transferred to Palmetto State, he and Riko were never seen in separate rooms. Their unconventional childhood led many to worry about their psychological well-being but also fueled a rabid obsession with the pair. Riko and Kevin were the face of the Ravens. To many, they were considered the future of Exy.

Last December, Riko and Kevin vanished from the public eye for weeks. When spring championships started in January, neither man was on the Ravens' starting line-up. It wasn't until the end of January that Tetsuji Moriyama addressed the topic at a press conference, and the news was a cruel blow to Exy fans everywhere: Kevin Day had broken his playing hand on a skiing trip. According to Tetsuji, Kevin and Riko were too devastated to face either the Ravens or their upset fans just yet.

The next day, Coach Wymack told the press Kevin was recuperating in South Carolina. Hearing Kevin would never play again was bad; finding out he'd left the Ravens was somehow worse for his obsessive fans. If Kevin was relegated to the sidelines as an assistant coach, he should at least lend his prestige and knowledge to his home team. Fans took offense on their beloved team's behalf, but most everyone assumed he'd transfer back as soon as his hand was finished healing. Except

[20]

Kevin Day signed with the Foxes in March—not as a coach, but a striker.

His fans went from feeling heartbroken to feeling betrayed. Palmetto State had borne the brunt of that rage since. The university and stadium had been vandalized upwards of a dozen times and there'd been numerous fights on campus. It would only get worse when the season started and people saw Kevin wearing the Foxes' colors. Neil wasn't looking forward to getting in the middle of that mess.

The apartment complex where Wymack lived was a twenty-minute drive from the airport. The parking lot was mostly empty, since it was mid-afternoon on a workday, but there were three people waiting on the sidewalk. Aaron was the first out and he aimed the key ring at the back of the car. Neil heard locks pop as he climbed out of the car. Aaron went to meet the others at the curb while Neil retrieved his duffel bag from the trunk. Neil slung it over his shoulder, relaxing a little at the familiar weight of it, and pushed the trunk closed. When he looked up he was the center of attention.

The twins were standing to either side of Kevin, dressed identically but easily distinguishable by the looks on their faces. Aaron looked bored now that he'd fulfilled his duty in getting Neil here. Andrew was smiling, but Neil knew his cheer didn't mean he was going to play nice. He'd been smiling when he smashed a racquet into Neil's stomach, too.

Nicholas Hemmick was the only one who looked genuinely happy to see Neil, and he stepped up to the curb at Neil's approach. Neil was glad for the distraction, since it kept him from looking at Kevin, and he readily accepted the hand Nicholas offered.

"Hey," the other man said, using his grip on Neil's hand to pull him up onto the curb. "Welcome to South Carolina. Flight go okay?"

"It was fine," Neil said.

[21]

"I'm Nicky." Nicky gave Neil's hand another hard squeeze before letting go. "Andrew and Aaron's cousin, backliner extraordinaire."

Neil looked from him to the twins and back again. Where the twins were light, Nicky was dark, with jet-black hair, dark brown eyes, and skin two shades too dark to be a tan. He also had the better part of a foot on them. "By blood?"

Nicky laughed. "Don't look it, right? Take after my mom. Dad 'rescued' her from Mexico during some la-di-dah ministry trip." He made a show of rolling his eyes, then jerked a thumb at the others. "You already met them, right? Aaron, Andrew, Kevin? Coach was supposed to be here to let you in, but he had to head up to the stadium real quick. The ERC called him, probably with more BS about how we haven't publicized our sub yet. In the meantime you're stuck with us, but we've got Coach's keys. Suitcases in the trunk?"

"It's just this," Neil said.

Nicky arched an eyebrow at him and looked at the others. "He packs light. I wish I could travel like that, but hell if I ain't materialistic."

"Materialistic is just a start," Aaron said.

Nicky grinned and caught Neil's shoulder, guiding him past the rest toward the front door. "This is where Coach lives," he said unnecessarily. "He makes all the money, so he gets to live in a place like this while we poor people couch surf."

"You have a nice car for someone who thinks he's poor," Neil said.

"That's why we're poor," Nicky said dryly.

"Aaron's mother bought it for us with her life insurance money," Andrew explained. "It's no surprise she had to die to be worth anything."

"Easy," Nicky said, but he was looking at Aaron when he said it.

"Easy, easy." Andrew lifted his hands in a careless shrug. "Why bother? It's a cruel world, right Neil? You wouldn't be here if it wasn't."

"It's not the world that's cruel," Neil said. "It's the people in it."

"Oh, so true."

They rode the elevator up to the seventh floor in silence. Neil watched the numbers tick above the door so he wouldn't look at Kevin's reflection. Unease over being so high off the ground was almost distraction enough. He preferred staying to lower levels so he could make an easy escape if need be. Jumping out the window here was definitely out of the question. He made a mental note to find any and all fire escapes.

Wymack's apartment was number 724. They gathered around the door so Aaron could dig the key out of his pocket. It took him two tries to remember which one he'd put it in. Neil didn't notice when he found it and unlocked the door. He was too busy staring at Aaron's pants pockets. They were much too flat to be hiding a pack of cigarettes, but Neil had seen Aaron put the pack away before crossing the street at the airport.

"Here you go, Neil," Nicky said, and Neil forced his gaze up to the open doorway. Nicky gestured for him to precede them. "Home sweet home, if anything involving Coach can be called sweet."

Neil had known since April he'd be crashing on Coach Wymack's couch for a couple weeks. He'd known, in the days following Wymack's visit, that it would be uncomfortable. He still wasn't prepared for the way his stomach roiled inside him now. He'd been on his own since his mother died, and the last man he'd lived with was his father. How was he supposed to let Wymack lock the door every night with both of them under the same roof? He couldn't possibly sleep here; every time Wymack breathed Neil would wake up and wonder who was after him. Maybe he should back out and check into a hotel, but how was he supposed to explain that to Wymack? Would he have to

[23]

explain? Wymack thought Neil's parents were abusive, so maybe he'd understand Neil's reticence.

He hadn't expected to lock up like this, and he'd hesitated too long. He saw the look Nicky sent Aaron, curious and confused, and knew he'd made a mistake. Still, it wasn't until Andrew stepped up alongside him to see what the holdup was that Neil could move again. Andrew was smiling, but his pale stare was intense. Neil met his eyes for only a moment and knew it was worse to stay out here with them than it was to cross that threshold. He'd figure it out, but not here and not now, not with Andrew and Kevin as witnesses.

Neil stepped over the threshold and started down the hall. The first doorway opened up into the living room Neil would be sleeping in. The couch Wymack had referenced was cleared off and even had a sticky note tacked to it saying that the blankets were in the coffee table drawer. It was the only clean surface in the room. Everything else was covered in paperwork and empty coffee mugs. Overflowing ashtrays were in unhealthy abundance as well.

Neil was halfway across the room to look out the window when Nicky spoke up behind him.

"What was that all about?"

Neil's blood turned to slush. It wasn't the words that got him but the language Nicky used. German was Neil's second language thanks to three years spent living in Austria, Germany, and Switzerland. He remembered more of Europe than he wanted to; most of their time there had been a cold mess. He knew the tang of blood in his mouth was just his imagination, but it was sharp enough to choke him. He could feel his heartbeat on every inch of his skin, going so fast it set him trembling head to toe.

How did they know he spoke German?

Neil had half a mind to run for it, but then Aaron answered, and Neil realized with a sick rush Nicky wasn't talking to him. No, they were talking about him, not intending for him to

[24]

understand. Neil forced himself to move, finishing his trip to the window. He pushed the curtains back and put his hands to the glass, needing something to steady him while his heart tried to ease back to a normal rhythm.

"Maybe he was savoring the moment," Aaron said.

"No," Nicky said. "That was pure fight or flight. What the hell did you say to him, Andrew?"

Neil looked back at them. Nicky wasn't looking at Andrew, maybe already knowing he wasn't going to get an answer, but was watching Neil across the room. When Neil turned, Nicky gave a bright smile and switched back to English. "How about a tour?"

Neil considered saying something, but he'd already given too much away. "Sure."

There wasn't much to look at. A bathroom and kitchen sat opposite each other, and the bedrooms were at the end of the hall. Wymack had converted the second bedroom into an office. The office made up for the bare living room walls: it was covered with newspaper articles, team photos, outdated calendars, and miscellaneous certificates. Two bookshelves lined the wall, one full of Exy books, the other a mishmash of everything from travel guides to classic literature. Wymack's desk was buried in paperwork, not an inch of wood visible, and Neil's file was on top. Holding down one corner was a hefty prescription bottle. Nicky scooped the bottle up with a triumphant sound and twisted the lid off.

"That's not yours," Neil said.

"Painkillers," Nicky said, ignoring that implicit accusation. "Coach shattered his hip a few years back, you know? That's how he met Abby. She was his therapist, and he got her the job here. Team's still split fifty-fifty on whether or not they're boning. Andrew refuses to vote, which means you're the tiebreaker. Let us know ASAP. I've got money riding on it."

He shook a couple pills into his hand, screwed the lid on, and put the bottle back. Neil looked to see what the others thought of this, but Andrew and Kevin had vanished. Only Aaron remained, and he didn't look at all concerned.

"You'll meet Abby tonight at dinner," Nicky said, stuffing the pills into his pocket. "We've got a couple hours to kill before then, so maybe we can take you by the court and let you gawk at it. We've got the perfect number for scrimmages now. Kevin's probably pissing himself in excitement."

"I doubt that," Neil said, thinking of Kevin's dispassionate expression downstairs.

"Kevin doesn't do excited," Aaron agreed, "but since Exy is the only thing he cares about, no one wants you on our court more than he does."

Neil's answer got stuck somewhere in his throat as he processed that. It was the same thing Aaron said in the car, almost, except Aaron sounded apathetic now where he'd been scornful earlier. Between that sudden change in attitude, the disappearing pack of cigarettes, and the matching outfits, Neil was starting to second-guess what was going on here. These were just small things, but Neil had learned to survive on the fine details.

"Isn't it difficult playing with him?" he asked, changing what he'd been about to say. "I mean, with him being a champion."

"Technically we haven't played with him yet," Nicky said. "He just started getting into drills with us last month. If he's anything on the line like he is as an assistant coach, you are going to have the most awful year ever." Despite his ominous words, Nicky sounded amused. "But he's worth it."

"Worth the fights, too?" Neil asked. "Like that one two weeks ago that Aaron said got completely out of hand. How many people got injured in that, again?"

There was a slight pause as Aaron thought, and for a moment Neil decided he'd imagined things. Then Aaron answered, "Eleven."

[26]

It was the right answer; Neil had read about the brawl in an article. But he and Aaron hadn't had that conversation in the car and Aaron should have known that.

Too late, Neil remembered Nicky's exasperated accusation in the living room: "What the hell did you say to him, Andrew?" Neil had assumed Nicky was referring to their first meeting in Millport, but Nicky had been talking about the car ride from the airport. It wasn't Aaron who picked Neil up from the airport after all.

Neil was annoyed by the trick and relieved he'd seen through it, but caution overrode both. Andrew wasn't cheerful naturally; his mania was drug-induced and court regulated. Two years ago some men attacked Nicky outside of a nightclub. Andrew was within his rights to defend Nicky, but he'd almost killed the four of them. The courts thought his violence to be a gross overreaction and tried to charge him. His lawyers struck a deal instead: Andrew would spend some time in intensive therapy, attend weekly counseling, and take medication.

After three years of this they'd let him off his medication long enough to assess his progress. Sobriety at any point before that was a violation of his parole. If the team nurse, Andrew's current psychiatrist, or the court psychiatrist who managed Andrew's parole suspected Andrew wasn't following the rules, they could request a urinalysis. If Andrew failed he'd be charged.

Andrew only had to hold out through spring, but apparently he couldn't wait that long. Neil couldn't believe Andrew would even risk sobriety when the consequences were so steep. He wondered if his arrival had to do with it, if Andrew wanted to meet his newest teammate without a hazy mind, or if Andrew just hated spending his summer break drugged to the gills.

As if on cue, Andrew appeared in the doorway with a bottle of whiskey in one hand and Kevin at his back. "Success."

"Ready, Neil?" Nicky asked. "We should probably beat it before Coach shows up."

[27]

"Why?" Neil pointed at the liquor. "Is this a robbery in progress?"

"Maybe it is. Will you tell Coach on us?" Andrew asked, sounding entertained by the notion. "So much for being a team player. I guess you really are a Fox."

"No," Neil said, "but I would ask him why you're not medicated."

There was a heartbeat of startled silence. The only one who didn't react was Andrew; even Kevin looked surprised.

Nicky was the first to find his tongue, but he reverted to German to ask Aaron, "Am I crazy? Did I just see that happen?"

"Don't look at me," Aaron said.

"I'd prefer an answer in English," Neil said.

Andrew put a thumb to the corner of his mouth and dragged it along his lips to erase his smile. "That sounds like an accusation, but I didn't lie to you."

"Omission is the easiest way to lie," Neil said. "You could have corrected me."

"Could have, didn't," Andrew said. "Figure it out for yourself."

"I did," Neil said. He tapped two fingers to his temple, copying Andrew's mocking salute from their first meeting. "Better luck next time."

"Oh," Andrew said. "Oh, you might actually turn out to be interesting. For a little while, at least. I don't think the amusement will last. It never does."

"Don't mess with me."

"Or what?"

There was a rattle as someone tested the knob on the front door. Andrew's smile was back in a heartbeat, bright and vacant. He turned to Kevin, and Kevin moved at the same time. The whiskey vanished somewhere between them in a practiced move.

"Hi Coach," Andrew called over his shoulder.

[28]

"Do you have any idea how much I hate coming home and finding you in my apartment?" Wymack demanded from out of sight.

Andrew held up his empty hands in an innocent gesture no one believed and stepped into the hallway. Aaron and Kevin went after him, presumably with the alcohol tucked between their bodies, and left Nicky and Neil in the office.

"I didn't break anything this time," Andrew said.

"I'll believe that after I've checked everything I own." The door slammed down the hall, and it wasn't long before Coach stepped into his office doorway. Clad in jean shorts and a faded tee, Wymack looked more like a garage band rocker than a university coach. Neil guessed he didn't have to look presentable on his home turf, but it was still disorienting.

Wymack gave Neil a once-over and nodded. "I see you made it all right. I was pretty sure Nicky's driving was going to get you killed."

Neil felt Nicky watching him and said, "I've survived worse."

"There is no surviving worse driving than that idiot's," Wymack said. "There's just open casket or closed."

"Hey, hey," Nicky said. "That's not fair."

"Life isn't fair, tweedle-dumb. Get over it. What are you still doing here?"

"Leaving," Andrew said. "Goodbye. Is Neil coming too?"

"Going where?" Wymack asked, looking suspicious.

"Jeez, Coach, what kind of people do you think we are?" Nicky asked.

"Do you really want me to answer that?"

"We're taking him to the court," Aaron said. "We can give him a lift to Abby's after. You didn't need him, did you?"

"Just to give him this," Wymack said, and Neil snagged the keys tossed his way. There were two rings looped together, two keys on one and three on the other. Neil eyed them as Wymack ticked them off on his fingers. "Long key is for when the front gate closes at night. Small one gets you into the apartment. The others are for the stadium: outer door, gear room, and court doors. Kevin has a matching set, so make him show you which is which. I expect you to make as much use of them as he does."

"Thank you," Neil said, clenching his fingers tight enough around them he could feel the teeth digging into his palm. He felt steadier with them in his hand. It didn't matter where he was sleeping or what tricks Andrew was up to. There was a court here and he had permission to play on it. "I will."

"Blatant favoritism, Coach," Andrew said.

"If you ever went to the court of your own volition, maybe I'd give you a set too," Wymack said. "Since I don't see that happening anytime this lifetime or next, you can shut up and share with Kevin."

"Oh, joy, joy," Andrew said. "My excited face begins now. Can we go?"

"Get out," Wymack said, and Andrew vanished. Kevin and Aaron followed. When Nicky reached the office doorway, Wymack put a hand in his path to stop him. "Don't you dare traumatize him his first day here."

Nicky looked from Wymack to Neil. "Neil's not traumatized, right?"

"Not yet," Neil said.

After a moment's debate, he shrugged his bag off his shoulder. The thought of leaving it behind made his skin crawl, considering what was hidden inside it, but he didn't trust Andrew's intentions. Neil didn't know why Andrew was sober or why he'd picked Neil up from the airport when it now seemed Wymack had tasked Nicky with that responsibility, but he didn't think Andrew was done playing yet. Neil trusted Wymack more than he did Andrew right now and hoped he wasn't making a mistake.

"Do you have someplace safe I can hide this?" he asked.

"There's space in the living room," Wymack said.

[30]

Neil glanced at Nicky, wondering how he could elaborate without making them curious enough to pry. He never walked away from his bag unless it was locked up somewhere, usually in his locker at Millport's stadium.

Before he could say anything, Wymack gave Nicky an impatient look. "Why are you still here? Get out."

"Rude," Nicky said, but he slipped past Wymack and disappeared down the hall.

Wymack looked at Neil again. "How safe is safe?"

Neil had never been an easy read before, but then, he'd never let the situation get so completely out of hand, either. On the run his mother had always stayed in control, weaving the perfect stories and choosing ideal marks to help them. Neil had fumbled his way through his transition to Millport, but he could have cut and run at any time if he didn't like the way things were going. This, he desperately wanted to make work, for however long he could hold onto it.

"It's all I have," Neil said at length.

Wymack motioned for Neil to get out of his way. Neil watched as he unlocked the bottom drawer on his desk. It was full of hanging files, but Wymack pulled them all out and stacked them on the floor nearby. The pile tilted over as soon as he let go, papers and folders sliding every which way. Wymack didn't even seem to notice, too busy digging a tiny key off his key ring.

"This is only a temporary fix," Wymack said. "When you move into the dorms, you're going to have to figure something else out."

He held the key out to Neil. Neil looked from him to the desk to the pile of papers and back again. He opened his mouth, closed it, and tried again. He'd only managed "Why" before Wymack got tired of waiting on him and pushed the key into his palm.

"Better hurry before Andrew sends someone looking for you," Wymack said.

Neil swallowed the rest of his question in favor of stuffing his duffel into the drawer. Luckily most of what was in the bag was clothes, so it fit into the cramped space with a couple shoves. Neil pushed the drawer shut and locked it. He tried to give the key back, but Wymack gave him a pitying look.

"The hell would I want that?" Wymack said. "Give it back when you move out."

Neil looked down at the key in his palm, at the security Wymack so easily and unquestioningly gave him. Maybe Neil wouldn't get any sleep tonight, and maybe he'd spend the next couple weeks waking up every time Wymack snored a little too loud, but maybe Neil really was okay here for now.

"Thank you," he said.

"Move along," Wymack said.

Neil left the office. The others had left the front door open and were waiting for him in the hallway. Neil slipped the key onto his key ring as he walked to meet them. Andrew led his cousins and Kevin to the elevator while Neil closed the door and locked it behind him. The elevator car arrived only seconds after Neil rejoined them, and they filed inside.

Neil's fleeting sense of safety vanished the second the doors closed behind him, because the others had arranged themselves in a ring around the walls of the elevator: Nicky and Aaron to his sides and Andrew and Kevin opposite him. All eyes were on Neil.

Andrew's smile vanished when the elevator started its slow crawl down. Neil returned his stare, every muscle tensed for a fight. At the fifth floor, Andrew pushed away from the back railing and started for Neil. He reached for Neil's keys, but Neil moved the ring out of reach. Andrew tried again, and Neil had to step back to dodge his grab. He backed right into the metal doors and realized a moment too late Andrew didn't care about his keys at all. He buried the ring in his pocket, feeling pinned in. How stupid, that someone so short could have such presence.

[32]

"How nice to meet you, Neil," Andrew drawled. "It will be a while before we see each other again."

"Somehow I don't think I'm that lucky."

"Like this," Andrew clarified, gesturing between their faces. "It will have to wait until June. Abby threatened to revoke our stadium rights for the summer if we break you sooner than that. Can't have that, can we? Kevin would cry. No worries. We'll wait until everyone's here and Abby has too many other Foxes to worry about. Then we'll throw you a welcome party you won't forget."

"You need to rethink your persuasion techniques. They suck."

"I don't need to be persuasive," Andrew said, putting a hand to Neil's chest as the elevator slowed to a stop. "You'll just learn to do what I say."

The doors slid open behind Neil. As soon as they'd parted enough Andrew gave Neil a small push. Neil tripped backward into the lobby. Andrew shoved past him, bumping him from shoulder to hip, and headed for the door. Kevin was a half-step behind him, and Aaron didn't even look at Neil on his way by. Only Nicky stayed behind long enough to smile at Neil.

"Ready for this?" he asked, and he went on ahead.

Neil remained behind for a few seconds longer to stare at their backs. He was starting to think Kevin wasn't his only problem at Palmetto State. It was almost a relief. Neil couldn't anticipate Kevin; he couldn't ask how much Kevin remembered about his past and he wouldn't know until too late what finally triggered Kevin into remembering him. But Andrew was just a psychotic midget, and Neil had grown up around violence. Handling him would be easy. Neil would just have to be careful.

"Ready," Neil said, and started after his teammates.

CHAPTER THREE

Neil spotted the Foxhole Court long before they made it to the stadium parking lot. Built to seat sixty-five thousand fans, it'd been placed on the outskirts of campus where it could tower over the shorter utilities buildings nearby. The paint job only made it stand out more: the walls were a blinding white with obnoxiously bright orange trim. A gigantic fox paw was painted on each of the four outer walls. Neil wondered how much it cost the university to build and how desperately they regretted the investment, considering the Foxes' miserable return.

They passed four parking lots before turning into a fifth. There were a couple cars already there, probably for maintenance staff or summer school students, but none were parked at the curb closest to the stadium. The stadium itself was surrounded by a barbed wire fence. Gates were placed equidistant down the length of the fence for handling a game night crowd, and all of them were chained shut.

Neil went up to the fence and stared through it at the outer grounds. It was deserted now, the souvenir stands and food stalls boarded up until the season started again, but he could imagine what it'd look like in a couple months. It made every hair on his body stand on end, and his heartbeat echoing in his ears sounded like an Exy ball rebounding off a court wall.

Nicky clapped a hand to Neil's shoulder. "All the orange grows on you," he promised.

Neil twisted his fingers through the metal links and wished he could break the fence down. "Let me in."

"Come on," Nicky said, and led him down the fence.

They'd reached the end of the gates—they'd parked by 24, and the next was 1. Between the two gates was a narrow door sealed with an electronic keypad. The door led to a hallway that cut the outer grounds in two; whoever made it as far as gate 24 would have to go into the stadium and through the stands to reach gate 1. The others were waiting for Nicky and Neil outside that door. Aaron had brought the whiskey with him.

"This is our entrance," Nicky said. "Code changes every couple months, but Coach always lets us know when it does. Right now it's 0508. May and August, get it? Coach and Abby's birth months. Told you they were boning. When's your birthday?"

"It was in March," Neil lied.

"Oh, we missed it. But we recruited you in April, so that should count as the world's greatest present. What'd your girlfriend get you?"

Neil looked at him. "What?"

"Come on, cute face like yours has to have a girlfriend. Unless you swing my way, of course, in which case please tell me now and save me the trouble of having to figure it out."

Neil stared at him, wondering how Nicky could care about such things when the stadium was right there. They knew the code to get inside, but they were standing around like his answer was the secret password. Neil looked from Nicky to the keypad and back again.

"What's it matter?" he asked.

"I'm curious," Nicky said.

"He means nosey," Aaron said.

"I don't swing either way," Neil said. "Let's go in."

"Bullshit," Nicky said.

"I don't," Neil said, and impatience put an edge in his voice. It wasn't quite the truth, but it was close enough. "Are we going in or not?"

In response, Kevin tapped in the code and pulled the door open. "Go," he said.

Neil didn't have to be told twice. He went down the hall, already turning his key ring over in his hands. The hall ended at

[35]

another door marked FOXES. He showed the key ring to Kevin in silent question. Kevin fingered the appropriate key.

It was strange sliding it into the knob and listening to the lock clack undone. Coach Hernandez occasionally let Neil sleep in the Millport High locker room, but it never occurred to him to give Neil a key. Instead he looked the other way whenever Neil broke in. Keys meant Neil had explicit permission to be here and do what he liked. They meant he belonged.

The first room was a lounge. Three chairs and two couches took up most of the space, forming a semicircle around an entertainment center. The TV was obscenely large, and Neil couldn't wait to watch a game on it. Posted above the TV on the wall was a list of sports and news channels.

The rest of the walls were covered in photographs. Some of them were official: team photos, snapshots of the Foxes' goals, and pictures obviously clipped from newspapers. The majority of the pictures looked like they'd been taken by one of the Foxes themselves. These were scattered anywhere they could fit and held up by tape. Taking up one entire corner was a clump of photos featuring the Foxes' three ladies.

Exy was a co-ed sport, but few colleges wanted women on their lines. According to Fox lore, Palmetto State refused to approve any of the women Wymack asked for his first year. After the Foxes' trainwreck first season, they were a little more willing to listen, and Wymack signed three women. On top of that, he made Danielle Wilds the first female captain in NCAA Class I Exy.

If Exy fans weren't kind to the Foxes, they were downright cruel to Danielle. Even her teammates were willing to shred her in public during her first year. The more outspoken misogynists blamed her for the Foxes' failings. Despite the controversy and with only Wymack at her back, Danielle held onto her position. Three years later, it was obvious Wymack made the right choice. The Foxes were still a mess but they fell in behind Danielle and slowly started racking up wins.

[36]

Neil's mental picture of Danielle was that of an aggressive and unrelenting woman, but the pictures he was looking at undermined that impression. Danielle was smiling in every photo, a toothy grin that was equal parts menace and mirth.

Nicky noticed his distraction and tapped the faces in the closest photograph. "Dan, Renee, and Allison. Dan's good people, but she'll work you to the bone. Allison's a catty bitch you should avoid at all costs. Renee's a sweetheart. Be nice to her."

"Or else?" Neil asked, because he could hear it in Nicky's tone.

Nicky only smiled and shrugged.

"Let's go," Kevin said.

Neil followed him out of the lounge. A hallway led from the lounge past two office doors labeled DAVID WYMACK and ABIGAIL WINFIELD. A door with a simple red cross on it was next. Further down two doors opposite each other were marked LADIES and GENTLEMEN. Kevin pushed open the GENTLEMEN door a bit, showing Neil a quick glimpse of bright orange lockers, benches, and tiled floor. Neil wanted to explore, but Kevin wasn't slowing on his way down the hall.

The hall dead-ended at a large room Neil dimly remembered from news clips. It was the room that opened into the stadium and the only place where the press could meet Foxes after games for interviews and photographs. Orange benches were set here and there, and the floor was white tile with orange paw prints. Orange cones were stacked in a corner, three deep and six high. A white door was on the wall to Neil's right, and an orange door was opposite him.

"Welcome to the foyer," Nicky said. "That's what we call it, anyway. By 'we' I mean whatever clever smartass preceded us."

Andrew straddled one of the benches and dug a bottle of pills out of his pocket. Aaron handed Kevin the whiskey they'd snitched. Kevin brought it to Andrew, waited while Andrew shook a pill onto the bench in front of him, and traded him the whiskey for the pill bottle. The medicine disappeared into one of Kevin's pockets, and Andrew swallowed the pill with an impressive swig of whiskey.

Kevin looked at Neil and gestured to the plain door across the room. "Gear closet."

"Can we—?" Neil started.

Kevin didn't let him finish. "Bring your keys."

Neil met him at the orange door and let Kevin pick out the right key. The other side of the doorway was darkness. There wasn't a ceiling, but Neil could see the walls rising up on either side. Neil followed Kevin into the shadows. Ten steps later he realized they must be in the stadium itself.

"You get to see the Foxhole Court looking its best," Nicky said behind him. "We made enough money off Kevin's presence we could get the floors refurbished and walls done. Cleanest this place has been since year one."

Light from the locker room bled into the stadium, the path to the inner court was too long for it to be much help. Inner court was mostly inky shadows with vague outlines. Neil closed his eyes and tried to imagine it. This space was reserved for the referees, cheerleaders, and teams. Somewhere around here were the Foxes' home benches. The plexiglass walls surrounding the court were invisible in the dark, as was the court itself, but knowing the court was there set Neil's heart racing.

"Lights," Aaron called from somewhere behind them.

Neil heard the hum of electricity before the lights came on, starting with emergency lights at his feet and cascading upwards. The stadium came to life before his eyes, row after row of alternating orange and white seats disappearing into sky-high rafters and the court lighting up in front of him. Neil was moving before the ceiling lights turned on, crossing the inner court to the court walls. He pressed his hands to the thick, cold plastic and looked up, where the scoreboards and replay TVs hung over the court's ceiling, then down to the glossy wood.

[38]

Orange lines marked first, half, and far court. It was perfect, utterly perfect, and Neil felt at once inspired and horrified by the sight of it. How could he possibly play here after playing on Millport's pathetic knockoff court?

He closed his eyes and breathed in, breathed out, imagining the way bodies sounded as they crashed into each other on the court, the way the announcer's voice would only come through in muffled, scattered bursts, the roar of sixty-five thousand people reacting to a goal. He knew he didn't deserve this, knew beyond a doubt he wasn't good enough to play on this court, but he wanted and needed it so badly he ached all over.

For three and a half weeks, it would be just the five of them, but in June the Foxes would move in for summer practices and in August the season would begin. Neil opened his eyes again, looked at the court, and knew he'd made the right decision. The risks didn't matter; the consequences would be worth it. He had to be here. He had to play on this court at least once. He had to know if the crowd screamed loud enough to blow the roof off. He had to smell the sweat and overpriced stadium food. He needed to hear the buzzer sound as a ball slammed inside the white goal lines and lit the walls up red.

"Oh," Nicky said, leaning against the wall a short ways down from Neil. "No wonder he chose you."

Neil looked at him, not really understanding the words, not really listening when his mind was still racing with the tick-tick-tock of a game clock counting down. Past Nicky was Kevin, who'd watched his father take a man apart and gone on to sign with the national team. Kevin was watching him, but the second their eyes met he pointed back the way they'd come.

"Give him his gear."

Aaron and Nicky brought Neil back to the locker room. Andrew hadn't followed them into the stadium, but he wasn't in the foyer either. Neil didn't care enough to ask but followed the cousins into the changing room. The front room was lined with lockers, each one marked with the players' numbers and names.

[39]

Through the doorway at the back Neil could see sinks and he assumed the showers were around the corner out of sight. He was more interested in the locker that had his name on it.

Coaches Hernandez and Wymack had spent the last few weeks of Neil's senior year arguing details on what sort of equipment Neil needed. Knowing that everything was going to be here for him wasn't half as good as seeing it. There were five outfits for workouts and a set of both home and away uniforms. Mounds of padding and armor took up most of the space in his giant locker, and his helmet was on the top shelf. Underneath the helmet was something neon orange and shrink-wrapped, and Neil carefully pulled it out to examine it. It opened to reveal a windbreaker that was almost brighter than the stadium paint. "Foxes" and "Josten" were printed on the back in reflective material.

"Satellites can pick these up in outer space," he said.

Nicky laughed at that. "Dan commissioned them her first year here. She said she was tired of everyone trying to look past us. People want to pretend people like us don't exist, you know? Everyone hopes we're someone else's problem to solve." He reached out and fingered the material. "They don't understand, so they don't know where to start. They feel overwhelmed and give up before they've taken the first step."

Nicky gave himself a small shake and smiled, melancholy instantly replaced by cheer. "You know we donate a portion of ticket sales to charity? Our tickets cost a little more than anyone else's because of it. Renee's idea. Told you she's pure gold. Now come on, let's get you looking foxy."

He turned away to find his own gear, so Neil pulled out what he needed and brought it to the bathroom. Changing out in a stall was awkward and uncomfortable, but he'd done it so many times he had it down to an art form. He traded out a t-shirt for shoulder and chest padding. He did a couple twists to make sure the straps were snug enough without being too tight, then tugged his jersey on overtop. He could put on shorts around the others, so he returned to the main room to finish dressing.

He traded jeans for shorts first, then sat on one of the benches to hook his shin guards into place. He covered those with long socks and put on scuff-free court shoes. He pulled thin cotton gloves on, snapping them closed just above his elbows, and strapped arm guards onto his forearms. He left his outer gloves by his helmet where he could carry them down to the court and pulled his bangs up under an orange bandanna. The last thing to put on was his neck guard, a thin band with a tricky clasp. It was a pain to deal with and occasionally made him feel like he was choking, but it was worth putting up with if it'd protect his throat from a stray ball.

They went back to the foyer, and Nicky had Neil unlock the gear door Kevin indicated earlier. Aaron got a bucket of balls while Nicky rolled out the stick rack. The racquets were arranged by numbers, a pair for each player with Neil's at the end. Neil unhooked one and gave it a slow spin, testing the weight and feel of it in his hand. It was dark orange with a single white stripe at the base of the head and white rope netting. It smelled brand new and felt like a dream, and it was all he could do to keep from smashing the taut net against his face. At Millport he'd used one of the older team racquets. This one had been ordered specifically for him, and the thought alone was enough to set his heart racing.

Kevin was right where they'd left him, waiting for them in the inner ring. He watched silently as they tugged on their helmets and gloves, and said nothing when Aaron led the way to the home court entrance. Neil used his last key to unlock the door and then stuffed the keys into his glove for safekeeping.

After the door closed behind them, Neil looked at Nicky and asked, "Is Kevin not going to play today?"

Nicky looked surprised that he'd ask. "Kevin only tolerates our court under two conditions: alone, or with Andrew on it.

He'll have to get over it this fall when Renee's in goal at games, but for now he can get away with being a snob."

"Where's Andrew?"

"He just dosed up, so he's out cold somewhere. He's going to crash and reboot into crazy mode."

"You don't think he's crazy now?"

"Crazy, nah," Nicky said. "Soulless, perhaps."

Neil looked at Aaron, waiting for him to defend his twin, but Aaron only led the way to half-court. Neil kept pace with Nicky, idly poking his fingers through the netting on his racquet. He looked at Kevin, who was still watching them through the court wall, and asked, "Kevin can't really play, can he? They said it'd be a miracle if he ever picked up a racquet again."

"His left hand's pretty much out," Nicky said. "He's playing as a rightie from now on."

Neil stared. "What?"

Nicky grinned, obviously pleased to have dropped that bombshell. "They don't call him an obsessive genius for nothing, you know."

"It's not genius," Aaron said. "It's spite."

"That too," Nicky said. "I wish I could see the look on Riko's face when he sees our first game. Rat bastard."

Kevin pounded on the wall in a demand for them to get moving.

Nicky waved a hand at him in dismissal. "We're doing this in our free time, you know!" he yelled, not that Kevin could hear him through the court walls.

"Thank you," Neil said belatedly.

"Huh? Oh, no. Don't worry about it. You can make it up to me some other time when the others aren't around."

"Can you try and get ass when I'm not standing right here?" Aaron asked.

"You could leave and let me and Neil get to know each other better."

[42]

"I'll tell Erik on you."

"Bald-faced lie. When's the last time you said a civil word to him?"

Neil didn't know any Foxes past or present with that name. "Who is Erik?"

"Oh, he's my husband," Nicky said happily. "Or will be, eventually. He was my home-stay brother for a year in Berlin and we moved in together after graduation."

Neil's heart skipped a beat. "You lived in Germany?"

He tried to do the math in his head, guessing Nicky's age against how long ago he'd been in high school. Chances were Neil had already moved on to Switzerland by the time Nicky made it to German soil, but it was such a close call Neil couldn't breathe.

"Ja," Nicky said. "You heard us earlier with the mumbo-jumbo, right? That was German. The little punks studied it at high school because they knew I could help them pass. If you take German as your elective here, just let me know and I'll tutor you. I'm good with my tongue."

"Enough. Let's play," Aaron said, putting the bucket of balls down.

Nicky gave an exaggerated sigh. "Anyway, remind me to show you his picture later. Our babies are going to be gorgeous."

Neil frowned, confused. "He doesn't live here?"

"Oh, no. He's in Stuttgart. Got a job he loves with great career potential, so he couldn't leave to follow me here. I was only supposed to stay long enough to get these kids through high school, but when Coach offered me a scholarship Erik said I should go for it. It sucks being apart for so long, but he came here last Christmas and I'll go there this year. If things ever die down around here I'll even get to spend next summer in Germany." Nicky sent a meaningful look toward the wall where Kevin was watching them.

[43]

They spent the next hour and a half teaching Neil drills. A lot of them Neil had done before, but there were a few he didn't recognize, and it gave him a thrill to learn something new. They ended with a short scrimmage, one striker against two backliners and an open goal. Aaron and Nicky weren't the best defense players in the NCAA by far, but they were far better than any of the high schoolers Neil was used to playing.

Aaron called them to a stop at last and Neil caught the ball on a rebound. When he dropped it into the bucket the others started unstrapping their helmets. Neil squished a flare of disappointment that they were done so soon, but he wouldn't push them to play any longer; Nicky had already said that they were giving up their summer break to play with him.

Nicky smeared his cheek against his shoulder, trying to wipe sweat off onto his jersey. He smiled at Neil. "How's that?"

"It was fun," Neil said. "You two are really, really good."

Nicky beamed, but Aaron snorted. "Kevin would kill himself if he heard that."

"Kevin thinks we're a waste of oxygen," Nicky said with a shrug.

"At least you're not going to completely drag us down," Aaron said. "It'll take most the season to get you where we need you to be, but I can see why Kevin picked you."

"Speaking of..." Nicky tipped his head toward the wall. "Someone's ready to get his hands on you."

Neil followed the gesture and looked through the wall toward the Foxes' benches. Andrew had reappeared and was lying flat on his back on the home bench, playing catch with a spare ball. Kevin had gotten his racquet at some point and was spinning it as he watched them. With half the court and a half-inch-thick wall between them, Neil could still feel Kevin's stare like a physical weight.

"Fear for your life," Nicky said. "He's not a forgiving tutor, and he doesn't know how to be nice. Kevin can piss anyone off on an Exy court, up to and including a drugged Andrew. Well, anyone except Renee, but she's not human so she doesn't count."

Neil looked at Andrew again. "I thought his medicine made that impossible."

"Spring was a learning experience." Nicky propped his racquet against his shoulder and started for the door. "Wish you'd seen it. Andrew would've taken Kevin's head off if Kevin hadn't already thrown Andrew's racquet halfway across the court. I can't wait to see how you handle it."

"Fantastic," Neil said, grabbing the balls bucket and following them off the court.

Andrew sat up as the court door banged closed behind them and tossed his ball to Nicky. He'd brought the whiskey with him and left it on the ground by his feet. Now he scooped it up and twisted the lid off.

"About time," he said. "Nicky, it's so boring waiting on you."

"We're done now," Nicky said, hooking his helmet over the end of his racquet so he could reach for the whiskey. "About time you stop that, don't you think? Abby's going to beat me senseless if she realizes you've been drinking."

"Doesn't sound like my problem," Andrew said with a brilliant smile.

Nicky looked to Aaron for help, but Aaron went ahead of them to the locker room. Nicky mimed blowing his own brains out and went with him. Neil meant to go after them, but he'd made the mistake of looking at Kevin. Once he met Kevin's eyes, it was hard to look away again.

Kevin's expression was indecipherable. Whatever it was, it didn't look particularly happy. "This is going to be a very long season."

"I told you I wasn't ready."

"You also said you wouldn't play with me, but here you are."

Neil didn't answer that accusation. Kevin got right in his face and tangled his fingers through the netting on Neil's racquet. When he started to pull it away, Neil held on tighter, silently refusing to let go. Kevin probably could have wrenched it away if he tried a little harder, but he seemed content just to hold on.

"If you won't play with me, you'll play for me," Kevin said. "You're never going to get there on your own, so give your game to me."

"Where is 'there'?" Neil asked.

"If you can't figure that out there's no helping you," Kevin said.

Neil gazed back at him in silence, pretty sure 'there' didn't apply to someone like him. Kevin must have seen that in the unimpressed look on his face because he reached up and covered Neil's eyes with his free hand.

"Forget the stadium," Kevin said. "Forget the Foxes and your useless high school team and your family. See it the only way it really matters, where Exy is the only road to take. What do you see?"

Imagining life in such simplistic terms was so ridiculous Neil almost laughed. He kept the vicious twist of his mouth off his face through sheer willpower alone. Something still must have shown, because Kevin gave his racquet a hard tug.

"Focus."

Neil tried to picture the world as if Neil Josten was really all there ever had been and would be. It was almost enough to make him despise the persona when he could see it in such easy terms, but he swallowed that distaste and turned his mental gaze toward Exy.

Had the game ever been his, or had it been pulling him to this point? Exy was the only bright point of his shattered childhood. He remembered his mother bringing him to little league Exy games, traveling an hour outside of Baltimore to where no one knew his father and the coaches would actually let

[46]

him play. He remembered her cheering for him as if their every move and word wasn't scrutinized by gun-toting bodyguards. The memories were fragmented and dreamlike, distorted by the bloody reality of his father's work, but he clung to them. They were the only times he'd ever seen his mother smile.

Neil didn't know how long he played with his little league team, but his hands remembered the weight of a racquet as well as they did that of a gun.

That thought was sobering, as it put him right back to square one and the fact that Neil Josten was a fleeting existence. It was cruel to even dream he could stay like this, but Kevin had escaped, hadn't he? Somehow he'd left that bloody room behind at Edgar Allan and become this, and Neil wanted the same so bad he could taste it.

"You," Neil said at last. Kevin pulled at his racquet again, and this time Neil let go.

"Tell me I can have your game."

It wouldn't do them any good, but Neil wasn't going to get into that. "Take it."

"Neil understands," Kevin said, dropping his hand and sending Andrew a pointed look.

"Congratulations are in order, I suppose! Since I have none to give, I will tell the others to respond appropriately." Andrew pushed himself to his feet and swallowed more whiskey on the way up. "Neil! Hello. We meet again."

"We met earlier," Neil said. "If this is another trick, just let it go."

Andrew grinned at him around the mouth of his bottle. "Don't be so suspicious. You saw me take my medicine. If I hadn't, I'd be keeled over somewhere by now puking from the withdrawal. As it is, I might puke from all the fanaticism going around."

"He's high," Kevin told Neil. "He tells me when he's sober, so I always know. How did you figure it out?"

[47]

"They're twins, but they're not the same." Neil lifted one shoulder in a shrug. "One of them hates your obsession with Exy while the other couldn't care less."

Kevin looked to Andrew, but Andrew only had eyes for Neil. Andrew took a second to process those words before he started laughing. "He's a comedian, too? An athlete and a comic and a student. How multitalented. What a grand addition to the Fox line. I can't wait to find out what else he can do. Perhaps we should throw a talent show and find out? But later. Kevin, we're going. I need food."

Kevin handed Neil his racquet back and the three went to the locker room. Aaron and Nicky were already in the showers when they arrived. Neil heard water running and sat on a bench in the changing room to wait.

"We're not taking you by Abby's like that," Kevin said. "Wash up."

"I won't shower with the team," Neil said. "I'll wait, and if you don't want to wait on me, just go on ahead. I'll find my way there from here."

"Nicky going to be a problem for you?" Andrew asked.

Neil didn't like the look of his manic smile, but he liked Andrew's veiled warning less. "It's not about Nicky. It's about my privacy."

Kevin snapped his fingers at Neil. "Get over it. You can't be shy if you're going to be a star."

Andrew leaned toward Kevin and put a hand to his mouth, but he didn't bother to lower his voice. "He has to hide his ouches, Kevin. I broke into Coach's cabinet and read his files. Bruises, you think, or scars? I think scars, too. Can't be bruises if his parents aren't around to beat him, right?"

Neil felt cold all over. "What did you just say?"

"I don't care," Kevin said to Andrew, ignoring Neil.

Andrew, in turn, ignored Kevin and gestured at Neil. "Showers aren't communal here. Coach put in stalls when he built the stadium. The board wouldn't pay for it—they didn't see

[48]

the point—so it came out of Coach's own pocket. See for yourself if you don't believe me. You don't believe me, do you? I know you don't. That's probably for the best."

Neil barely heard him. "You had no right to read my file!"

He regretted not flipping open the folder when Wymack put it down by him at the stadium. He couldn't believe Hernandez had said such things in his letters to Wymack. He knew Hernandez had to explain his situation, or at least as much as Hernandez understood it to be, to prove Neil was a fit for the Foxes' halfway-house team. Neil still felt betrayed, and on its heels was anger that Andrew had dug up those papers about him.

Andrew laughed, sounding delighted to have crossed such a personal line. "Relax, relax, relax. I made that up. We were locked in Coach Arizona's office to watch your game on the local TV station, and he said our secret meet-and-greet would be easy since you always shower alone last. Told Coach he still couldn't find your parents. Coach asked if they'd be a problem, and Arizona said he didn't know because he hadn't met them a single time. Said they spent a lot of time commuting to their jobs in Phoenix and no time at all checking in on you. But I'm right, aren't I?"

Neil opened his mouth, then closed it before he gave Andrew a piece of his mind. Andrew wanted him to react, so Neil had to reel it in. He sucked in a slow breath through gritted teeth and counted to ten. He only made it to five before Andrew's smile was too much.

Neil didn't believe Andrew about the showers, but it was better to investigate than stay here and take a swing at Andrew. He got off the bench and went to the bathroom. The sinks with their ceiling-high mirrors were the connecting section between the toilets and the showers, and the showers were around the corner out of sight. He edged around for a quick look. Andrew was telling the truth for once. The walls were lined with stalls, tall enough to afford complete privacy and outfitted with locking doors.

"Weird, right?" Andrew said at Neil's ear. Neil hadn't heard his approach over the sound of the cousins' showers. Lashing out was instinctive, but Andrew caught the elbow Neil would have slammed into his ribs. Andrew laughed and retreated a couple steps. "Coach never explained it. Maybe he thought we'd need to grieve our disastrous losses in private. Only the best for his rising stars, right?"

"I didn't think Wymack recruited rising stars," Neil said, pushing past Andrew for his locker.

"No," Andrew agreed. "The Foxes will never amount to anything. Try telling Dan that, though, and she'll box your ears." He scooped up his whiskey and started for the door. "Kevin, car."

Neil watched the door close behind them before gathering his clothes and heading to the showers. He washed as quickly as he could and grimaced as he got dressed again. Vents kept the air moving, pulling moisture out to cut back on mildew, but the room still felt heavy and wet. Neil felt sticky as he tugged his clothes on. He raked his fingers through his hair as he met up with the cousins in the main room. They showed him where to put his armor so it could air dry and his uniform to be washed. Aaron got the lights on their way out, Neil locked the doors, and they found the other two waiting by the car.

Nicky took the keys from Andrew and shook them at Neil. "It's your first day, so you get shotgun again. Enjoy it while you can. Kevin hates sitting in back."

"I don't have to sit up front," Neil said, but Kevin and the twins were already piling into the backseat with Kevin in the middle. The way they sat put Andrew behind Neil's seat, so Neil hoped the ride was short.

Abigail Winfield lived in a one-story house about five minutes from campus. Nicky parked at the curb since there were already two cars in the driveway when they arrived. The front door was unlocked, so they let themselves in without knocking, and they were greeted by the thick smells of garlic and warm tomato sauce.

Coach Wymack and Abigail were in the kitchen already. Wymack was grumbling as he dug through the silverware drawer and Abigail ignored him in favor of stirring something at the stove. Coach spotted the Foxes first and stabbed a finger at Nicky.

"Hemmick, get over here and be useful for once in your mangy life. Table needs setting."

"Aww, Coach," Nicky complained as Abigail turned. "Why do you always have to pick on me? You already started it. Can't you finish?"

"Shut your face and get to work."

"Can't you two behave when we've got a guest?" Abigail asked, setting aside her spoon and coming to greet them.

Wymack raked the group with a look. "I don't see any guests. Neil's a Fox. He's not going to get any special treatment just because it's his first day. Don't want him thinking this team is anything but dysfunctional or June will be a rude wake-up call."

"David? Shut up and make sure the vegetables aren't boiling over. Kevin, check the bread. It's in the oven. Nicky, table. Aaron, help him. Andrew Joseph Minyard, that had better not be what I think it is." She made a grab at the whiskey, but Andrew laughed and ducked out of the doorway. Abigail looked like she wanted to go after him down the hall, but Neil was in her way. He stepped neatly to one side to let her through, but she settled for flicking Nicky a murderous look.

"What was I supposed to do?" Nicky asked, avoiding her eyes as the three split up to their various chores. "Take it from him? No way in hell."

Abigail ignored him in favor of facing Neil. "You'd be Neil, then. I'm Abby. I'm nurse for the team and temporary landlord to this lot. They're not harassing you too much, are they?"

"No worries," Andrew called from out of sight. "He'll actually take work to break, I think. Give me until August, maybe."

"If you dare give us a repeat of last year—"

"Then Bee will be here to pick the pieces up," Andrew interrupted, reappearing in the doorway at Neil's side. He'd lost the whiskey along the way and he splayed his empty hands at her in a calming gesture. "She did so well with Matt, didn't she? Neil won't even be a blink on her radar. You did invite her over, didn't you?"

"I invited her, but she declined. She thought it would make things awkward."

"Things aren't anything but awkward when Andrew and Nicky are around," Coach said.

Andrew didn't even try to defend his honor but looked at Neil. "Bee's a shrink. Used to work in the juvie system, but now she's here. She deals with the really serious cases on campus: suicide watch, budding psychopaths, that sort of thing. That makes her our designated handler. You'll meet her in August."

"Do I have to?" Neil asked.

"It's mandatory once a semester for athletes," Abby confirmed. "The first time is a casual meet-and-greet so you get to know her and find out where her office is. The second session is in spring. Of course, you're free to visit her any time you like, and she'll talk to you more about scheduling while you're there. Counseling services are included in your tuition, so you might as well make use of it."

"Betsy's amazing," Nicky said. "You'll love her."

Neil doubted it, but he let it slide for now.

"Let's eat, shall we?" Abby asked, motioning for Andrew and Neil to enter the room.

Neil had just about lost his appetite, but he sat at the table as far as he could get from Kevin and Andrew's seats.

[52]

Conversation died as everyone got settled and served up what they wanted, but it started up again as they dug into chunks of steaming lasagna. Neil tried as best as he could to stay out of it, more interested in seeing the way they interacted.

From time to time the table split as Kevin and Wymack got caught up talking about spring training and recruits at other schools and Nicky regaled the other half of the table with gossip about movies and celebrities Neil didn't know. Andrew watched Kevin and Wymack, but he had nothing to contribute to the conversation. Instead he hummed to himself and pushed his food around his plate.

It was after ten when Wymack decided it was time to go, and Neil left with him. Getting in the car alone with him was the hardest thing Neil had done all day. Andrew was crazy, but Neil had an ingrained distrust of men old enough to be his father. He spent the entire ride frozen and silent in the passenger seat. Maybe Wymack noticed the rigid set to his shoulders, because he said nothing to Neil until they were back at his apartment.

When Wymack closed and locked the front door behind them, he asked, "Are they going to be a problem?"

Neil shook his head and discreetly put more space between them. "I'll figure it out."

"They don't understand boundaries," Wymack said. "If they cross a line and you can't get them to back off, you come to me. Understand? I don't have perfect control over Andrew, but Kevin owes us his life and I can get to Andrew through him."

Neil nodded and went down the hall to get his bag from Wymack's desk. It'd been locked up all day, but he unloaded it onto the couch anyway to check his things. The second his hands closed over the binder at the bottom of his bag, his heart kicked into overdrive. He wanted to go through it and make sure everything was there, but Wymack was watching him from the doorway.

"You plan on wearing the same six outfits over and over again this year?" Wymack asked.

[53]

"Eight," Neil said, "and yes."

Wymack arched an eyebrow at him but didn't push it. "Laundry room is in the basement. Detergent's in the bathroom cabinet under the sink. Use what you need, and take what you want from the kitchen. It'll piss me off more if you act like a skittish stray cat than it will if you eat the last bowl of cereal."

"Yes, Coach."

"I've got paperwork to go over. You good?"

"I might go running," Neil said.

Wymack nodded and left. Neil set his running pants to one side and stuffed his sleeping pants and tee under the couch for later. He changed in the bathroom and went around Wymack to lock his bag up again. Wymack didn't even look up from the papers he was perusing, though he grunted what might have been a goodbye as Neil left again. Neil locked the door behind him, stuffed the keys to the bottom of his pocket, and took the stairs down to ground level.

He didn't know where he was or where he was going, but that was all right. If he gave his feet a direction, they'd take him running past all of his thoughts, and he'd be happy to let them.

CHAPTER FOUR

Neil spent the following morning exploring the campus and memorizing its layout. When he was sure he knew his way around, he left school grounds and went for a long run. Gradually he looped his way back around. He had an hour to stretch out and eat lunch before he met the others at the stadium, and he made sure to show up early enough to change in private.

When the others arrived, Neil was waiting for them on the court. He watched as Kevin propelled Andrew toward the home goal. Andrew was laughing about something, but Neil couldn't hear what Kevin was saying to him. Aaron and Nicky scattered balls down the first-fourth line, and Nicky rolled a couple Neil's way. Neil spaced them out at half-court around him.

They started with drills, some of which Neil practiced yesterday and a few more he didn't know. The exercises gradually increased in difficulty and Neil grimaced a little as Andrew deflected every shot Neil aimed his way. It was only a little comforting that neither Aaron nor Nicky was scoring, either, but Kevin landed almost a third of his shots. It was a poor show from a former national champion, but it was also intensely humbling as Kevin had grown up playing left-handed. Seeing him take on Andrew right-handed was ballsy enough; seeing him actually score was surreal.

Kevin kicked them off the court for a water break after an hour and a half of drills, but instead of following the backliners and Neil to the locker room, he stayed behind with Andrew to keep practicing. Neil watched them over his shoulder.

"I saw him first," Nicky said.

"I thought you had Erik," Neil said.

"I do, but Kevin's on the List," Nicky said. When Neil frowned, Nicky explained. "It's a list of celebrities we're allowed to have affairs with. Kevin is my number three."

Neil pretended to understand and changed the topic. "How does anyone lose against the Foxes with Andrew in your goal?"

"He's good, right? But Andrew sat out most of last year." Nicky shrugged. "Coach didn't need a third goalie when he signed us, so Andrew was a bench warmer up until November. Then the ERC threatened to revoke our Class I status and fire Coach if we didn't start winning more often. Coach bribed Andrew into saving our collective asses with some really nice booze."

"Bribed?" Neil echoed.

"Andrew's good," Nicky said again, "but it doesn't really matter to him if we win or lose. You want him to care, you gotta give him incentive."

"He can't play like that and not care."

"Now you sound like Kevin. You'll find out the hard way, same as Kevin did. Kevin gave Andrew a lot of grief this spring," Nicky said as they pushed their way into the locker room. Aaron went ahead of them to the water fountain and Nicky propped himself against the wall to watch Neil. "Andrew walked off the court for an entire month. He said he'd break his own fingers if Coach made him play with Kevin again."

The thought of Andrew willingly destroying his talent made Neil's heart clench. "But he's playing now."

Nicky took a couple quick sips from the fountain as soon as Aaron stepped out of the way and smeared a hand across his mouth. "Only because Kevin is. Kevin got back on the court with a racquet in his right hand, and Andrew wasn't far behind him. Up until then they were fighting like cats and dogs. Now look at them. They're practically trading friendship bracelets and I couldn't fit a crowbar between them if it'd save my life."

"But why?" Neil asked. "Andrew hates Kevin's obsession with Exy."

"The day they start making sense to you, let me know," Nicky said, moving so Neil could get a drink. "I gave up trying to sort it all out weeks ago. You could ask, but neither of them will answer. But as long as I'm doling out advice? Stop staring at Kevin so much. You're making me fear for your life over here."

"What do you mean?"

"Andrew is scary territorial of him. He punched me the first time I said I'd like to get Kevin too wasted to be straight." Nicky pointed at his face, presumably where Andrew had decked him. "So yeah, I'm going to crush on safer targets until Andrew gets bored of him. That means you, since Matt's taken and I don't hate myself enough to try Seth. Congrats."

"Can you take the creepy down a level?" Aaron asked.

"What?" Nicky asked. "He said he doesn't swing, so obviously he needs a push."

"I don't need a push," Neil said. "I'm fine on my own."

"Seriously, how are you not bored of your hand by now?"

"I'm done with this conversation," Neil said. "This and every future variation of it. Look, Nicky, I have no problems with your sexuality, but I'm here to play. All I want from any of you is the best you can give me on the court."

The stadium door slammed open as Andrew showed up at last. He swept them with a wide-eyed look as if surprised to see them all there. "Kevin wants to know what's taking you so long. Did you get lost?"

"Nicky's scheming to rape Neil," Aaron said. "There are a couple flaws in his plan he needs to work out first, but he'll get there sooner or later."

"You're such an asshole," Nicky said as he started for the door.

"Wow, Nicky," Andrew said. "You start early."

"Can you really blame me?"

Nicky glanced back at Neil as he said it. He only took his eyes off Andrew for a second, but that was long enough for

[57]

Andrew to lunge at him. Andrew caught Nicky's jersey in one hand and threw him hard up against the wall. Nicky grunted at the impact but made no move to shove Andrew off when Andrew leaned up against him. Neil looked from Nicky to Aaron, but Aaron appeared unmoved and unsurprised by the sudden violence. Neil looked back at Andrew and waited to see how this played out.

"Hey, Nicky," Andrew said in stage-whisper German. "Don't touch him, you understand?"

"You know I'd never hurt him. If he says yes—"

"I said no."

"Jesus, you're greedy," Nicky said. "You already have Kevin. Why does it—"

He went silent, but it took Neil a moment to realize why. Andrew had a short knife pressed to Nicky's jersey. Where he'd pulled it from, Neil didn't know, but he refused to think Andrew wore one onto the court under his uniform. There had to be rules and regulations against that. The last thing Neil wanted was for Andrew to stab someone in the middle of a game. The Foxes would be banned from the league in an instant.

"Shh, Nicky, shh," Andrew said, like he was soothing a troubled child. "Why the long face? It's going to be okay."

Neil was no stranger to violence. He'd heard every threat in the book, but never from a man who smiled as bright as Andrew did. Apathy, anger, madness, boredom; these motivators Neil knew and understood. But Andrew was grinning like he didn't have a knife point where it'd slip perfectly between Nicky's ribs, and it wasn't because he was joking. Neil knew Andrew meant it. If Nicky so much as breathed wrong right now, Andrew would cut his lungs to ribbons, any and all consequences be damned.

Neil wondered if Andrew's medicine would let him grieve, or if he'd laugh at Nicky's funeral too. Then he wondered if a sober Andrew would act any different. Was this Andrew's psychosis or his medicine? Was he flying too high to understand

[58]

what he was doing, or did his medicine only add a smile to Andrew's ingrained violence?

Neil looked to Aaron, waiting for him to interfere. Aaron was tense but quiet as he stared at Andrew's knife. Neil gave him another second, but he couldn't wait forever. He didn't know what would finally set Andrew off and he didn't want to find out.

"Hey," Neil said, looking back at Andrew. "That's enough."

"Quiet," Nicky said in English, barely louder than a breath of air. "Quiet. It's fine."

"Hey," Neil said again, ignoring him, but he wasn't sure what to say. Questioning Andrew's sanity or calling his bluff would end with Nicky in the hospital. He wouldn't pretend to accept Nicky's advances just to calm Andrew down. What Neil needed was a distraction, something more important to Andrew than Nicky. That left only one thing that Neil knew of. One person, rather.

"Are we playing or what?" he said. "Kevin's waiting."

Andrew looked at Neil as if that hadn't occurred to him. "Oh, you're right. Let's go or we'll never hear the end of it."

Andrew let go of Nicky and spun away. His knife vanished under his armor before he reached the door. Aaron squeezed Nicky's shoulder on his way out. Nicky looked shaken as he stared after the twins, but when he realized Neil was watching him he rallied with a smile Neil didn't believe at all.

"On second thought, you're not my type after all," Nicky said when the door closed behind his cousins. "You need some more water before we hit the court for round two?"

"That's not okay," Neil said, pointing at the door.

"That's nothing," Nicky said.

Neil caught his arm as Nicky passed and hauled him to a stop. "Don't let him get away with things like that."

Nicky considered him for a moment, his smile fading into something small and tired. "Oh, Neil. You're going to make this so hard on yourself. Look," he said, tugging free and turning

Neil toward the door. "Andrew is a little bit crazy. Your lines are not his lines, so you can get all huff and puff when he tramps across yours but you'll never make him understand what he did wrong. Moreover, you'll never make him care. So just stay out of his way."

"He's like this because you let him get away with it," Neil said. "You're putting all of us at risk."

"That was my fault." Nicky opened the door and waited for Neil to precede him out. "I said something I shouldn't have, and I got what I deserved."

Neil wasn't convinced, but he couldn't demand better explanations for an argument that had happened in German, so he led the way to the inner court. Neil looked first to Andrew, who was jogging to the half-court line, and then to Kevin, who was standing on the fox paw logo at the court's center. Aaron was at the door waiting for Nicky and Neil, and the three entered the court together.

Kevin barely waited for them to stop at his side before dividing them up with a flick of his fingers. "Aaron is with me. Nicky and Andrew get the child. Two-man team scrimmage with an empty away goal."

"I'm not a child," Neil said. "You're only a year older than I am." Two, really, but he wasn't about to tell them he'd lied about both his birthday and his age.

Kevin ignored that, but Nicky spoke up, "Shouldn't Andrew be with you and Aaron? Then Neil can practice shooting on him."

Kevin looked bored by the suggestion. "If I thought he could make it to the goal, I would have set it up that way."

"Them's fighting words," Nicky said, grinning at Neil. "Bring it, kid."

There were only five of them, but they set up as if they had two full teams: Neil and Kevin spaced out on the half-court line, Nicky at first-fourth, and Aaron at far-fourth. Andrew acted as dealer from his place in home goal and slammed the ball all the way to the other end of the court. The second Neil heard the crack of Andrew's racquet, he started moving, pushing up before Aaron could close him out.

Kevin should have done the same and pushed up the court toward Nicky, but he stayed on the half-court line. Likewise, Aaron let the rebound go past him. Neil didn't stop to think about it but scooped the ball out of the air. He only had it for two seconds before Kevin appeared out of nowhere. Kevin smashed their racquets together so hard the ball popped one way and Neil's racquet flew the other. Neil swore at the sharp pain that stabbed up his arms.

"Keep count," Kevin said before going after the ball.

Neil scrambled for his stick and hurried after him, but Kevin's head-start was too much. Nicky tried to fend Kevin off, but Kevin faked him out and scored a few seconds later. Andrew, who should have been guarding their goal, was using his oversized racquet as a prop. He looked over his shoulder as the goal lines lit up red but didn't react otherwise.

"You could at least try," Kevin said.

Andrew thought about it, then said, "I could, couldn't I? Maybe next time!"

Nicky caught the ball and tossed it to Andrew, who caught it with his goalie glove. The four set up to go again, and Andrew started them off with another vicious serve. This time Kevin jogged to meet Nicky, leaving Neil to get past Aaron. Neil ran for the ball and Aaron fell in alongside him on his way by. As soon as Neil was close enough to catching the ball that body-checking was a legal move, Aaron slammed into him full-force. Neil stumbled, off-balance, and ground his racquet into the floor to stop himself from tripping over his own feet. Aaron caught the ball and threw it right over his head to Kevin. Andrew watched as Kevin scored again.

"What's Andrew doing?" Neil asked.

"Nothing," Aaron said, as simple as it was obvious, and they set up for another serve.

[61]

At the twenty-minute mark, Kevin checked Neil into the wall and pinned him there with a gloved hand to his chest long enough to demand, "Are you even trying?"

Neil shoved him, but Kevin was already leaving, off to grab the ball and score again.

The court seemed so much larger when he only had one teammate to rely on, and the rules that only let them carry a ball for ten steps made them rely heavily on the court's walls. Neil wasn't used to playing like this. He didn't like it and his unfamiliarity with this style only made it easier for Aaron and Kevin to completely dominate the court.

Each set forced Neil to try harder and go faster, but this wasn't Millport. His childhood experience and his speed weren't enough when facing athletes of this caliber. Neil was frustrated, then amazed, then frustrated all over again as the scrimmage wore on. He scored a couple times during the scrimmage, but his goals felt worthless when he didn't have a goalkeeper to contend with.

After forty minutes, Kevin called them to an abrupt halt and swept his racquet at the backliners. "Get out. Both of you get out right now."

"Thank God," Nicky said, and ran for the door.

Kevin waited until Aaron pulled the door closed behind them, then grabbed the grated front of Neil's helmet and dragged him toward Andrew's goal. Andrew finally took an interest in the proceedings and stood up straight. Kevin let go when Neil reached the fox paw marking the foul line.

"Ball," he said, and Andrew tossed it over. Kevin pushed it against Neil's chest until Neil took it. "You stay here and fire on Andrew until he's tired. Maybe you'll score once."

"Uh oh," Andrew said with a laugh. "This won't end well."

Kevin turned around and left, slamming the door behind him on his way out. Neil collected the bucket of balls from the north home corner where they'd stored it during their scrimmage. He set the bucket on first-fourth and went back to the foul line for his first shot.

Andrew, who hadn't lifted so much as a finger to stop Kevin from scoring on him, didn't have the same consideration for Neil. He swept his massive racquet around in one long swing and hit the ball so hard Neil heard it bounce off the away court wall behind him. Neil looked over his shoulder, then took another ball from the bucket and tried again.

Neil lost track of time after that. Swings and minutes blurred in an exhausting mix. He kept going long after his arms started burning because he didn't know how to stop. Eventually the pain faded in favor of a heavy sense of numbness. He knew Andrew should be tired by now since Andrew had such a heavy racquet and was hitting every ball like he wanted to score a home run, but Andrew didn't even slow down.

He knew he'd gone too far when he took a swing and lost his grip on his racquet. Andrew laughed as it clattered against the ground and skidded toward the goal. Andrew knocked the ball straight back at Neil, and Neil didn't have a racquet to defend himself with. He brought up his arms to block his face instinctively, but he felt that sharp smack on his forearms even through his arm guards. He stumbled back a step under the impact and shot Andrew a dirty look.

"Let's go," Andrew said. "Tick tock. I won't wait forever for you."

Neil knew it was a bad idea, but he went for his racquet anyway. Picking it up hurt, and when he tried to lift it high enough for a swing, his right arm gave a sharp spasm and he lost his grip. His stick hit the court at his feet.

"Oh no," Andrew said. "I think Neil's in trouble."

Neil crouched and reached for his racquet. It felt like his muscles were unraveling inside of him, twisting into tight balls around his elbow and wrist, but Neil wrapped his fingers around the stick and picked it up. Andrew stood his racquet up in front of him and propped his arms on top of it, waiting and watching as Neil stupidly tried another shot on goal. Neil only got his racquet shoulder height before he dropped it again. The ball rolled harmlessly away.

"Can you or can't you?" Andrew asked.

Defeat tasted sour as Neil crouched by his racquet. "I'm done."

Andrew left the goal to meet him but stopped with one foot on Neil's racquet. Neil tried to pull it out from under him, but he didn't have the strength. He was even less successful in his attempt to push Andrew off, and that hurt so much his vision crackled black.

"Get off my racquet."

"Make me?" Andrew said, spreading his arms in invitation. "Try, anyway."

"Don't tempt me."

"Such fierce words from such a little creature," Andrew said. "You're not very bright. Typical of a jock."

"Hypocrite," Neil said.

Andrew gave him a thumbs-up and pushed past Neil. Neil tried to catch himself before he tipped over, but his hand wouldn't hold his weight. He fell flat on his back and didn't even try to get up. He was too tired to care anymore, so he laid there and listened as Andrew left the court. The door banged closed behind him. Neil rolled his head to one side and watched through the walls as they left.

When he was sure they were gone he painstakingly cleaned up the court. His arms were throbbing as he peeled his uniform off, and getting dressed again was almost too much to handle.

"Damn," he whispered. He'd gone too far today in his determination to keep up with his teammates. If he couldn't control himself and take it one step at a time, there was no way he'd be able to play by the time August rolled around.

He ran back to Wymack's place, keeping his pace slower than usual, and took the stairs up to the seventh floor. The apartment door was unlocked, and Wymack was waiting for him in the hall with a can of coffee grinds in his hand.

"Kevin called ahead to say you wouldn't be on the court tomorrow and that I should entertain you with clips of past games. He said you tried to blow your arms out against Andrew. I said you weren't that stupid. Which one of us is right?"

"I might have gotten carried away," Neil said.

Wymack tossed the coffee to him. Neil caught it instinctively, but he couldn't hold onto it. It bounced off the floor at his feet and the lid popped off to spill grinds everywhere. Wymack stalked toward Neil with a snarled, "You idiot."

Retreating from a furious older man was so instinctive Neil didn't realize he'd flinched until Wymack froze. Wymack's face went almost dangerously blank and Neil dropped his gaze. He was careful not to look away from Wymack entirely. He needed to see when Wymack started moving again. He waited for Wymack to say something. After an endless, brittle silence, he realized Wymack wouldn't speak until he did.

"Today was my mistake," Neil said quietly. "It won't happen a second time."

Wymack didn't answer. He didn't come closer, either. At length he pointed at the ground in front of him. "Come here. No," he said when Neil started to reach for the mess at his feet. "Leave it."

Neil stepped over it and went to stand in front of Wymack: within arm's reach but just barely. He'd perfected that trick as a kid. He could look at anyone's arms and judge the safe distance from them in a heartbeat. If they had to move to hit him, he had enough time to dodge. Either way he wouldn't catch the full intended force of their blow.

"Look at me," Wymack said. "Right now."

Neil dragged his stare up from Wymack's chest to his face. Wymack's expression was still too blank for Neil to feel safe, but he knew better than to look away again.

[65]

"I want you to understand something," Wymack said. "I am a loud, grouchy old man. I like to yell and throw things. But I don't throw punches unless some punk is dumb enough to try me first. I have never, ever hit someone without provocation, and I'm sure as hell not going to start with you. You hear me?"

Neil didn't believe him, but he said, "Yes, Coach."

"I'm serious," Wymack said. "Don't you dare be more afraid of me than you are of Andrew."

Neil could have told him it was Wymack's age that made him such a problem, but he didn't think Wymack wanted to hear it. There was no solution to that problem. "Yes, Coach."

Wymack gestured over his shoulder and stepped aside. "I already ate, but I haven't put the leftovers away yet. I'll take care of this. You take care of you."

Neil ate to the sound of the vacuum. Wymack was in his office by the time Neil was done, and Neil retired to the couch early. He wanted to get his bag and go through his folder, but he didn't want to intrude on Wymack's space, so he stared at the ceiling until he finally fell asleep.

-

It took Neil two weeks to decide he'd never meet Kevin's standards. It got to the point where he saw Kevin's look of cool disapproval every time he blinked. Half of the time Neil didn't know what he was doing wrong and the other half he couldn't change. He clocked a faster mile than any of them, but they were better and stronger than he was. Kevin knew Neil was inexperienced, but he didn't forgive Neil for his mistakes. Neil didn't want pity, but he did want understanding. When he caved and asked Nicky for advice on how to deal with Kevin, Nicky only smiled and said, "I warned you."

It did nothing for Neil's fraying patience. Luckily being angry at himself and loathing Kevin's condescending version of coaching meant he didn't have time or energy to be afraid. Two weeks of playing with the dysfunctional group and Kevin still gave no signs of recognizing him. All Kevin cared about was

[66]

how short Neil fell on his court—and as far as Neil could tell, it was shorter and shorter by the day. Two weeks of Kevin's scornful dismissal and rude commentary wore away at Neil's resolve to take it easy. He didn't care if he blew out his arms again if it meant Kevin would stop riding him like he was an incompetent preschooler.

Everything was for Exy, from his early morning run to the hours he clocked at the gym to the afternoon scrimmages to the longer run he took in the evenings after dinner. He made loops around the campus and went up and down the stairs in the stadium. No matter what he did he was too slow, and he went to sleep in so much pain every night he could barely change for bed. By the time his third week started, he couldn't even sleep because he was too busy analyzing the day's mistakes.

One night he cast aside his blankets in disgust and left the apartment. It was pitch black out, probably somewhere around two in the morning, and it was just cool enough he should've changed out of his pajama pants. He warmed up quickly as he set off for Palmetto State. There were few street lights around Wymack's neighborhood, but when Neil reached Perimeter Road, the winding street that surrounded Palmetto State, the path was better lit.

Neil knew the way to the stadium by heart even in the dark. There were a couple cars in the parking lot, as usual, and Neil thought he saw the moving figure of a security guard in the next lot. He punched in the code for the Foxes' entrance and opened the door, then stilled with his hand halfway to the light switch. The lights were already on.

Belatedly he realized he'd passed the cousins' car. He was so used to seeing it here when they met for scrimmages he hadn't thought it out of place. He frowned over his shoulder at it, wondering if Wymack had heard him leave and called the others to check on him, then pulled the door closed and jogged for the locker room.

He checked every room but found no sign anyone was there. He stretched out in the foyer before pushing through the back door. He heard the sound of a ball ricocheting off the wall, but with the stadium seating rising up to either side of the Foxes' entry hall, he couldn't see where on the court the others were. He was almost to the inner court before he finally spotted Kevin. Kevin was alone at first-fourth with a bucket of balls, and he was systematically heaving them at the wall. Neil watched in silence, wondering what odd sort of drill he was doing. It took Kevin a dozen shots before Neil realized he was trying to rebound them all from the same spot. Kevin was honing his right-handed aim.

Watching Kevin going at it in the middle of the night, fierce and merciless, was almost enough that Neil forgave him. Kevin was more demanding of himself than he was of anyone around him. He set his standards impossibly high and tried for them with everything he had, and he didn't understand why others wouldn't do the same.

Neil was watching Kevin, but it didn't take him long to realize someone else was watching him. He didn't have to look to know who it was; the intensity of the other man's stare set his nerves on edge with its weight. He didn't turn to see where Andrew was but raised his voice enough that Andrew would hear.

"Won't you play with him?"

"No," Andrew said, somewhere to Neil's left.

Neil waited, but Andrew didn't elaborate. "I think he'd benefit more if you did."

"And?"

Neil slowly turned, dragging his gaze along the empty home bench to the seats behind it. Andrew was sitting in the first stairwell about ten steps up. He was leaning forward, arms folded across his knees, as he stared Neil down. The blank expression on his face was startling. It'd been weeks since Neil last saw him sober and he'd gotten used to Andrew's drugged mania. Neil almost accused him of violating his parole again before he remembered what time it was. Andrew had likely come off his drugs to sleep.

More interesting than Andrew's calm demeanor was the baggy t-shirt and sweatpants Andrew was wearing. Andrew wore long sleeves to pick Neil up from the airport, and Neil had only seen him in court gear since then. Now, without bulky armor and gloves in the way, Neil could finally see Andrew's trademark accessories: black bands that covered his arms from his wrists to his elbows. From what Neil heard, they were a sarcastic joke meant to help people distinguish the twins from one another. Why he had them on in the middle of the night, Neil didn't know.

He didn't have to ask. Andrew knew what he was looking at. He tucked two fingers into the band on his opposite arm and slid free a long, slim blade. Metal glinted in the overhead lights as Andrew pushed it back under the dark cloth a few seconds later.

"Is that your slow attempt at suicide or do you actually have sheaths built into those?" Neil asked.

"Yes."

"That's not the one you tried to cut Nicky with. How many knives do you carry?"

"Enough," Andrew said.

"What happens when a referee catches you with a weapon on the court?" Neil asked. "I think that's a little more serious than a red card. You'd probably get arrested, and they might even suspend our entire team until they think they can trust us again. Then what?"

"I'd grieve forever," Andrew dead-panned.

"Why do you hate this game so much?"

Andrew sighed as if Neil was being purposefully obtuse. "I don't care enough about Exy to hate it. It's just slightly less boring than living is, so I put up with it for now."

"I don't understand."

[69]

"That's not my problem."

"Isn't it fun?" Neil asked.

"Someone else asked me that same thing two years ago. Should I tell you what I told him? I said no. Something as pointless as this game is can never be fun."

"Pointless," Neil echoed. "But you have real talent."

"Flattery is uninteresting and gets you nowhere."

"I'm just stating facts. You're selling yourself short. You could be something if only you'd try."

Andrew's smile was small and cold. "You be something. Kevin says you'll be a champion. Four years and you'll go pro. Five years and you'll be Court. He promised Coach. He promised the school board. He argued until they signed off on you."

"He—what?" Neil stared at him, blood rushing in his ears as he tried to make sense of Andrew's words. Andrew had to be lying to him; Kevin couldn't have said such things about him. Kevin could barely stand to be on the same court with him as far as Neil could tell. What good did it do Andrew to say such obvious lies? Was he trying to rile Neil up?

"Then Kevin finally got the okay to sign you and you hit the ground running," Andrew said. "Curious that a man with so much potential, who has so much fun, who could 'be something' wouldn't want any of it. Why is that?"

If Andrew was telling the truth, then Kevin had definitely lied to all of them, and Neil could only guess at one reason why he'd go to such great lengths. Maybe Kevin remembered him after all and was saying whatever he had to in order to recruit Neil. But if that was so, how much did Kevin know? How much did he understand or remember about what happened eight years ago? Did he know Neil's name? Did he know what that name meant?

"You're lying," Neil said at last, because he needed that to be the truth. "Kevin hates me."

[70]

"Or you hate him," Andrew said. "I can't decide. Your loose ends aren't adding up."

"I'm not a math problem."

"But I'll still solve you."

Neil turned away without another word. Kevin was gathering his balls, finished with practice. When Kevin started for the door, Andrew moved behind Neil. Neil heard cloth rustle as Andrew stood, and Andrew's shoes tapped quietly on the stairs as he came down to inner court.

"You are a conundrum," Andrew said.

"Thank you."

"No, thank you," Andrew said as he slipped past Neil without a look back. "I need a new toy to play with."

"I'm not a toy."

"I guess we'll see."

Kevin had his helmet off as soon as the court door closed behind him. He looked right past Andrew to Neil. Neil stared back at him, looking for the truth on Kevin's face, looking for some reason behind Andrew's big words. Kevin couldn't have heard their conversation all the way out on the court, but Neil still expected him to call Neil by his real name.

Instead Kevin said, "Why are you here?"

"I wanted to practice."

"As if it will help you any."

It was rude, but it was exactly what Neil needed to hear. Andrew had lied to him. Neil could breathe a little easier as he watched Kevin set the bucket of balls on the ground at his feet. Kevin set his racquet and helmet on the home bench to undo his gloves and arm guards. Andrew took them as Kevin peeled them off, tucking the gloves under his arm and looping his fingers through the straps of the guards. He snagged Kevin's helmet by the safety grating across the front and watched Kevin collect his racquet again.

"Andrew?" Kevin asked.

[71]

"Ready already," Andrew said, and started for the locker room.

Neil didn't watch them leave. He sat on home bench and stared at the court, listening to the door close behind them. He reached over and picked a ball out of the bucket, turning it over and over in his fingers.

"Court," Neil whispered, then gave himself a violent shake.

He squeezed the ball until his fingers ached, mentally retracing his steps backward. He went to Arizona, then across Nevada to California. He remembered the black sands beach along California's lost coast where his mother finally gave up the fight. He hadn't even realized she'd been injured so badly after running into his father in Seattle. She'd bled most of the way through Oregon, but he hadn't thought it was serious. He hadn't known she was bleeding out on the inside, a kidney and her liver ruptured, her intestines bruised beyond repair.

He didn't know when she figured it out, if she'd known by Portland that something was seriously wrong but was too scared to stop or if she hadn't seen her death coming until they crossed the California border and she started losing consciousness. She should have gone to a hospital, but she'd turned them down the treacherous path to the lost coast instead. They stopped six feet from the tide and she made him repeat every promise she'd ever dragged out of him: don't look back, don't slow down, and don't trust anyone. Be anyone but himself, and never be anyone for too long.

By the time Neil understood she was saying goodbye, it was too late.

She died gasping for one more breath, panting with something that might have been words or his name or fear. Neil could still feel her fingernails digging into his arms as she fought not to slip away, and the memory left him shaking all over. Her abdomen felt like stone when he touched her, swollen and hard. He tried pulling her from her seat only once, but the sound of her dried blood ripping off the vinyl like Velcro killed him.

He burned the car instead, dumping every emergency case of gasoline they'd bought along the way onto the seats so it'd scorch her down to the bone. He hadn't cried when the flames caught, and he hadn't flinched when he pulled her cooling bones out. He filled her backpack with everything that was left of her, carried her two miles down the beach, and buried her as deep as he could. By the time he found the highway again he was numb with shock, and he lasted another day before he fell to his knees on the roadside and puked his guts out. Somehow he'd made it to San Francisco, but he only stayed a day before setting off for Millport. He took it one step and one mile and one day at a time because anything else was too much for him to handle in his grief.

Neil stared at the court in front of him and swallowed once, twice, against the nausea that was crawling up his throat. This was why Wymack's contract, Kevin's lofty ambitions, and Andrew's words meant nothing in the end. It didn't matter what they offered or promised him. Neil wasn't like them. He was nothing and no one, and he always would be. Court wasn't for people like him. He'd take what he could learn and enjoy it while he could, but this was a dream he'd have to wake up from eventually. Wanting anything more than that would just make it harder to walk away.

He dropped the ball back into the bucket and went up to the locker room. After making sure Kevin and Andrew really were gone, he changed into his uniform and headed to the court for drills. He wore himself out, putting every thought he had into the moves he was making so he couldn't think about the Foxes or Court or his past. When he was finally done and had cleaned everything up, it was after dawn. He was too tired to go back to Wymack's and knew he'd just get back when Wymack was watching the morning news, so he showered and dressed and fell asleep on one of the Foxes' couches.

[73]

He woke up again around noon and headed back to the apartment. His keys got him into the building, but Wymack's door was unlocked again. Neil considered bringing up Wymack's lax security with the coach and then forgot all about it. Even with the door just a couple inches open he could hear furious voices arguing. He put an ear to the crack and held his breath, straining to make out the words.

"Damn it, Kevin, I said sit down!"

"I won't!" Kevin shot back. If Wymack hadn't said his name already, Neil wouldn't have recognized his voice. Kevin's voice was twisted with fear and panic. "How could you let him do this?"

"I don't have any say in this and you know it. Hey!"

There was a hard thud as bodies hit the wall, and Neil took advantage of the struggle to slip inside. He closed the door as quietly as he could, but his stealth was a wasted effort. It sounded like Wymack and Kevin were knocking over everything Wymack owned, and Neil winced at the sharp sound of shattering glass.

"Look at me," Wymack demanded. "Look at me, god damn you, and breathe."

"I warned Andrew he was going to come for me. I told him!"

"It doesn't matter. You signed a contract with me."

"He could pay off my scholarship in a heartbeat. You know he would. He'd pay you off and take me home and I—I can't go back there. I can't, I can't, I won't, I—I have to go. I have to go. I should go now, before he has to come for me. Maybe he'll forgive me if I go back. If I make him hunt me down any more than I have already he'll kill me for sure."

"Shut up," Wymack said. "You're not going anywhere."

"I can't tell Riko no!"

"Then don't say a word," Wymack said. "Keep your mouth shut and let me and Andrew do the talking. Yes, Andrew. Don't tell me you forgot about that psycho. I've got Betsy's number on

[74]

speed dial. Want me to put you through to her office so you can talk to him? Want to tell him you're thinking about going back?"

Silence followed that. Neil waited, holding his breath, until Wymack spoke again. He was quieter this time, but concern made his voice more gruff than comforting.

"I'm not letting you go back there," Wymack said. "Nothing says I have to. Your contract says you belong to me. He can send us all the money he wants, but you have to sign off on it before it means anything, and you're not going to. Okay? You let me and Andrew worry about Riko fuck-face. You worry about getting your game and team where they need to be. You promised me you could get us past the fourth match this year."

"That was before," Kevin said, miserable. "This is now."

"The ERC is giving us until June before they break the news. They saw how many security issues we had over your transfer, so they're waiting until everyone's here where I can keep an eye on them. I told you because you need to know, but I need you to keep it from Andrew until then. Tell me you can see Andrew today and not completely freak out."

"Andrew will figure it out. He's not stupid."

"Then you have to be the better liar," Wymack said in a hard voice. "The ERC is looking for a reason to take him away from us, and you know they won't give him back. Then where will you be?"

They were quiet for so long Neil thought they might be done. Finally Kevin said, "Give me your phone."

"If you think I'm going to let you use my phone to call him, you—"

"Jean," Kevin cut in. "I have to call Jean. I have to hear him say it."

Apparently that was an acceptable compromise, because Wymack stopped arguing. Neil looked over his shoulder, wondering if he should make a break for it. He didn't know what was going on, but it had to be awful if it'd brought Kevin this far off his condescending perch. He was debating how quietly he

[75]

could slip out the door when Kevin spoke. Kevin's bleak tone brought Neil up short, as did the French Kevin was speaking.

"Tell me it isn't true," Kevin said. "Tell me he didn't."

Neil couldn't hear the answer, but the sharp slap of the phone snapping shut again said it wasn't the one Kevin wanted. The couch creaked under someone's body weight and Neil imagined Kevin sinking onto the cushion in despair.

"Wait here," Wymack said, and a few seconds later he stepped into the hallway. He started a little when he spotted Neil at the end of the hallway but said nothing. Neil watched as he disappeared into the kitchen. He recognized the sound of Wymack's liquor cabinet by now, the click of the lock and the soft clink of the glass doors. Wymack returned with a handle of vodka and dropped it off with Kevin.

"Drink," he said from out of sight. "I'll be right back."

Wymack came back to the hallway. Neil pointed over his shoulder at the door in a question. Wymack followed Neil out of his apartment and closed the door behind him. Neil looked down the hall for stray eavesdroppers, but the other doors were closed.

"I wasn't going to tell anyone else until June," Wymack said. "How much did you hear?"

"Kevin's having a nervous breakdown," Neil said. "I don't know why."

"Edgar Allan put in a transfer request with the ERC and it was approved this morning. They're part of the southeastern district effective June 1st."

It took a minute for Wymack's words to make sense. When it clicked, Neil's stomach bottomed out. It'd been hard enough facing Kevin in Arizona. How could Neil risk meeting Riko too? Just because Kevin didn't remember Neil didn't mean Riko wouldn't either. Neil didn't want to find out the hard way if Riko had the better memory of the two.

"That's impossible," Neil said.

"Not really. They're the only NCAA Exy team in West Virginia, so it was as easy as a vote and a couple signatures."

[76]

"That's impossible," Neil said again. "We can't play the Ravens. What sane board pits the best and worst teams against each other?"

"One that knows there's a lot to gain from it," Wymack said. "Kevin's transfer created a lot of backlash, but it also generated a lot of new interest in Exy. The ERC wants to follow it through to the natural conclusion: Kevin and Riko's reunion on the court, but this time as rivals for the first time ever. It doesn't matter who wins. They know what publicity and funding they can score with such a move."

"I can't play against Riko," Neil said. "I'm not ready."

"Riko isn't your problem," Wymack said. "Leave him to Matt. Your problem is getting around his backliners and goalkeeper."

"Can't you protest?" Neil said. "They're setting us up for a match everyone knows we can't win."

"I could, but it won't do any good," Wymack said. "The ERC doesn't do take-backs, especially when it means spurning a Moriyama. There's something you need to know about the Moriyamas, but I didn't want to have this conversation with you yet. I wanted you settled a bit more, or at least hoped you'd get to know the team better before I dropped this on you. Now that the ERC is forcing my hand, I don't have a lot of choices.

"What I'm going to tell you is an open secret. That is, we know it," he waved a finger in a circle, likely meaning the Foxes, "but no one outside our team does. It has to stay that way no matter what, do you understand? People could get hurt if this gets out. People could die."

Neil waved over his shoulder at the apartment doors. "What about them?"

"I'm the only one on this floor," Wymack said. "They built this complex around the same time we started construction on the Foxhole Court. Thought our team would be something and people would want to live in the area to be close to the stadium for games. Then we couldn't perform, so the apartments didn't

[77]

fill. The lower floors are pretty full, and the middle floors get rented out during football season, but top two floors are pretty bare. And no, you can't break into any of them, so don't even think it."

Neil let that accusation go without comment. "You're stalling, Coach."

Wymack folded his arms across his chest and stared at Neil. "Do you know why Kevin came to Palmetto State?"

"He broke his hand," Neil said. "He couldn't play, so he transferred here as an assistant coach. I assumed he was following Andrew."

"I brought him here," Wymack said. "He showed up at my hotel room at winter banquet with his hand a bloody mess. He didn't want us to notify the Ravens or take him to a hospital, so Abby bandaged him up as best she could and I put him on the bus back to South Carolina with us."

"That doesn't make sense," Neil said. "How'd he get from the ski resort to your hotel?"

"He wasn't in the mountains," Wymack said.

"But he broke his hand in a skiing accident," Neil said.

"Bullshit," Wymack said. "It wasn't an accident."

Neil stared blankly at him, and Wymack gave a short nod before explaining.

"The ERC had an end-of-year meeting a few days before the southeastern district's winter banquet. The NCAA advisors got everyone talking about Riko and Kevin. They had some concerns about the season, they said. They were sure Riko was holding Kevin back, that Kevin was selling himself short so as not to outshine Riko on the court. They wanted to know if it was Coach Moriyama's doing. In response Moriyama pitted Riko and Kevin against each other.

"Riko won," Wymack said, "but I'm thinking he didn't get it fair and square. If he had, maybe things would have turned out differently. As soon as Coach Moriyama dismissed them for the night Riko broke Kevin's hand."

[78]

It was like getting punched in the gut. "What?"

Wymack dragged his thumb along the back of his hand, tracing the path of Kevin's injury. "Kevin doesn't talk about his time at Evermore, but I could tell it wasn't the first time Riko or Moriyama laid a hand on him. It was just the first time Kevin was smart enough to pack his bags and walk away. So much for family, hm?"

"I don't believe in family."

"Neither do I."

He meant it. Neil finally understood that look Wymack sent him in Millport, that perfect understanding that undid Neil's defenses. Neil searched his face, looking for the story behind that exhaustion. Whatever broke Wymack happened so long ago he wasn't even bitter over it anymore, but he was definitely still cracked if he poured so much time into the Foxhole Court.

"Why doesn't anyone else know what Riko did?" Neil asked.

"Because Riko is a Moriyama," Wymack said tiredly. "This is where it starts getting messy."

He thought for a minute, then held up his index fingers. "The Moriyama family is broken in half: the main family and the branch family. The main consists of the first-born sons and the branch is for everyone else. Coach Moriyama—Tetsuji—heads the branch family and his older brother Kengo heads the main. Kengo has two sons, Ichirou and Riko. Because Ichirou was born first, he stayed with Kengo in the main family. Riko was born second, so Tetsuji became his legal guardian and Riko became part of the branch family. Follow?"

"I think so."

"The families are estranged," Wymack said. "Kengo and the main family are up in New York City, where Kengo is CEO of an international trading company. One day he'll pass the business to Ichirou. Tetsuji and Riko get a kickback of the profits, but they're considered unimportant and have no say in any business decisions. That's how Tetsuji had the freedom to study in Japan and develop Exy. So long as he doesn't do anything to damage the family's reputation, he is free to do what he likes, and what he likes is to create the most awful and powerful team in the nation. This all is public knowledge."

Neil looked past Wymack at the door, thinking of Kevin's freak-out. "And the truth?"

"The real Moriyama family business is murder."

Neil shot a quick look at him. Wymack held up a hand to ward off any questions, his expression grim. "The Moriyamas are an immigrated yakuza group. Do you know what the yakuza are? They're Japanese mafia. Kengo's father brought the group to America a couple decades ago and set up shop up north. I don't know what all they're involved in and I don't want to know. I don't know how much even Kevin knows, since he's attached to Riko and the branch family, but Kevin knows the main family uses Raven games as a cover for big meetings. So many people go in and out of Edgar Allan that it's a convenient way to bring in their far-flung contacts. They've got VIP lounges along the upper floors where they make deals."

"They're a gang," Neil said slowly.

Wymack nodded, watching him carefully and waiting to see how Neil took it. Neil barely noticed the attention. He was thinking back to the last time he'd seen Kevin and Riko together. He remembered scrimmaging and arguing footwork with them. Their game came to an abrupt halt when they were called upstairs. If Neil closed his eyes now he could remember every detail of the room they went to, from its floor-to-ceiling tinted windows to the heavy conference table dominating it. The floor was carpeted, but someone had laid a tarp down on top of it to catch all the blood.

Neil finally knew where he'd been and why. He'd never understood how they went from Exy practices to murder or why Kevin and Riko were there too. But if the Moriyamas were a gang, it made sense. Neil's father worked out of Baltimore and held the eastern ports with an iron grip. His territory's western border would have ended at West Virginia. In that sense he was Tetsuji Moriyama's neighbor, and that would have brought him to Kengo's attention. Neil's father and Riko's father were business partners; that's why Neil was allowed to practice at Edgar Allan's stadium.

Wymack interpreted his long silence as fear. "I'm telling you this because everyone else here already knows the story from Kevin, but don't worry about the yakuza. Like I said, Kengo and Ichirou mostly keep to New York and couldn't give a flying fuck what Tetsuji and Riko do. The only way it's relevant to us is explaining why Tetsuji and Riko are violent and rotten. They have a lot of power behind their name and a rather twisted view of their place in the world. And we happen to have something of theirs."

"Kevin," Neil said.

"I'd hoped they'd thrown him away," Wymack said. "Everyone said Kevin would never play again. Edgar Allan had to release Kevin from his school contract because of the severity of his injuries and Tetsuji didn't argue when I took Kevin on as an assistant coach. I thought they were ready to let him go. But Tetsuji didn't take Kevin in out of the goodness of his heart. He raised Kevin to be a star. He put a lot of time and money into Kevin's development on the court. As far as Tetsuji is considered, Kevin is valuable property. Any profit Kevin makes is rightfully the Moriyamas'."

"But Kevin's handicapped."

"He's still a name," Wymack said.

Neil's head was spinning as he tried to sort it all out. "He wants Kevin to transfer back?"

"If he wanted Kevin to transfer, he'd just say so," Wymack said.

"Kevin wouldn't really go back," Neil said, disbelieving. "Not after what Riko did."

Wymack gave him a pitying look. "Tetsuji never formally adopted Kevin. Do you know why? Moriyamas don't believe in

[81]

outsiders or equals. Tetsuji took Kevin in and took over his training, but he also gave Kevin to Riko—literally. Kevin isn't human to them. He's a project. He's a pet, and it's Riko's name on his leash. The fact he ran away is a miracle. If Tetsuji called tomorrow and told him to come home, Kevin would. He knows what Tetsuji would do to him if he refused. He'd be too afraid to say no."

Neil thought he'd be sick. He didn't want to hear anymore of this; he'd already heard too much. He wanted to run until it all started making sense in his head, or at least until the ice left his veins. "Then why go through all the trouble of changing districts?"

"The Moriyamas are ready to cash in on their investment," Wymack said. "No one honestly expects Kevin to make a comeback, but he signed with us to play. His arrogance is inspiring, and this year he's still a star. If he can't keep up and perform, the fans and critics will move on and forget about him. Tetsuji thinks he'll burn out, so he has to seize the moment now.

"Our teams are going to make a fortune this season. People are going to be hounding us every step of the way and gambling on our games. There'll be TV spots and merchandise and all kinds of publicity stunts. Tetsuji is pitting Riko and Kevin against each other knowing how it'll end. He'll put it all on the table and let his Ravens destroy us on the court. Rake in the winnings, establish Riko as the superior player forever, and relegate Kevin to the has-beens."

Neil swallowed hard. "What if Coach Moriyama told him to stop playing?"

Wymack was quiet for an endless minute, then said, "Kevin only had the strength to leave because Riko destroyed his hand. That was finally one injustice too many. Because of that I'd like to think Kevin would defy Tetsuji, but it's just as likely we'd never see him with a racquet again. But the day Kevin stops playing forever is the day he dies. He has nothing else. He

[82]

wasn't raised to have anything else. Do you understand? We cannot lose to the Ravens this year. Kevin won't survive it."

"We can't win against them," Neil said. "We're the worst team in the nation."

"Then it's time to stop being the worst," Wymack said. "It's time to fly."

"You don't really think we can," Neil said.

"If you didn't think you could, what are you doing here? You wouldn't have signed the contract if you'd already given up on yourself." Wymack half-turned away. "I need to make sure Kevin's not cutting his wrists open in there. It's probably best if he doesn't see you right now. I can call Abby to come get you if you want to hang out with the others, but I need you to keep this a secret from your teammates until June. I need time to figure out how we're going to handle this season."

"I won't say anything," Neil said, taking a couple steps back. "And don't worry about me. I'll go for a run or something."

"Kevin should be out of here by four," Wymack said. "That's when Andrew's done with Betsy, so Nicky will pick him up on his way over to her office."

Neil nodded and left, taking the stairs back down to the ground level.

Neil thought it would be awful if Kevin remembered the boy with the murderous father, but this was worse. This was Kevin maybe remembering that boy when Kevin belonged to an equally horrific family. Neil didn't remember the Moriyamas, but they'd definitely remember him if they'd done business with his father. The Butcher of Baltimore wasn't a man easily forgotten. Neither was his wife, who'd stolen five million dollars the night she ran away with the Butcher's only son. The Butcher turned his people inside-out for years hunting them down. All of his contacts would have heard of it.

Somewhere the ERC was reworking and finalizing a schedule that put the Moriyamas in Neil's near future. Neil

[83]

would quit before that match. He had no choice. He'd play up until their game against the Ravens and then run. If he was lucky, the match would come at the end of the fall season so he wouldn't jeopardize the striker line too much by taking off.

It was stupid and suicidal to stay even that long. Neil knew he should go now, before he met his teammates or the ERC publicized his name or he ever stepped on a court with Kevin Day at his side. It'd seemed an acceptable risk before, since none of his father's people were into sports. The chance of one of them seeing him on TV during a match was negligible so long as Kevin didn't figure him out and give him away. Now that he knew who the Moriyamas were and knew they would be watching him, it made absolutely no sense to stay.

Neil had grown up wondering why Kevin and Riko were in that room eight years ago and how they'd overcome it. He'd wondered why their luck and circumstances were so different that they could become international stars while Neil's life spiraled so quickly out of control. He'd hated and worshipped them all his life, jealous of their successes and desperate for them to excel. Now it seemed he'd been wrong all along; Kevin hadn't escaped either.

No matter what they did or who they became, maybe they never would.

Neil shoved the stairwell door open so forcefully it banged against the wall and was running before he was even halfway across the lobby. He hit full speed before he reached the street, going so fast he was nearly falling over, but he couldn't outrun his thoughts.

CHAPTER FIVE

The Foxes weren't scheduled to start their practices until Monday, June 10th, but they were required to move into campus the day before so they had time to get settled in the athletes' dormitory. Neil found their estimated arrival times on a list hanging on Wymack's fridge. The first of them wasn't expected to arrive until two in the afternoon and the last not until five. Neil was impatient to have the whole team together at last. Once they were here, Kevin would have an entire team to yell at and would have to leave Neil alone.

Kevin was successful so far in keeping his cool in front of Andrew. Neil attributed it to years of smiling at the press and pretending things were fine when he was living with abusive gangster rejects. That stress needed an outlet, though, and Neil was the most convenient target. The two weeks between the ERC's vote and the official start of summer practices were so hard to tolerate that Neil almost learned to hate both Exy and Kevin. Kevin had gone from impossible to please to completely horrible to be around. For the most part, the cousins let Kevin do as he wished with Neil and pretended there was nothing wrong with it.

Neil was much better at instigating fights than winning them, but it'd be worth losing if he could just put a fist through Kevin's face once. Starting a fight was too out of character for who he portrayed "Neil" to be, though. As much as Neil hated coming across as a pushover, he didn't have a choice. He couldn't let Kevin or Andrew see the real him. So he gritted his teeth and tried as hard as he could to behave.

Now he only had to survive a few more hours. He and his duffel bag caught a ride with Wymack to the stadium, where

Wymack collected a package of dorm keys for the team. Neil took his and the paperwork regarding appropriate dormitory behavior. He skimmed over it before signing all the dotted lines. Wymack traded the papers for a school catalogue. Neil had missed the athletes' early registration window because he signed so late, so he'd have to register with the rest of the freshmen class in August. Neil wasn't in any rush; he still didn't know what he was supposed to declare his major as.

He took the catalogue to the Foxes' lounge and curled up in one of the chairs to flip through it. He knew he should just pick one at random, since he wouldn't even last the semester here, but it was interesting to see how many options Palmetto had. He toyed with the idea of studying something outrageous, but he was too practical to commit. If he wanted something useful, there was only one obvious choice.

Foreign languages were the keys to freedom he couldn't live without. Neil was fluent in German. He was second-best at French, thanks to eight months in France and ten months in Montreal. His grasp on them was fading with disuse, though he watched and read foreign news online to keep from losing them entirely. Neil could ask the cousins for help with German, but he didn't want them to know he understood their private conversations. How much French Kevin knew, Neil wasn't sure, but he didn't want to spend more time with Kevin than he had to.

He perused the modern languages section, debating. There were five languages available as majors and another three that could be minored in. The smart choice was to go with Spanish. Neil's Spanish had never been good and it was long gone by now, washed out by the German and French that followed. If he could pick it up again, it opened up a world of opportunities in the southern hemisphere.

He wasted an hour going through the list of requisite courses, looking up class times, and figuring out an ideal schedule. As soon as he thought he had a couple classes nailed down, he found a timing conflict and had to backtrack and start over. The problem was in how much time Neil needed open for practices. When the school year started the Foxes would meet for two hours in the morning and for five hours in the afternoon. Neil also needed to fit in the five weekly hours of tutoring time Palmetto required of all their athletes. It took him six drafts before he found a schedule that worked.

He checked the clock, saw he still had half an hour to kill, and considered running laps. He'd just gotten up when Abby walked in.

Neil had seen Abby a couple times this summer, mostly when Wymack was feeling too lazy to cook and wanted Abby to do it for him. Neil never sought her company of his own volition, since seeing her meant seeing Andrew's lot. How she could stand having them under her roof, he didn't know.

"Hey, Neil," Abby said. "You're a little early for the meeting."

"Coach won't let me into Fox Tower until Matt gets here."

She checked her watch. "He'll be here before you know it. Since you've got time to spare, we might as well get your physical over with."

"Physical?"

"Just a general check-up: weight, height, all that good stuff. We have to do it today instead of tomorrow because there's blood work involved. I can't let you on the court until you've slept it off. When's the last time you saw a doctor?"

"A long time ago."

"Don't like doctors?"

"Doctors don't like me. Is it necessary?"

"You're not playing until I sign off on you, so yes," Abby said, unlocking the medical room door and pushing it open. She flicked on the light on her way inside, seemingly oblivious to the way Neil hadn't moved. It took her a couple minutes before she came looking for him. "Sometime today, preferably. I've got a lot of you to get through."

Neil eased off the chair, grabbed his bag, and went into her office. He left his duffel on the ground at his feet and sat on the bed. The first part of Abby's test was easy like she'd said it would be. He weighed in and let her run through a series of tests from reflexes to blood pressure. She took two vials of blood from his left arm, labeled them, and locked them in a drawer. Then she motioned at him and said, "Shirt off."

Neil stared at her. "Why?"

"I can't check track marks through cotton, Neil."

"I don't do drugs."

"Good on you," Abby said. "Keep it that way. Now take it off."

Neil looked past her at the closed door and said nothing. Abby looked at him and said nothing either. After five minutes of this, she was the first to give in. "I want to make this as painless as possible, but I can't help you if you can't help me. Tell me why you won't take off your shirt."

Neil looked for a delicate way to say it. The best he managed was, "I'm not okay."

She put a finger to his chin and turned his face back toward her. "Neil, I work for the Foxes. None of you are okay. Chances are I've seen a lot worse than whatever it is you're trying to hide from me."

Neil's smile was humorless. "I hope not."

"Trust me," Abby said. "I'm not going to judge you. I'm here to help, remember? I'm your nurse now. That door is closed, and it comes with a lock. What happens in here stays in here."

"You won't tell Coach?"

"This isn't his business," Abby said, gesturing between them with her free hand. "I only report to him if I think it'll affect your performance on the court or if you're breaking the law and I need an intervention."

Neil stared at her, wondering if he could believe her and knowing he didn't have a choice. His skin was already crawling

[88]

in anticipation of her reaction. "You can't ask me about them," he said at last. "I won't talk to you about it. Okay?"

"Okay," Abby agreed easily. "But know that when you want to, I'm here, and so is Betsy."

Neil wasn't going to tell that psychiatrist a thing, but he nodded. Abby dropped her hand, and Neil pulled his shirt over his head before he could lose his nerve.

Abby thought she was ready. Neil knew she wouldn't be, and he was right. Her mouth parted on a silent breath and her expression went blank. She wasn't fast enough to hide her flinch, and Neil saw her shoulders go rigid with tension. He stared at her face as she stared at him, watching her gaze sweep over the brutal marks of a hideous childhood.

It started at the base of his throat, a looping scar curving down over his collarbone. A pucker with jagged edges was a finger-width away, courtesy of a bullet that hit him right on the edge of his Kevlar vest. A shapeless patch of pale skin from his left shoulder to his navel marked where he'd jumped out of a moving car and torn himself raw on the asphalt. Faded scars crisscrossed here and there from his life on the run, either from stupid accidents, desperate escapes, or conflicts with local lowlifes. Along his abdomen were larger overlapping lines from confrontations with his father's people while on the run. His father wasn't called the Butcher for nothing; his weapon of choice was a cleaver. All of his men were well-versed in knife-fighting, and more than one of them had tried to stick Neil like a pig.

And there on his right shoulder was the perfect outline of half a hot iron. Neil didn't remember what he'd said or done to irritate his father so much. Likely it was after another one of the local police's visits. The police and feds had nothing concrete to pin on his father, but they came around as often as they could in hopes of finding something. Neil's job was to stay quiet and still until they left again. Neil guessed he'd twitched a little too much, because as soon as they were gone his father ripped the

[89]

iron from his mother's hands and smacked Neil with it. Neil still remembered how his skin looked as it peeled off with the metal.

Neil twisted his hands in his shirt and lifted his arms, baring his forearms to her. "Do I have track marks?"

"Neil," Abby said softly.

"Do I or don't I?"

Abby's mouth thinned to a hard line as she forcibly redirected her attention back to his physical. The second she gave him the okay to put his shirt on again, Neil yanked it over his head. Abby filled out the rest of her forms in silence.

"We're done," Abby said. "Neil—"

"No." Neil grabbed his duffel and escaped her office as quickly as he could.

He half-expected her to follow him, but Abby stayed in her office and left him alone. Neil flipped through his catalogue, trying to work off his agitation. He wanted a cigarette so bad his fingers ached. He wanted something that would make him feel a little less alone. He shoved his catalogue aside again and checked himself, making sure everything was covered under his shirt. All of his shirts were at least a size too big, since baggy clothes hid his scars better, but Neil still felt raw and exposed.

Neil shoved the catalogue into his bag, hooked the strap over his shoulder, and went down the hall with every intention of waiting the rest of the afternoon in the inner court. He made it as far as the foyer when a door opened behind him. Neil hesitated at the exit and looked back as someone stepped into the lounge at the other end of the hall.

The new arrival seemed startlingly tall compared to the Foxes Neil had put up with so far this summer. Nicky was almost six feet and Kevin was an inch or two taller, but this man looked halfway to seven. Part of the illusion Neil blamed on his black hair, which he'd gelled up in short spikes around his skull.

The hairstyle was also what kept Neil from recognizing him immediately, as the man hadn't sported such a brazen look last year. By the time he put a name to the man's face, the

[90]

stranger had crossed the hall to him and put a hand out. Neil accepted his hand and did his best to keep his stare on Matthew Boyd's face. It was difficult; Matt's short sleeves did nothing to hide the faded but obvious track marks on both arms. No wonder Abby was so adamant about that part of the check-up.

"Matt Boyd," the man said, giving Neil's hand a firm shake. "I'm a junior this year, and I'm the Foxes' starting backliner. You must be Neil."

Neil was saved the trouble of answering. Wymack had heard Matt's arrival and he came out of his office to hurl a key ring at Matt's head. The jangling got Matt's attention and he turned in time to get smacked on the cheek with the keys. Matt snagged the ring as it fell and made a face at his coach.

"Jesus, Coach, good to see you too. When did we move past a simple 'hello'?"

"I could say the same for you, stomping past my open door like that without so much as a by-your-leave," Wymack said.

"You looked busy."

"I'm always busy. That's never stopped you pricks from interrupting me before."

Matt shrugged and looked around. "Where are the monsters?"

"Probably razing Fox Tower to the ground as we speak. You met Neil?"

"I was trying." Matt sent Neil a knowing look. "I can't believe you put up with Coach this long. How did you survive?"

"I wasn't around much," Neil said.

"Neil's been training with Kevin and Andrew every day," Wymack said.

"Oh god," Matt said with feeling. "You're awful, Coach."

"He knows it," Abby said, stepping in her office doorway and propping her shoulder against the doorframe. "Welcome back, Matt. Did you have a safe drive?"

"Safe enough, but I drank so much coffee I probably won't sleep for a week." Matt looked to Neil again. "Already settled?"

"Coach wouldn't let me move in without you," Neil said.

"Way to keep him waiting," Wymack said. "Take him and get out of here."

"Come on," Matt said. "I'll swing you past Coach's place to get your things."

"This is it," Neil said.

Matt looked at his bag, then around the room for suitcases that didn't exist. He flicked a questioning look at Wymack, who shook his head, and turned back on Neil. "That's a joke, right? You should see how much I crammed into my truck—and how much I had to leave behind—and you expect to last a year with one bag? That thing have magical expanding powers I don't know about or something?"

"You get to take him shopping later this week," Wymack said. "On your time, not mine. I'm sick of seeing him in the same clothes over and over. Just let me know when you're going and I'll give you the p-card so we can expense it."

Neil was mildly offended. "I have money."

"Good for you," Wymack said. "I thought you two were leaving."

"Didn't miss you at all," Matt said, but there was no heat in his voice. "Let's go, Neil."

Matt's truck was parked two spaces down from Wymack's and Abby's cars, a monstrous blue thing that looked like it could eat a hole through the stadium without slowing. Matt hadn't been joking about how many things he owned: the truck bed was stuffed with furniture and only a dozen taut cords kept anything from falling out. The back seats in the extended cab were also full of suitcases and crates. Matt took a backpack out of the passenger seat and tossed it in back with the rest so Neil could fit. The truck came to life with a quiet roar Neil felt more than heard, and the radio blasted to life a half-second later. Matt cut it off and yanked his door closed.

"We're not all bad, just so you know," Matt said as he pulled out of the parking lot. "Dan hated that your first impression of us would be the do-nothings. She was pretty sure you wouldn't stick around long enough to meet the rest of us. She thought about coming back to campus early to be a buffer, but Coach told her not to bother. Said you had to deal with them eventually."

"They're interesting," Neil said.

"Interesting," Matt repeated. "That's the tamest description of them I've ever heard. Seriously, though. If they give you any trouble, just let me know. I'll kick Kevin's ass for you."

"Thanks, but I can handle them on my own."

"I thought I could handle them, too." Matt raked a hand through his hair, skewing his spikes every which way. "Andrew made it pretty clear he wasn't going to be handled by anyone. You change your mind, you know where to find me. My offer's good through graduation."

Neil wouldn't need Matt's help, but he said, "Thanks."

Matt pointed out the windshield. "There it is."

Most of Palmetto State's buildings, offices, and dormitories were inside the giant loop known as Perimeter Road. Fox Tower was one of the few exceptions, but only because a stray hill forced Perimeter to hug the campus green near the clock tower. The hill might have been a nice spot for students to picnic between classes, except someone thought to build the athletes' dormitory on the peak. It stood four stories tall and had its own computer lab and parking lot.

The parking lot was out back, and Andrew's car was the only one parked there. Matt skipped all the lined spaces in favor of pulling up at the curb. It took both of them to unload the truck onto the sidewalk, and Neil waited with the pile while Matt parked. Getting everything inside and up to the third floor was a nightmare, especially since several pieces of furniture wouldn't fit in the elevator. The stairwell was too narrow to make it easy on them, and the handrail kept getting in their way as they tried to turn corners at the landings. It was made only more difficult by the serious height difference between them and the fact Neil had his duffel bag on him. He didn't want to leave it either in their room or Matt's truck, so he carried it up and down on every trip.

Their suite was room 321. A kitchenette was off to one side right inside the door and the front room was a spacious living room. Three bare desks lined the walls, waiting to be covered in schoolwork and books. A short hall dead-ended at the bathroom and branched off into the bedroom. Two beds were bunked against one wall and a third bed was raised chest-height against the other to fit shelving and dressers under it. There was only one closet, but hanging dividers hung off the empty pole.

It was trial and error to make everything fit. Eventually they pushed all the desks to the wall by the window, almost close enough to be touching, so Matt could put his couch against one long wall and a coffee table in the middle of the living room. He'd taken the shelves out of his entertainment center for the drive, but most of the bolts were still in place. It took only a couple minutes to put it together again, and Matt promptly filled it with a TV and game systems. Neil left him to organize his movies and went back to the bedroom.

The mattresses were bare, which meant Neil was going to have to buy sheets. He hadn't slept in a real bed since he left Seattle. He'd broken into cars to borrow backseats in California, slept on the bus to Nevada, and dozed in passenger seats while hitchhiking with truckers to Arizona. His house in Millport had been unfurnished, so he'd slept on the floor with shirts as his pillow. Wymack's couch was the nicest thing he'd had in over a year, but now he had a bed.

Sleeping alone would be disorienting. He'd gotten in the habit of sleeping in his mother's bed, as her paranoia didn't want him out of her reach. They slept back to back, guarding each other, the guns under their pillows uncomfortable but reassuring lumps.

"I'm heading out to get Dan and Renee from the airport," Matt said from the doorway. "Want to come with?"

[94]

"I've got to run by the store," Neil said. "Do you care which bed you sleep in?"

"I'm too tall to sleep up top," Matt said, "and Seth keeps weird hours, so unless you've got a thing with heights you're better off in the loft. I'll be back in an hour or so, and you can hitch a ride with us to the court when the girls are settled. Dan won't believe you're okay until she sees you with her own eyes."

"I'll be back by then," Neil said, so Matt left.

Neil waited until the door closed behind him before shrugging his bag off his shoulder. He walked laps around the dorm room again, this time with a sinking feeling in his gut. His locker was on the other side of campus, and Wymack's locked cabinet was even further away. The only quasi-secure place in the entire room was his dresser, and that was just because the drawers closed all the way. Nothing had a lock on it except the front door.

He could bring the duffel with him, seeing how it was only two miles to the store, but he needed to buy so many things he knew he couldn't carry it all back. He ran through the timing in his head instead, adding up Matt's drive to the airport, the wait for the girls' luggage to show up at the belt, and the trek back. Even if Matt was only gone an hour, he and Neil should get back to the dormitory around the same time. The suite's lock was going to have to be enough for now. Neil could look for a better solution at the store.

He dug his wallet out of the duffel's end pocket and stuffed the bag into his dresser's bottom drawer. It barely fit, but at least it closed. He pressed his fingers to the wood for a second, looking for the courage to walk away, and triple-checked the lock on his way out.

The next room down was the girls', and the cousins' room was after that. Nicky was lounging in his doorway. He smiled when he saw Neil.

"Hey, stranger," Nicky said. "What'd you think of Matt?"

"He seems fine," Neil said, not slowing on his way by.

[95]

"He is fine," Nicky called after him with a laugh.

Neil took the stairs down, checked his watch at the front door, and ran to the store. The conditioned air felt like heaven on his warm skin as he paced the aisles, taking what he needed without lingering long over the details. He stocked up on everything from bed sheets to hair dye and groceries, and then backtracked for a messenger bag. His duffel bag was the perfect size for everything he owned, which meant there was no spare room for schoolbooks and notepads. He checked the small hardware section, didn't find a lock he thought he could install on anything in his room, and went back to the office and school supplies.

At the end of the row were fireproof safes: too small to fit his bag, definitely too small to fit his clothes, but large enough for what he needed to hide most. Neil lugged one with him to checkout and piled everything onto the belt. The safe made his trip back to the dormitory more than a little awkward, since it was too heavy fit into a bag without tearing it.

He knew he made good time, but the girls' flight must have landed ahead of schedule, because Matt's truck was in the parking lot when Neil returned. Neil detoured past it and put a hand to the hood, but he couldn't tell if the heat was from the sun or the engine. He shouldered his way inside and ran upstairs with his heart hammering in his chest.

Nicky's door was closed, but now the girls' was partly open. Neil heard voices on his way past but didn't slow to say hello. He hurried to his room. Only when he tested the knob and found it still locked could he breathe a little easier.

He dumped his bags on the bedroom floor to sort through his new things. The sheets went up onto his loft still in their packaging and he piled his scant groceries on top of the dresser. He ripped the cardboard padding off his small safe, skimmed the directions and warnings, and pushed everything else aside to get his bag. It took work to get the drawer open, since his duffel was such a tight fit, but he finally pried the duffel loose and dropped

[96]

it in front of him. He unzipped it in one long move, folded the flap out of the way, and froze.

On first glance, his bag looked undisturbed. Everything was still in there in the same order he'd left it in, folded but crinkled from recent rough treatment. But Neil got his paranoia from his mother and he packed his clothes in a very specific way. Even a cautious thief would be fooled, since Neil folded everything the same. Neil's code was in the tags. He always bent the tags twice on a shirt in the top layer.

Someone had gone through Neil's things and put it all back—the same order, the same layers, the same neat folds—but the tags were all pressed flat by a too-careful hand.

Neil yanked his clothes out and threw them, digging frantically for the binder buried underneath it all. From cover to cover it looked like a stalker's journal. Plastic sheet protectors were stuffed full of newspaper clippings, photographs, and anything else he could find on Kevin and Riko. The clippings were glued to computer paper, which Neil put back-to-back in the plastic slips to create a hidden inner pocket. In those pockets were Neil's most important possessions.

Most slips hid money: certificates for five-digit amounts he could cash out when he needed them, numbers detailing where he and his mother had hidden money while on the run, and rubber-banded stacks of bills. A list of emergency contacts, coded as an immature nursery rhyme, was toward the back. Only one of them lived in the United States. His mother married into an American crime family, but she'd been raised in a British one. Her brother, Stuart Hatford, gave her the list when she ran away from her husband. She in turn gave it to Neil when she died.

Stuart's phone number was on the next page, buried in a sheet covered top to bottom with random numbers. Neil could only find it using his birth name. It was down as many rows as there were letters in his first name and over as many as there were in his last. Neil had never called it, and he hoped he never had to. There was no point in running away from a murderous family if he just ran into the arms of another one.

The last slip in his binder contained a forged optometrist's note. Neil didn't need a prescription, but he couldn't buy colored contacts without a measurement of his eyes' diameter and curvature. Tucked in with it was a box of brown lenses.

Neil thumbed through the money and did the math in his head. He came up with the right amount, but that didn't make him feel better. If someone had gone through his things and found this binder, then found what it was hiding, how was he supposed to explain himself? Just in cash and certificates Neil was carrying a quarter of a million dollars.

The fact someone had deliberately come in here and dug through his bag made his stomach hurt with hot anger. The smart thing to do was pretend to not notice anything amiss and wait for the thief to come to him. That was what his mother would do. Unfortunately, Neil had inherited his father's temper, and he'd finally had enough.

It could have been Matt, but Neil doubted it. It wasn't that he trusted Matt; Neil didn't trust anybody, especially not a man he'd just met. Timing cleared Matt because there was no way he could get to the airport and back, help the girls get their things upstairs, and still have time to unpack and repack Neil's bag. That left one obvious suspect.

Neil slipped a finger into the spine of his binder and pulled out the two thin needles that remained of his mother's set of lock picks. He held them between his lips so he wouldn't lose them and set the lock on his safe. He stuffed his binder inside, slammed it closed, and hooked a second lock through the safe's handle. He gave the handle a couple fierce yanks to make sure the locks caught and shoved the safe under his pile of clothes. He spit the picks into his palm and stormed out of his room, slowing just long enough to lock the door behind him.

Neil checked Andrew's door and was unsurprised to find it locked. Neil crouched and got to work, but it didn't take long. It

[98]

was a cheap lock and easier to handle than the one at his old locker room. Whoever built the dormitory hadn't counted on people like Neil and Andrew, it seemed. Neil rose to his feet, stuffed his picks in his pocket, and shoved the bedroom door open.

Andrew's group was scattered around the living room. Aaron and Nicky were half-sunk into matching beanbag chairs as they played a video game, Kevin was reading a magazine at one of the desks, and Andrew was sitting on the desk closest to the window so he could smoke. They all went still when the door opened and stared at Neil.

Andrew was the first to react. He flicked his cigarette out the window and smiled. "Try again, Neil. You're in the wrong room!"

Aaron paused the game with a stab of his finger and looked at Nicky. "We locked that," he said in German, not quite a question.

"Last I checked," Nicky answered. He switched to English to offer Neil a friendly, "Hey, sounds like Matt's back. You meet Dan and Renee yet?"

The double deceit in their words and Nicky's smile just further infuriated Neil. If the cousins were going to keep using German thinking they could go behind everyone's backs with it, Neil would keep his fluency a secret until the last possible moment. That didn't mean Neil couldn't hit back, so he switched to French and focused his anger on Kevin.

"Stay out of my things," he snapped. He wished he could take some satisfaction in the shell-shocked looks the language and his furious tone earned, but he felt nothing. "The next time one of you goes where you don't belong I swear I'll make you regret it."

It was an age before anyone responded. Nicky was too busy gaping at Neil to say anything, and Aaron was staring at Kevin as he waited for a translation. Andrew's surprise gave

[99]

way to what a fool might mistake for delight, and he leaned forward on the desk.

"Wow, another one of Neil's many talents. How many can one man have?"

Neil ignored him in favor of Kevin. "Tell me you understand."

"I understand," Kevin said in French, "but I don't care."

"Start caring. I've let you push me around for two weeks because I know how scared you are about the district change, but I've had enough. Andrew's going to find out about it at tonight's meeting. You should be prepping to handle that explosion instead of harassing me."

"You worry about your incompetence. I'll worry about Andrew."

"You'd better," Neil said. "Put a leash on your pet monster or I will."

"A frightened child like you?"

"Fuck you, cripple."

Across the room Kevin's face went white. "What did you call me?"

"I called you a deadweight has-been," Neil said.

Kevin was out of his chair so fast he knocked it over. Neil backed out of the room and slammed the door closed between them. He'd only made it two steps back toward his room when Kevin yanked the door open again.

Kevin got his hands on Neil's neck in an instant and slammed Neil up against the opposite wall. Neil dug his fingers into Kevin's wrists, trying to loosen Kevin's grip enough that he could breathe. He tried to knee Kevin, but Kevin crushed him against the wall with his own body.

"What the fuck did you call me?" Kevin demanded again.

Neil didn't have the breath to answer. It didn't matter; Kevin's angry voice and the loud smack of Neil's body against the dormitory's concrete walls was enough to fill the hall with Foxes. Andrew was the first to show up in the cousins' doorway, but Matt was the one who went for Kevin. He wrapped an arm around Kevin's throat and wrenched Kevin's head back at a dangerous angle.

"Get off him, Day," Matt snarled.

"Whoa, whoa, calm down," Nicky said over Andrew's shoulder. "Come on, Matt."

Kevin let go of Neil with one hand and drove an elbow into Matt's ribs. Matt grunted and tightened his grip, forcing Kevin to release Neil entirely if he hoped to breathe anytime soon. Matt hauled Kevin away from Neil, but Kevin wiggled free two steps later and swung at Matt. Matt deflected it with one swipe and punched Kevin hard enough to send him sprawling.

The look on Matt's face said he was just getting started, but Andrew stepped between them before Matt could go after Kevin again. Andrew was smiling and his stance was casual, but Matt knew better than to try his luck against the short psychopath. Matt took a step back, silently conceding the fight, and shot Neil a worried look. Kevin got to his feet behind Andrew and glared at Neil. Neil refused to look at anyone at all and pretended the far wall was the most interesting thing he'd seen in years.

The girls chose that moment to step in. One moved up alongside Matt, expression tight with anger. She swept a dark look between Andrew's group and Neil and said, "What do you think you're doing? It's our first day back. Why are we fighting already?"

"Technically we never left," Andrew said, "and Neil's been here a couple weeks, so it's your first day back, not ours." He leaned to one side, looking past her to her roommate. "Hello, Renee. About time!"

The first girl didn't give Renee a chance to answer. "Explanation now, Andrew."

"You're looking at me like it's my fault." Andrew wagged a finger at her. "Look again, why don't you? Neil's at our room, which meant he brought the fight to us. Dan, your bias is cruel and unprofessional."

Danielle Wilds turned on Neil next. The Foxes' captain was taller than he was, but not by much. Her brown hair was cut mercilessly short and was disheveled from moving in. She swept Neil with a quick head-to-toe, brown eyes narrowed. "What's the problem?"

"There isn't one," Neil said. When Dan jerked a hand between him and Kevin, Neil shrugged. "Just a difference of opinions. Nothing that matters."

"We're getting along splendidly," Andrew said. "Neil even agreed to ride to the stadium with us."

"Oh did he?" Dan asked, obviously skeptical.

They all looked at Neil. The fact it was suicidal didn't mean much anymore, not when Andrew's lot had been through his things. Neil had massive damage control to do.

"Yes," Neil said. "I figured Matt's truck would be full, so I took them up on their offer."

Dan looked ready to argue, but Matt quieted her with a touch on her arm. Dan sent Andrew a suspicious glare, then shook her head. "I don't know who started this, but the fighting stops now."

"Always the optimist," Andrew said, and gave Neil his two-fingered salute. "See you soon. Don't run off, okay?"

"Wouldn't dream of it," Neil lied.

Andrew vanished into his room. Aaron and Nicky followed. Kevin was the last to move. He sent Neil a chilly look in parting and slammed the door behind him. Neil was left staring after them and wondering how he was supposed to survive that car ride.

CHAPTER SIX

Neil left reality behind when he stepped into Dan's room. Spending a month with Andrew's cracked lot and a volatile Wymack had almost irreparably damaged his image of the Foxes. Now he was sipping on a glass of sweet iced tea and eating cookies Renee had brought with her from home. They asked him about the fight only once more, and when Neil brushed it aside, didn't press him. Now the girls were going over charity projects they wanted to involve the Foxes in this fall.

Dan sat propped against Matt's shoulder, fingers twined with his, and nodded as Renee ticked ideas off on her fingers. She seemed friendly enough now that Andrew was out of sight, but Neil had already noted her spine. She was made of sterner stuff, his mother might have said. Neil guessed she had to be to captain a ragtag team like this.

Her roommate Renee was a mystery. The Foxes' senior goalkeeper had bright white hair cut to her chin. The bottom two inches of her hair were dyed in alternating pastel colors. It was interesting enough to warrant a second look, but downright odd when paired with her scant make-up, conservative clothes, and delicate silver cross necklace. Nicky had called her the sweetheart of the team. Neil understood why as he listened to her talk. He had no idea how she qualified for the Foxes' halfway-house team.

At five Wymack called to let them know Seth and Allison were on their way to campus from the airport. They were clearing away their glasses when Nicky showed up for Neil.

"I'm timing you," Dan said, showing Nicky her watch. "I know how long it takes to get to the court from here, especially with the way you drive. You take him straight there, you get me?"

Nicky waved her off. "Have a little faith in a guy, Dan."

"That's Renee's job, not mine. Mine is to make sure we start the year with ten working bodies."

"It's not like we're going to kill him."

"Kevin already tried," Matt pointed out.

"Nah, that was just a love tap." Nicky beckoned to Neil. "Can we go? These people are making me feel extremely unwelcome."

He didn't wait for Neil but vanished into the hallway. When Neil stepped out of the girls' room, Nicky was jogging to the stairwell. Neil had to hurry after him. Nicky waited until they were in the stairwell to slow. He arched his eyebrows at Neil in exaggerated surprise. "So you speak French."

"Yes," Neil said.

Nicky waited a beat to see if he'd elaborate on his own. "Why French?"

"My mother's family is French." It was a lie that probably had his British mother rolling over in her sandy grave. "She didn't really give me a choice on which language to study at school. How did Kevin learn?"

"You don't know?" Nicky asked. "You knew he'd understand you."

"I heard him use it once," Neil said.

"Jean taught him," Nicky said. "Jean Moreau? He's a backliner the Ravens imported from Marseille. He and Kevin were tight, and he taught Kevin French on the sly. Hey, maybe you can teach me a couple good pickup lines. Kevin refuses to help."

"I'm pretty sure I never learned the things you want to say."

"What a waste," Nicky complained.

Andrew was leaning against the car waiting for them. Kevin was already in the passenger seat, and Aaron was in the backseat alone. Andrew was between Neil and the door, so Neil

[104]

had to stop in front of him. Nicky kept going around the car to the driver's seat, leaving Neil to Andrew's nonexistent mercy.

"You waited for us," Andrew said with feigned surprise. "A liar who practices occasional honesty. Clever. Keeps people guessing. Very effective. I would know. I do it myself, you see. Come on, then. After you."

Neil climbed into the backseat. Andrew followed him in, sandwiching Neil between him and his brother. Nicky already had the engine going. As soon as Andrew yanked his door shut Nicky peeled out of there like he wanted to take the asphalt with him. Neil automatically reached for his seatbelt, but one of the brothers was sitting on it.

Andrew sprawled against his side. "After everything we've done for you, you have to start a fight with us. For shame, Neil."

"You started this fight a month ago," Neil said. "If you want it to stop, leave me alone."

"I like fighting. It's just troublesome when Coach and Abby and the other busybodies start crying foul. Show some consideration."

"You show some consideration and stay out of my things."

"How do you know it was us, anyway? Maybe it was Matt. Innocent until proven guilty fails on an Exy court."

"I haven't heard you deny it yet."

"You wouldn't believe me anyway."

"I don't believe anything you say."

"Believe this, Neil: you can't put a leash on me. Don't think you can, okay? And don't be stupid enough to tell other people you will. It's not safe. You'll make me want to break you."

"You?" Neil said. "You can't."

Andrew's smile curved wider. "Ohhh, that sounds like a challenge. Mother may I?"

"Your mother's dead. I don't think she cares what you do."

"I know for sure she never did," Andrew said. "Well, she had to take offense to the dying part, but I thought that was rather fun. But you're right." He slapped the heel of his palm against his temple as if something obvious had just occurred to him. "I do as I please. Consider this your official invite, you suicidal wretch. I'm bringing you to Columbia with us this Friday."

He let go of Neil and held up five fingers, smiling at Neil through them. "You have five days to meet the others. Five days of practices and all of Coach's ridiculous bonding nonsense. Then it's our turn on Friday. You can get to know us off the court."

"We'll take you out to dinner," Nicky said over his shoulder. "We used to live in Columbia, so we know all the best spots. Even better, we've got a free place to crash so we don't have to worry about driving back drunk or exhausted. It'll be a blast."

"I don't drink or dance," Neil said.

"That's all right," Andrew said. "Kevin doesn't dance anymore and I never do. You can drink soda and talk to us while the others make fools of themselves. We can't get through this year with this little misunderstanding between us, so we'll take a night off and fix it."

'Fix' was a strange choice of words. Neil knew one of them would have to break for them to get along, and he was pretty sure Andrew understood that too. It was obvious Andrew expected him to be the first to give ground.

Neil knew he should. It was past time to concede. But Neil wanted to prove him wrong, no matter how stupid it was. "If I go, promise me you'll never touch anything of mine ever again."

"So possessive," Andrew said.

"Of course I am," Neil said. "Everything I own fits in one bag."

Andrew considered that, then answered with a mad grin. "Okay. One night with us, and no more break-ins. Friday night will be fun."

Neil highly doubted that.

They reached the stadium a full minute ahead of their more law-abiding teammates and waited on the curb for Matt's truck to arrive. As soon as the upperclassmen parked and got out, Andrew pointed at Neil.

"Look, one piece."

"Are you bleeding anywhere?" Matt asked.

"Nowhere vital," Neil said.

Renee intervened before her friends could react. "Why don't we wait inside for Seth and Allison? We've got a while and it's a little warm out here."

"Maybe they'll get in a crash and won't make it," Nicky said hopefully.

"Really, Nicky," Renee said. "That's a little inappropriate, don't you think?"

She said it gently, with the hint of a smile on her face, but Neil still felt the rebuke. It was subtler but somehow deadlier than the dirty looks Matt and Dan were sending Nicky, maybe because she was so sweetly disappointed in Nicky's attitude. Nicky dropped his gaze from hers and gave an uncomfortable shrug.

"Let's go," Dan said, and led the way into the locker room.

Wymack and Abby were perched on the entertainment center in the lounge when they arrived. Dan's annoyance faded under real warmth as she greeted the pair. Andrew's group went straight to one of the couches while Matt waited for the girls on the other. Neil picked a chair where he could keep an eye on everyone. After Renee's friendly greetings, she retired to Matt's couch. They left a space between them for Dan. Dan stayed with Wymack a while longer, chatting animatedly about the summer Exy major leagues.

It took almost twenty minutes for the final two Foxes to arrive, and Neil felt the tension in the room change when the door banged open. Neil noted his teammates' reactions and mentally divided the team into four groups: Dan's three, Andrew's four, the new arrivals, and himself.

Seth Gordon was the first into the room and he brought an attitude problem with him. He didn't look happy to see any of them again after only a month apart and he barely grunted at the staff in greeting. He took a second to scowl fiercely at Neil, but that was it. He threw himself into one of the open chairs, all long limbs and black anger, and glared at the doorway as he waited for his companion to arrive.

Allison Reynolds was only a few seconds behind him. She stopped in the doorway to glower across the room at her surly teammate. Neil had seen pictures of Allison when researching the Foxes, but she still required a second look. The Reynolds were billionaires thanks to their world-class luxury resorts. Allison grew up a modern-day princess and a celebrity through her association with her family's clients. Rumor had it she lost her inheritance when she chose Exy and public schools over joining the family business, but Allison still looked like a catwalk star. Everyone else was in jeans and rumpled from moving in. Allison looked ready for a photo shoot with perfect platinum curls, spiked heels, and a skintight dress.

"Nice to see you two, too," Wymack said dryly.

Allison skipped him to nod at Abby. "You survived the summer."

"By the grace of God," Abby said. "It doesn't get easier, that's for sure."

Allison swept the room with a look, lip curling a little in scorn as she spotted Andrew's group. Her gaze settled on Neil and she studied him a moment, expression calculating.

"I'm going to sit with you," she said.

She crossed the room to perch on the arm of his chair. There wasn't really room for her there; she had to lean against him to keep her balance. She wound an arm around his shoulders to keep from sliding off and crossed her legs at the knee. The move slid her short hem further up, showing off a healthy stretch of toned, tanned thighs.

[108]

Neil saw it in his peripheral vision but kept his gaze on Allison's face. His skin stung with the memory of his mother's heavy blows. Life on the run meant no time for friends or relationships, but that didn't stop Neil from checking out girls as he grew older. His mother's watchful eye noticed his lingering looks and increasing distraction. Afraid he'd spill their secrets over a childish crush, she beat him like she could kill his hormones with her bare hands. A few years of this violence and Neil finally got the hint: girls were too dangerous to consort with. Allison was beautiful but off-limits.

"I can move if you want to sit here," Neil said.

"No, this is fine." She smiled, but it had a smug edge to it, probably because Seth was glaring at them like he could kill them with willpower alone. Allison looked back at Wymack and flicked her fingers in an impatient gesture. "This will be quick, won't it? It was a long flight and I'm exhausted."

"You're the ones slowing this down," Wymack said, and stabbed a finger at Neil. "First order of business: Neil Josten, our new striker sub. Got anything to say?" When Neil shook his head, Wymack jerked a thumb between Allison and Seth. "You already met everyone else. Here's the last of them: Seth Gordon, starting striker, and Allison Reynolds, our defensive dealer. Questions, comments, concerns? Anyone?"

Seth pointed at Neil and said angrily, "I'm fucking concerned—"

Neil guessed Wymack had heard this argument before, because he spoke over Seth like he didn't hear him. "All right, then. Moving on. Abby?" Abby got down from her perch and passed out stapled packs of paper. "Same boring forms as always. Sign your name on the appropriate lines and give these back to me first thing tomorrow. You can't practice until I have these on file.

"Summer practices start at 8:30. Enjoy sleeping in while you can, because we're moving to 6:00 when the semester starts. We're meeting at the gym. I repeat, we're meeting at the gym. If

[109]

you're late because you came here instead of there I will put my shoe through your face. You've only been gone for a month. I know you all know how this works."

"Yes, Coach," the team chorused.

"Physicals get done before you leave today. Andrew, you're first. Seth, you're going second. The rest of you draw straws or something. It's up to you. Don't even think of leaving before you've seen Abby." He gave Andrew's lot the evil eye. Andrew and Nicky affected innocent looks that fooled no one.

Abby went to stand behind Kevin. Wymack hesitated before reaching for the papers stacked facedown at his side. "Last order of business from me today is our schedule."

"Already?" Matt asked. "It's only June."

"We don't have dates yet, but the ERC's made some changes that will make this spring look like a cakewalk. They're notifying the coaches in our district one by one to try and control the fallout. It has potential to get ugly."

"How could it be worse than the shit we dealt with last year?" Seth asked.

Matt counted off on his fingers. "The break-ins, threatening phone calls, rabid press, vandalism..."

"Personal favorite was when someone told the police we were running a meth lab out of the dorm," Dan said sourly. "Police raids are awesome."

"The death threats were creative, though," Nicky said. "Maybe this time they'll follow through and actually kill one of us. Let's vote. I nominate Seth."

"Fuck you, faggot," Seth said.

"I don't like that word," Andrew said. "Don't use it."

"I would say 'fuck you, freak', but then you wouldn't know which one of you I was talking to."

"Don't talk to us at all," Aaron said. "You never have anything useful to say."

"Enough," Wymack said. "We don't have time for petty bullshit this year. We've got a new school in our district."

[110]

Neil glanced at Kevin where he sat white-faced and rigid. Four men on one couch meant Andrew's group was sitting crushed together with Kevin and Andrew in the middle. Even on drugs Andrew couldn't miss the way Kevin went tense, but with his medicine in his veins he thought it was funny. He grinned up at Kevin, but the smile evaporated off his face when Wymack spoke.

"Edgar Allan's come south."

Shock silenced the team, but not for long.

"No way," Dan said sharply. "That isn't funny, Coach."

Seth apparently thought otherwise because he started laughing. Aaron, Nicky, and Matt drowned each other out as they demanded explanations. Allison made a shrill noise of disbelief that left Neil's right ear ringing. Renee, like Neil, watched Andrew and Kevin and said nothing.

Wymack tried explaining the ERC's logic, but he kept his attention on Andrew. It didn't take the team long to notice his distraction. The hubbub slowly died out. As it did, Andrew's smile returned. This time it was all teeth. Andrew's drugs made him manic, but they didn't make him any less vicious. Neil knew what that smile meant and braced for violence.

"Hey, Kevin," Andrew said. "Hear that? Someone really misses you."

"The ERC shouldn't have approved it," Kevin said, so quietly Neil barely heard him.

"You said he would come for you."

"I didn't know it would be like this."

"Liar," Andrew said, and Kevin flinched.

Andrew twisted to sit sideways on the couch so he could see Kevin better. It put his back against Nicky's side. Nicky leaned away from his deranged cousin, knuckles white where he was holding onto the arm of the couch. Andrew either didn't notice or didn't care how uncomfortable he was making Nicky. He had eyes only for Kevin. Kevin looked sick to his stomach, but he wasn't panicking over this bombshell. Andrew had no problems interpreting that pseudo-strength.

"You did know about this," Andrew said. "How long? One day, two days, three four five?"

"Coach told me when it was approved in May."

"May. May, Day. Mayday. A little curious, Kevin Day. When were you going to tell me?"

"I told him not to," Wymack said.

"You picked Coach over me?" Andrew asked, and laughed. "Ohhhh my. Favoritism, deception, betrayal, how familiar. After all I've done for you."

"Andrew, knock it off," Abby warned him.

"Help me," Kevin said, almost a whisper.

Andrew clucked his tongue and cocked his head to one side. "Help you? Help a man who lies to my face for a month? How?"

"I want to stay," Kevin said. "I'll ask you again: don't let him take me away."

"You're the one who would tell him yes," Andrew said. "Maybe you forgot."

"Please."

"You know how much I hate that word."

Kevin stared down at his hands where they were clenched in his lap, eyes on the scar that ran across the back of his hand. Neil had only gotten glimpses of it, since he didn't want Kevin to catch him staring. It was a jagged mess along the thin bones of his hand. However Riko broke his hand, it hadn't been a clean strike. Andrew heaved an exaggerated sigh and held his hand out, blocking Kevin's view of his scar.

"Look at me," Andrew said.

Kevin turned a haunted look on him. Neil wasn't sure how Andrew could smile at such an empty stare, drugs notwithstanding. Neil felt Kevin's despair all the way across the room, and it was such a familiar feeling he thought he'd be sick.

[112]

"It'll be fine," Andrew said. "I promised, didn't I? Don't you believe me?"

It took a while, but at last Kevin visibly relaxed. The dead edge melted out of his eyes as he absorbed every ounce of strength Andrew could give him. The unwavering trust Kevin had in Andrew was amazing. How Kevin thought one psychotic midget could protect him against a family as twisted as the Moriyamas, Neil didn't know. Neil thought he should be impressed, but all he felt was bitterness. He swallowed hard against the churning in his stomach and looked away.

Wymack watched them a minute longer, then nodded. "The ERC will make their official announcement later this month. They agreed to wait until you were all here where it's easier for us to protect you. That doesn't mean you can be careless. Chuck—that's our university president Charles Whittier, Neil—has reissued orders that reporters stay off our campus without a police escort this summer. You'll see twice as many campus police around, and I need all of you to save their number to your phones just in case. Understand?"

Neil didn't own a phone, but he joined the others in saying, "Yes, Coach."

The room went quiet, and Neil couldn't stand it anymore. "Anything else, Coach, or are we finished?"

"This is a big deal," Dan said. "It changes everything. You don't understand."

"Neil found out when Kevin did," Wymack said. "I already had the talk with him, so he understands just fine. And no, there's nothing else. Abby, they're all yours. Do with them what you will."

Neil got to his feet and started for the door without a backward glance. Dan tried to call him back for his physical, but Abby quieted her.

Renee caught up with him outside. "Unfortunately this news means Andrew can't give you a ride back to the dorm," she said. "Kevin needs him right now and that trumps whatever

[113]

agreement you two had. If you're okay with waiting a bit, though, you're more than welcome to ride with us. There's plenty of room in Matt's truck."

Neil meant to say no, but what came out was, "Why does Kevin trust Andrew?"

Renee smiled. "Because he knows he can."

"With so much at stake," Neil pressed, as if she didn't understand what was going on as well as he did. Maybe she didn't. Maybe she couldn't understand what Kevin was risking and what he would face if Andrew failed. She wasn't like them. She was normal, or as normal as the Foxes could hope to be. Gangs and blood feuds were things out of movies. Neil hated that she couldn't understand, but he hated more that he did. "With so much at stake he honestly thinks Andrew is enough?"

Renee held out her hand to him. "Neil," she said, so gently he wondered if she'd even heard him. "Neil, please wait for us."

"No," Neil said, taking a step back. "I know the way. Thank you."

He rolled his papers into a tube and jogged away. She didn't call after him, but he felt her stare on the back of his head. As soon as he reached the far edge of the parking lot he sped up to a full-out run.

The run did nothing to calm the restless anxiety gnawing at his stomach. He reached the dorm in worse spirits than he'd left the stadium. He tried to distract himself by putting his things away, but he ended up pacing the room with his empty duffel bag in his hands. His fifth time around he couldn't take it anymore. He fell to his knees and yanked at his dresser, hurriedly unloading his few outfits so he could get to his safe. He punched the code in and undid the combination lock, needing to see his binder. He went through it cover to cover, checking and recounting everything.

He shouldn't have come here. He shouldn't have stayed once he heard about the district change and found out who the Moriyamas were. Andrew getting into his things should be the

[114]

last straw, even though Andrew hadn't said anything yet about what was in Neil's folder. Maybe Andrew wasn't smart enough to check the slips, or maybe he'd written the folder off the second he realized it was basically a shrine to Kevin and Riko. But Neil couldn't just assume Andrew hadn't found his money. For all he knew Andrew was waiting to throw it in his face later.

Panic told him to go now, but Neil couldn't move. A quieter voice beneath his fear kept him from getting up again. Neil still remembered Kevin's breakdown at Wymack's last month. Kevin's fear cut him wide open because Neil knew that feeling. Every day Neil woke up and relearned how to breathe. He gave himself two minutes every morning to calculate his chances of getting caught, weigh the benefits of staying wherever he was, and talk himself through his fear.

Did Kevin do the same? The dead look Kevin turned on Andrew today was the same look Neil saw in his reflection. When Neil stopped acting, when he stopped worrying about who was watching, when he let go of the lies that kept him alive, that was the only expression he could make.

Neil repacked his safe and dug out the cigarettes he'd bought at the store earlier. He went to the window, undid the two locks that kept it closed, and shoved the pane up as far as he could. A screen kept him from leaning out, but he pressed against it so hard it creaked. He lit a cigarette and watched it burn. The acrid smell of smoke and fire took the edge off his nerves, but the familiar and quiet grief that followed made everything worse.

No matter how alike he and Kevin really were, the critical difference between them made Neil feel worlds away from all of this. Kevin had Andrew to lean on, and Neil had no one at all to confide his hopelessness and loneliness in. Whether Neil left today or tomorrow or next week, he'd leave alone. Two, five, ten years from now, if Neil was even still alive, he'd still be alone. He could be anyone, anywhere in the world, but he'd be alone until the day he died. He'd never trust anyone enough to let them in.

And that was why Neil couldn't go.

Even if everything in Neil screamed at him to run, Neil couldn't do it, not after seeing that little show between Kevin and Andrew today. Maybe he was pathetic, or maybe he was too jealous to walk away. Maybe Neil just needed to understand.

Why did Kevin always get more? Kevin lived with an awful family, but he had a home and a reputation and a following. He grew up in the spotlight while Neil was left looking over his shoulder in a dozen countries around the world. Kevin lost his hand but gained his freedom. He was stubborn enough and skilled enough to pick up where he'd left off, even if it meant learning how to play with his weaker hand. He had a coach and a teammate willing to defy the Moriyamas for him. Why? Why did Kevin deserve all that?

Why did he deserve Neil? Why should Neil hesitate here and worry about him when Neil's own life was on the line? After the way Kevin treated him this summer, Neil should be happy. This was the perfect time to duck out. The team would assume Neil was a scared kid who couldn't deal with the Moriyama truth and the press would be too busy following Kevin and Riko to dwell on another failed Fox. Neil should send Riko an anonymous thank-you card and go over the border to Mexico.

But Neil couldn't, not yet.

He shook a clump of ash off onto the windowsill and pushed his finger against it, smearing it into a dark streak on the white paint. He looked up at the clouds and searched them for his mother's furious face. "One of us has to make it, Mom."

It wasn't going to be Neil. It was obvious he was too stupid to survive without his mother if he let himself get into messes like this. But maybe Kevin could do it. Maybe he'd get through this somehow, riding his talent and Andrew's psychotic obsession and Wymack's fierce protection. Maybe he'd get

[116]

through this season on the Foxes' roster and be safe. He'd recover and he'd be free. Neil couldn't leave until he knew Kevin would be okay. He didn't want to find out from half the world away.

He sucked in a slow, deep breath, trying to inhale as much smoke as he could, and watched as his cigarette burned down to the filter. He went through two more cigarettes before his roommates showed up. Neil stubbed the third out when he heard the front door open and scraped ash off the windowsill onto the carpet. He ground the ash in with a shoe, stuffed what was left of the butt into his pack for later, and kicked his things into some semblance of order. His safe was closed and locked, so he went out to greet his teammates. He felt distant as he watched them walk in. Maybe he was already dying, his stupid soul fading from his short body in preparation for a brutal end.

Seth came in first and heaved his suitcases off to one side. He was mid-rant and needed his hands free for angry gesturing. Matt was behind him with a tolerant look on his face and a third bag in his hands. Matt pushed the door shut and passed the bag to Seth, who threw it after the others.

Neil wasn't sure who Seth was angriest at: Abby, Allison, or Andrew's group. His rant went back and forth between all of them without a logical pattern. He stopped only when he ran out of colorful language. Finally he threw his hands up in disgust and turned on Neil. "And to make it all worse, I get stuck with a fucking amateur as a sub!"

"Kevin approved him," Matt said.

"Like that makes me feel any better." Seth glared at Neil. Neil stared back, unimpressed by his rage. His apathy only served to incense Seth further. "We were a bad joke; now we're a practical one. When the others find out about this, we're going to win our games only because they'll be too busy laughing to take us seriously. We were supposed to make it this year. I trusted him to pick our sub because he said he could get us past the championships death match. But this is repulsive."

[117]

"At least give Neil a chance," Matt said.

"Day's fucking with us," Seth said. "It isn't right."

"This attitude isn't right," Matt said, pointing at him. "Kevin would never recruit someone just to make us look bad— we do that well enough on our own. If you want us to win this year, act like it. We need a cohesive offensive line. Since you and Kevin are a lost cause, you're going to have to make it work with Neil."

"He's short, he can't play, and he looks like he has an attitude problem."

"Coach says he's got potential." Matt looked at Neil. "Andrew says you're fast."

Neil frowned. "When did he say that?"

"When do you think, wiseass?" Seth asked. "We talked all kinds of shit about you after you booked it."

"Dan asked what they thought of you," Matt said before Neil could react. "Nicky thinks you need more time with us. Aaron says you have to be more aggressive. Kevin didn't say anything, which would normally be weird since Kevin's not known for mincing words, but I guess he's distracted. But Andrew bets you can outrun everyone on this team. Coach said you clocked a four-minute mile back in Arizona. That true? You're a little short to run so fast."

"I like running," Neil said.

"Fuck running," Seth said. "Learn to score. Word is you still can't score on Andrew."

"No," Neil admitted. "Not yet."

"When you do, you can talk to me," Seth said. "Until then, stay out of my way and try not to drag down my line too much."

"Welcome to the Foxhole Court," Matt added dryly as Seth grabbed his suitcase and stormed into the bedroom. "Hey, let's hit downtown for dinner tonight. We might as well enjoy ourselves before this blows up in our faces, and I don't want to be here when Andrew's between doses. Can you two handle each other while I check with the girls?"

[118]

"Probably," Neil said.

He and Seth managed to get along until Matt came back, but that was only because they ignored each other. Seth was busy moving in and Neil was happy to stay out of his way. When Seth was done with the bedroom and had moved on to the living room, Neil tidied up the mess he'd made earlier. Matt set up his computer at one of the desks and killed time online until it was time to rendezvous with the others.

"Downtown" referred to a long street of shops branching off the campus just a short ways from Fox Tower. Mostly the stores sold campus gear, but there were a couple bookstores and a half-dozen pubs. It was like a ghost town now with so few students around. Half of the places they passed had signs up that they'd reopen closer to fall. The rest stayed open in hopes of drawing in the summer school students and the athletes that would be filtering in over the next couple weeks.

They ended up at a place that was half-bar, half-pizza joint. The L-shaped corner booth was perfect for Neil, who could take an end spot on the bench and watch his teammates. He expected the same loud madness he'd seen at Wymack's house his first night in South Carolina, especially after seeing the tension Seth and Allison added to the team, but he was pleasantly surprised. Whatever their differences, the upperclassmen had had years to get used to them, and they carried a table-wide conversation for most of dinner. Even Seth and Allison made attempts to get along, though Neil attributed that civility to the beer.

He stayed out of all of it, and for the most part they let him. He'd done the meet-and-greet thing with Dan's group after his fight with Kevin, and Seth and Allison simply didn't care to know him better. The only times anyone asked him anything at dinner was when Dan or Matt wanted his opinion on the matter at hand.

They were halfway through dinner when Dan and Matt ducked out. Neil saw them leave, but aside from Allison nudging Renee meaningfully, no one said anything about it. No one mentioned the district change, either, though it had to be on everyone's mind. They pretty much had the restaurant to themselves, but the lack of other chatter meant their voices carried easier.

Dan and Matt came back eventually, looking a little worse for wear. Dan picked up their check from the bartender on her way back to the table. Seth toasted Matt with what was left of his beer, but his eyes were on Allison when he did so.

Dan and Matt led the way back to the dorm hand in hand. Renee walked behind them with Seth and Allison. Neil was happy to take up the rear. When they made it back to their floor, Nicky was waiting for them in the hallway.

"Hey, Renee," Nicky said. "You mind calling Andrew's phone?"

"Did he lose it?" Renee asked, pulling hers out of her small purse.

"I did," Nicky said. "And, uh, the man carrying it. He's not answering any of my calls."

"Jesus, Nicky," Matt said. "Coach told you to keep an eye on him tonight."

"I know what he said." Nicky made a face at Matt. "You try it sometime."

"Where's Kevin?" Dan demanded.

"Hasn't left his bed since we got back," Nicky said. "Aaron's watching him."

Renee held up a hand to ask for quiet. Everyone fell silent immediately to watch her. She had her phone at her ear but said nothing, likely listening to it ring on the other end. Neil knew someone picked up by the way Renee smiled, but he didn't know how Renee could smile so warmly when she was speaking to Andrew.

"Did I wake you?" she asked in lieu of hello. "I was hoping to talk to you tonight, but Nicky says you've wandered off. Oh? All right, then. I'll try again tomorrow. Lunch, perhaps? Okay. Good night."

[120]

She hung up and put her phone away. "He's at Coach's. Maybe Coach wanted to make sure he took his medicine tonight." Renee gave Nicky's shoulder an encouraging squeeze. "He's safe. Kevin's safe. Get some rest. There's nothing else we can do tonight except lock our doors and pray."

"Thanks," Nicky said, and he disappeared back into his room.

They split up to their rooms to prep for bed. Neil climbed up the wooden ladder to his loft and stretched out on the mattress. The simple pleasure of having a real bed didn't last long. After the lights were out and his roommates had quieted down, Neil was left with just the darkness and his thoughts. He lay awake long into the night thinking about Kevin, and when he slept, he dreamed of his father waiting for him on the Foxhole Court.

CHAPTER SEVEN

By Neil's third day on the court, he had no idea how the Foxes made it to championships last spring. His guess that the team was made up of four groups was partially accurate, but the lines he'd drawn were flexible. Whenever Allison and Seth were fighting, Allison ended up with the girls and Seth retreated to Matt. It seemed Allison and Seth didn't believe in middle ground: either they were slinging vile insults at each other or they were making out in the locker room regardless of whoever might be around. Neil didn't know what triggered the abrupt and constant change in emotions. He hoped he never understood.

The entire first week of summer practices was eaten up by in-fighting as the court hierarchy fell into place again. When Dan was acting as their captain, she ruled them with the same angry spine Neil saw that first day. She didn't hesitate to push people into line and the Foxes let her have the final say in everything. Even Andrew followed her orders, though Neil guessed it was because he was amused by her supposed fearlessness.

Kevin knew more about the sport than any of them ever would and he had some lingering authority from his stint as their assistant coach, but his cold personality was a turn-off and his approach made it hard for the others to listen to him without snapping back. He caused the majority of the arguments that week, and most of those fights were between him and Seth. Kevin and Seth hated each other with a loathing second only to what Seth and Nicky felt for each other. It took only one wrong word to turn their arguments into physical brawls. The fighting hit a peak on Wednesday afternoon when Andrew left practice early for his weekly therapy session. The second he vanished, Seth went for Kevin with fists flying.

Matt was the brute force that kept them in line when Dan's words weren't enough. Because of Kevin's injury and Andrew's apathy, Matt was also the best player the Foxes had. Neil privately thought Matt should have been named captain because of the solidarity he could bring the team. Whatever happened between him and Andrew last year, he seemed to have an understanding with the cousins, which meant the Foxes had a solid defense line. His relationship with Kevin was harder for Neil to figure out. His skill and commitment meant Kevin was willing to work with and listen to him, but the two of them went from perfect understanding to outright antagonism constantly. It reminded Neil a little of Allison and Seth, except without the desperate sexual undertones.

Renee was next in line and the eye of the storm. She doled out friendly advice, encouraged her teammates' efforts, and played mediator occasionally. She didn't get involved in the others' fights, either to take sides or preach peace, and no one argued with a word she said. Even Andrew seemed quite taken with her. Neil saw them talking off to the side several times throughout the week. It was obvious no one else approved of their odd friendship, but neither goalkeeper paid any mind to the unhappy looks sent their way. Neil wasn't sure what to make of it. He was less sure what to think about Renee, so he avoided her whenever he could.

The rest of the Foxes fell in under them in an ever-shifting order. Seth's position on the team varied the most. He was the team's only fifth-year, since everyone else from his starting line had quit or flunked out by now, but he was too much of an isolationist to make much of a difference on the court. His mood was so volatile Neil was sure he had to be on something. Why Abby and Wymack hadn't put an end to it, Neil didn't know. Allison carried weight because of her seniority and her aggressive attitude on the court, but she absolutely loathed the cousins and didn't like working with them.

Aaron was a better player than Nicky was, but he kept a clinical distance from it all. Nicky gave it everything he had, but he liked dramatic plays and liked picking fights with Allison and Seth even more. Andrew's position was hard to figure out. His influence over Kevin and his skill made him useful, but he put in as little effort as Wymack let him get away with.

Neil didn't have a place in that hierarchy yet. His teammates held so little regard for him he didn't even have the dubious honor of being dead last. He wasn't surprised, since he was an inexperienced newcomer to their mess, but that didn't make it easier to deal with. Dan tried her hardest to include him, checking on him anytime she was near him on the court, but she had her hands full managing the rest of her team. Allison didn't take Neil seriously, Matt was too far away to help, and Neil didn't want to deal with Renee. The cousins were keeping their distance this week. That left Seth and Kevin.

Kevin and Seth had to deal with Neil since he was on their line, but Neil would rather they ignored him entirely. Nothing he did was right in their eyes. They tore him apart and kicked him aside as useless no matter how hard he tried. Neil hated their attitudes, but he was determined not to lose his temper in front of the team again. Luckily the strikers were as willing to fight over him as they were with him, so he took what comfort he could in watching Seth and Kevin duke it out with fists and sticks.

Wymack rarely interfered in the fighting. He let them brawl and then punished them with intense cardio and excruciating drills. Seemed he'd long ago decided his team could only function by testing themselves against each other and establishing their own ranking. Neil thought it madness at first, but as the week progressed he could see the team finally figuring out the limits and alliances between them.

By the time Friday rolled around, Neil was desperate for the weekend. The stress of worrying about Kevin and Riko, the irritation and exasperation over his teammates' behavior on the court, and Kevin and Seth's unending, angry condescension were wearing him down. He couldn't deal with it any longer, but he couldn't escape from it, either. He spent all day with the Foxes at practice, then went back to the dorm and saw them all evening too. Neil was being suffocated by their very presence. All he wanted to do was vanish from campus for the weekend. He had to find some breathing room before he cracked.

He'd forgotten about Andrew's plans for him. When Neil left the shower after Friday's practice he expected everyone else to be gone. Neil rode to practices with the team, sharing the bed of Matt's truck with Allison, Seth, and Renee, but he always ran back to the dorm alone afterwards. The others caught on within a couple days that Neil liked leaving after them, and none of them had asked him why. They didn't try to change his mind and stopped waiting on him after the second day. Maybe it was a Fox thing, knowing when there were boundaries they really shouldn't cross and questions they'd never get answers to. Neil wasn't sure, but he appreciated it.

Friday was different, though. Neil lugged his dirty uniform into the locker room and saw Nicky waiting on one of the benches with a black gift bag.

"You survived your first week," Nicky said. "Did you have fun?"

"Is it going to be like this all summer?"

"Pretty much," Nicky said. "At least it's never boring, right?"

Neil dropped his uniform in one of the laundry baskets, checked his locker to make sure it was secure, and turned to find Nicky standing right at his back. Neil put a hand up to shove Nicky out of his space. Nicky was expecting it and pushed the black bag into Neil's open palm.

[125]

"This is for you," Nicky said. "Andrew said you don't have anything appropriate for where we're going. He told me what size to get you, and I picked it out. Trust me, it's awesome."

Neil stared at him, thrown. "What?"

"You didn't forget about our party, did you? Here." Nicky hooked the twine handle over Neil's fingers. Neil watched him do it, trying to remember the last time someone gave him a gift and coming up blank. That his first one should be from Andrew was unsettling.

Nicky misinterpreted his discomfort as suspicion and laughed. "No catch. It's more for us than you, honestly. We can't be seen with you in public if you look like a raggedy hobo. No offense." He waited a beat before finally realizing something wasn't right. "Neil?"

"Thank you," Neil said, but even he heard the uncertainty in it.

Nicky studied him. Neil stared back, refusing to give anything else away. Finally Nicky tweaked Neil's hair. "We'll pick you up at nine, all right? I suggest napping until then. We'll be out all night. We've got all the right contacts to keep the party going until dawn." Nicky grinned and gave Neil's hair another tug. "Speaking of, ditch them tonight. Your contacts, I mean."

Neil's stomach roiled. "Shut up."

Nicky gave an exaggerated look around as if checking for eavesdroppers. "Look, it's not like they're a secret. Anyone who's looking can see the ring in your eyes that means you're wearing lenses. I saw 'em day one. I just didn't think they were fashion lenses until Andrew said so. And seriously? Brown? How boring can you be?"

"I like brown."

"Andrew doesn't," Nicky said. "Take them out."

"No."

"Please," Nicky said. "No one's going to see you but us, and we already know they're a lie. Don't wear them."

"Or what?" Neil asked.

Nicky's silence was answer enough. Neil was ready to brush that warning off, but he caught himself. He was sure he could hold his ground against Andrew, but he wasn't facing Andrew alone. He was going out with Andrew's entire group half the state away from here. Nicky was honestly trying to help him get the night off on the right foot. Neil didn't think much of that consideration. He knew which side Nicky would take if things got ugly.

"Nine," Nicky said again, when Neil didn't answer, and left.

Neil gave him a few minutes' head start. When he was sure the cousins were long gone, he jogged across campus to the library and killed a few hours scouring the news in the computer lab. He picked up a small dinner on the way back to the dorm at one of the university's three convenience stores.

His dorm room was empty. He dimly remembered Matt saying something about going to the movies with Dan. Neil didn't know where Seth was, but luckily he was still gone when it was time for Neil to get ready. He was alone, but Neil checked the lock on the dorm door before gathering his clothes. The bedroom didn't have a lock, which bothered him, but the bathroom did. He shut himself in there to get ready.

When he was finished changing, he took a long minute to study his reflection. He wasn't sure what to make of the result. No matter how many times he and his mother changed their identities and languages, one thing stayed the same: they aimed for nondescript fashion that would blend in with an everyday crowd. Neil wore faded tees and plain jeans and worn sneakers, generally in pale colors that helped wash him out further.

This outfit was the complete opposite, and every piece of it was black. The cargoes were light and cut to accommodate a pair of heavy boots. The shirt was long-sleeved, tight, and fashioned to look like it'd torn through in places. A charcoal inner layer peeked out through the gashes, hiding Neil's skin, but he ran his hands over the cloth a dozen times to make sure there weren't any open holes. He was sure he could feel his scars through the thin cloth.

There was only one thing left to change. Neil's stomach churned a little with nerves when he took his contacts out. He blinked a couple times, adjusting to their absence, and flushed the brown lenses down the toilet. A glance at the mirror almost took his breath away. It'd been over a year since Neil had seen his real eyes, since he never left bed without putting his contacts in. His eyes were a chilly shade of blue that only looked brighter against his black hair and clothes. He couldn't look at them for long; they were his father's eyes.

Neil gathered his clothes and left the bathroom. As he turned into his bedroom to drop his clothes off, he caught a glimpse of Andrew's group in the living room. Andrew had picked his lock again. Neil debated how much damage the thick heels of his new boots would do against Andrew's face and liked what his mind came up with.

He put his laundry into the bottom drawer of his dresser, which he'd decided to use in lieu of a hamper, and turned to see Andrew in the doorway to the bedroom. Andrew lounged against the doorframe, arms folded over his chest, and studied Neil. Neil took the chance to look him over, noting first and foremost the lack of an expression on Andrew's face. Andrew was sober tonight. Neil wondered if Andrew understood the terms of his parole or just didn't care.

Neil couldn't leave with Andrew in the way, so he stopped as close to Andrew as he dared and waited for Andrew to move. Andrew did, but only to reach out for Neil with one hand. Neil tensed as Andrew's fingers wrapped around the back of his neck, but Andrew only wanted to pull Neil's head down. Neil focused on Andrew's cheekbone so as not to go cross-eyed and let Andrew study his eyes.

"Another bit of unexpected honesty," Andrew said. "Any particular reason?"

"Nicky asked nicely. You might try it sometime."

[128]

"We already talked about this. I don't ask." Andrew gave Neil another slow once-over and let go. "We're going."

Nicky perked up as the two stepped into the living room, but his happy expression faltered when he got a look at Neil. "Oh, man. Neil, you clean up good. Can I say that, or is that against the rules? Just—damn. Aaron, don't let me get too drunk tonight."

Andrew stopped by Nicky long enough to pull a pack of cigarettes out of his pocket. He lit one, never mind that the dormitory rooms came equipped with smoke detectors, and put his lighter in Nicky's face.

"Don't make me kill you," Andrew said.

Nicky held up his hands in self-defense. "I know."

"Do you?"

"Promise," Nicky said weakly.

Andrew put his lighter away and left the room. Kevin and Aaron followed. Nicky raked Neil with a last appreciative look and went out to the hall. He waited with Neil while Neil locked the door. They trailed the others downstairs to the car in silence.

Neil ended up in the same spot as last time, stuck between Aaron and Andrew in the backseat. Neil expected trouble, but the brothers propped themselves against their respective windows and dozed off within minutes of leaving campus. Neil couldn't sleep in such company, so he spent the hour wondering how many things could go wrong tonight. It was an extensive list.

When the car's headlights first started flashing over exit signs for Columbia, Nicky motioned over his shoulder at Neil. "Wake Andrew up, will you? Preferably without touching him."

"What?" Aaron asked sleepily, rousing at Nicky's voice.

"I can't remember which exit we decided was the shortcut. You?"

Aaron answered by reaching around Neil and pushing Andrew's shoulder. Andrew's reaction was immediate and violent. Aaron got his hand out of the way in time, but there was nowhere for Neil to go. Andrew's elbow slammed into his diaphragm hard enough to double Neil up over his knees. Aaron, completely unsympathetic, snapped his fingers over Neil's head at Andrew.

"Exit," he said.

Andrew braced himself on Neil's back and leveraged himself between the front seats. He watched until they passed a sign and said, "Not yet. It's the exit that has Waffle House."

"This is South Carolina," Nicky said. "Every exit leads to Waffle House. Still breathing, Neil?"

"Yes," Neil said hoarsely. "I think."

Andrew dropped back into his seat and let go of Neil. Neil managed to sit up, but he couldn't help pressing a hand to his shirt. It felt like Andrew's elbow had blown a hole right through him. He flicked a look at Aaron, who shrugged at his silent accusation, and then at Andrew. Andrew didn't return it, too distracted by his hands. He had them up in front of him, but it wasn't until a car passed going the other direction that Neil realized what he was looking at. In the flash of light from passing headlights Neil saw Andrew's fingers were trembling.

"Nicky," Andrew said.

Nicky glanced back. He couldn't see tremors in the darkness, but he saw where Andrew was looking. Nicky swept across lanes toward their exit. "We're almost there."

"Pull over."

"We're on an exit ramp."

"Now."

Nicky didn't argue again. He pulled off onto the almost nonexistent shoulder, braking so hard Neil expected the car to fishtail. Horns blared as a car whipped past them. Andrew shoved his door opened, leaned out of the car as far as he could, and dry-heaved into the weeds alongside the road. Neil was sitting close enough to him to feel the way Andrew's entire body shook with the effort. It sounded like Andrew was tearing his esophagus to shreds.

[130]

"Where are your crackers?" Nicky asked when Andrew was left gasping for breath.

"He took them earlier," Kevin said.

"All of them?" Nicky asked, horrified. "Jesus, Andrew."

"Shut up," Andrew said, and spat a couple times. He reached blindly for Kevin's headrest, found it on the third try, and pulled himself back inside the car. "Just get us there."

Nicky floored it, but once they entered the outskirts of Columbia night traffic slowed them down. Their first destination was a restaurant called Sweetie's. It was too late for dinner, but the parking lot was packed. Nicky dropped them off at the door so he could circle and look for a spot. There were four groups ahead of them waiting for seats. Andrew detoured to the salad bar and grabbed two handfuls of cracker packets from a bucket on the end. Kevin watched as Andrew methodically ate his way through them. Andrew answered with a baleful look.

He finished his snack before Nicky joined them. A few minutes later they were finally seated at a booth in the back. Before the host could leave Andrew stuffed his empty cracker packets into the man's apron. The host didn't even bat an eye at such rudeness but left them with their menus. Their waitress wasn't far behind him, and Nicky handed the menus back unread.

"We're just here for the ice cream special," Nicky said.

"No problem," she said. "I'll get that right to you."

Nicky's smile disappeared the second she left and he turned a concerned look on Andrew. Andrew sat cradling his face in one hand. The other hand was flat on the table in front of him, and his shaking was more pronounced now. A shudder passed through Andrew's frame. Andrew sucked in a long breath through clenched teeth.

Kevin pulled a bottle of pills out of his pocket and set them on the table, halfway between himself and Andrew. "Just take it."

[131]

Andrew went perfectly still as he stared at the bottle. "Fuck you."

Neil finally understood. "You're going through withdrawal."

Andrew ignored him. "Put that away before I shove it down your throat."

Kevin frowned but did as he was told.

It didn't take long for their ice cream to arrive. Their waitress passed out bowls and set a pile of napkins in the middle of the table. As soon as she left, Andrew scattered the napkins with an impatient hand. Underneath them all was a pile of packets full of pale yellow powder.

"We're in public," Aaron said.

Andrew ignored him in favor of ripping open two bags and upending them into his mouth.

Nicky nudged Neil. "Try the ice cream. You'll love it."

Neil obediently dipped into the mound he'd been served, but he didn't let Nicky or the food distract him from Andrew. Andrew collected the rest of the packets and hid them in one of his pockets. Moving was a mistake, judging by the tight look on his face. Andrew pressed the side of his hand hard against his mouth and swallowed so hard Neil heard it across the table.

It took Andrew another minute before he relaxed enough to start eating. Whatever he'd taken must have dulled the edge of his withdrawal, because he was back to a calm façade by the time he finished eating. When the bill arrived, Andrew pushed it Aaron's way, and Aaron clipped a small stack of twenties to the check. Neil looked back as they left, seeing first the people taking cracker packets from the salad bar and second the waitress pocketing the money they'd left her.

It was a short drive from the restaurant to their real destination of the night. Eden's Twilight was a two-story nightclub a couple blocks from the main road. There was a line of people waiting to get in, and the clothes they wore made Neil's outfit look plain. Most of the men wore leather, half the

[132]

women had corsets, and a good number of both genders were covered in buckles and chains.

Neither the line nor the fashion deterred the cousins. Nicky pulled up the curb by the door and let them out. The pair of bouncers at the entrance perked up at their arrival, and Aaron greeted them with a complicated fist bump and handshake Neil didn't try to understand. One of the bouncers dug an orange tag out of his back pocket and handed it over, and Aaron brought it to Nicky. Nicky attached it to the rearview mirror and drove away to park the car somewhere.

Andrew saluted the bouncers on his way by and led the way into the club, bypassing the line entirely. Kevin followed, and Aaron motioned for Neil to go ahead of him.

A second set of doors opened into a madhouse. The four were standing on a dais that wrapped around the floor and was crowded with tables. Stairs led down to a packed dance floor. Somewhere stairs led up to the second floor, which was more a balcony than anything else. The DJ was off the floor on a platform of his own, positioned halfway between floors. Speakers taller than Neil lined the walls, and Neil could feel the bass crunching against his bones.

Neil stopped staring so he wouldn't fall behind and followed Kevin around the room. It took a bit of searching before they found a table. It was covered with glasses, but the stools were abandoned, so they claimed it. Andrew cleared away the cups while Aaron hunted down two more chairs. As soon as they were set, Andrew snagged his fingers in Neil's collar and pulled Neil after him toward the bar.

Three bartenders were on staff, but Andrew was interested in a specific one and willing to wait for him. When the man finally made it to them, he flashed Andrew an easy smile. "Back so soon, Andrew? Who's your newest victim?"

"A nobody," Andrew said. "It's the usual for us."

The man nodded and looked at Neil. "And for you?"

"I don't drink," Neil said.

[133]

"Soda, then," the man said, and pushed away to put their order together. He returned with a tray of drinks. Andrew wielded it with an easy expertise that made Neil wonder if he'd ever worked here before. When the bartender slid Neil his glass of soda last, Andrew led the way back through the crowd, pushing drunks out of his way with his free hand. Nicky was waiting for them at the table and leaned out of the way for Andrew to put the tray down past him.

"Cheers," Nicky yelled, and they drank as one.

Neil went through his soda quicker than he meant to. The others were drinking at an unhealthy speed and Nicky prodded at Neil to keep up. The soda made him feel dehydrated and the caffeine went to his head faster than he expected. He'd mostly given up soda when he tried out for the Millport Dingos last year, so he wasn't used to it anymore. When he got up to help Andrew get the second round of drinks, he thought about switching to water, but the bartender poured his soda before he could ask.

Andrew's packets from Sweetie's reappeared as soon as they made it back to the table. Andrew waggled one at Neil in taunting invitation. When Neil just looked at him, Andrew smirked and passed them out to the others instead. Even Kevin took one, which Neil found disappointing for some reason.

"Cracker dust," Nicky said as he ripped his packet open. "Heard of it? Tastes like sugar and salt and gives you a small rush. Sure you don't want in?"

"Drugs are stupid."

"Ouch," Andrew said with a cold smile. "That's judgmental."

"I'm not going to apologize for thinking you're being idiotic."

"Is your spine the spine of the righteous?" Andrew wondered. "Are you trying your best to step on my toes because you're feeling the tragic weight of the holier than thou?"

"Righteousness is for people who don't know any better."

"Easy, easy," Nicky said, distributing shots around the table. The bartender had put a bit of soda in a shot glass for Neil for this round, and Nicky set it down in front of Neil. "Dust isn't bad. It just makes the night more interesting. You think Kevin would risk his future over a night out at the club?"

"What future?" Neil asked.

Kevin shot Neil a black look, but Nicky intervened before he could say anything. "Drink with us if you won't dust with us," Nicky said, holding his open packet in one hand and his shot in the other. "Down the hatch on three."

Arguing would be fruitless when the four had left their common sense at the door, so Neil picked up his glass in silence. Nicky counted them off, and Neil knocked his shot back. As soon as it hit the back of his throat, Neil knew he'd made a serious mistake.

His sodas had tasted sweet, but this shot was almost unbearably so, and the aftertaste on Neil's tongue wasn't sugar. Neil lurched to his feet, but Andrew grabbed him by his hair and slammed him back into his seat. A cruel twist pulled his head back at a dangerous angle, and Andrew slammed Neil's hand flat against the tabletop. Neil lifted his other hand to pry Andrew's fingers off, but Nicky caught his wrist.

"Just noticed, did you?" Andrew asked. "You're an idiot."

"Y-you—" Neil sputtered.

"Did you think you were safe because you were up there ordering your own drinks? Roland knows what it means when I bring outsiders here."

Neil wrenched his hand out from under Andrew's, but Andrew gave his head a warning yank. A bolt of heat went down Neil's neck. Neil hissed in pain and went still. Andrew slid out of his chair and leaned against Neil, letting Neil take his weight while he checked Neil's eyes.

"Almost there," he said. "Give it a minute and then it'll really hit. Until then, why don't you go have a little fun? The night is still young."

[135]

Neil hadn't seen Aaron get up, but he was waiting behind Neil when Andrew let go. Neil reached for Andrew with lethal intent, but Aaron grabbed the back of his chair and pulled hard enough to topple it over. The world spun in a sickening rush even after Neil hit the ground. When Aaron tried to pull Neil to his feet, Neil swung at him and missed. Neil could feel the drugs eating through his system. His heart pounded harder than the bass did, shaking him apart from the inside out.

It took both Nicky and Aaron to get Neil up. They hauled him away from the table. Neil stumbled more than once, unable to feel the ground under his feet. He tried pulling out of Aaron's grip, but he didn't succeed until they'd reached the stairs down to the dance floor. Then Aaron let go without warning. Neil tripped down the stairs with only Nicky to break his fall. Nicky looped an arm around his waist and dragged him deeper into the writhing throng.

Bodies and lights blurred around him, making Neil nauseous. He clawed bloody lines down Nicky's arm as he fought to get free. Nicky didn't let go until they'd reached the middle of the dance floor. He pulled Neil up against him and caught Neil's chin in his fingers to force his head back.

Nicky's kiss was harder than Neil expected it to be, and there was more than just tongue in it. Beneath the burn of vodka Nicky shared with him was the sweet tang of cracker dust. Neil didn't mean to swallow, but it hurt too much to hold it in his mouth.

"This is how the game goes," Nicky said against his lips. "Stop fighting if you want to survive."

"Fuck you," Neil snarled.

"Good luck, Neil."

Nicky let go and vanished into the throng of dancers too fast for Neil to follow. The sudden loss of support made him fall. He couldn't feel his legs. It took serious work to get into a crouch, and a couple strangers had to help him up from there. Neil used the momentum to stumble away, but he didn't know which way he was supposed to be going. He couldn't see the exit through all these people, especially with the lights flashing all around him.

A hand came up against the small of his back and shoved. The push got him free of the crowd and sent him crashing into the back wall. Andrew propped his shoulder against the dark paint just out of arm's reach. Neil wanted to rip his throat open, but it was taking everything he had to just stay standing. He settled for channeling his hatred into a fierce look.

"Such ingratitude," Andrew said. "Those drinks were expensive."

"I hate you."

"Take a number and get in line with the rest of this team. I won't lose any sleep over it."

"Don't sleep. I'll kill you."

"Will you?" Andrew asked. "Will you do it yourself, or will you pay someone else to handle the mess? You certainly have enough money to outsource it to a proper hit man. One wonders what a no-one like you is doing with such a fortune."

"I found it on the sidewalk."

"Really," Andrew drawled. "Is that why you won't spend it, or do you just like looking like a homeless person? The team is split, you know. Most of them think you're trailer trash like Dan. Renee knows better. So do I. I think you're something a little more like us." Andrew leaned toward him and enunciated every syllable. "Runaway."

If Neil was sober, he'd be better steeled to hear that word. With cracker dust in his system and angry music drumming his skin to bits, he couldn't hide his flinch. "Mind your own business."

"Tonight is Mind Neil's Business Night," Andrew said. "Didn't you notice? Give me something real or I won't let you stay here."

"This isn't your team. It isn't your say."

"Don't tempt me to prove you wrong. How about I call the police and ask them to run a real check on you? You think they'll find anything interesting?"

"That's a hollow threat," Neil said. "The police would never do favors for someone like you."

"I know a cop who would," Andrew said. "If I called him tonight and told him you're a serious problem child, he'd make it a priority. How cold is your trail?"

"Shut up," Neil said. "Why can't you leave me alone?"

"Because I don't trust the way you look at him," Andrew said. "Edgar Allan is in our district and you are on my team. You, a know-nothing from Arizona who somehow managed to catch Kevin's eye. You, a lie from head to foot, with a bag full of money and a hard-on for everything Kevin and Riko. Do you understand?"

Neil did, but he was as baffled as he was furious. "I'm not a mole. Are you kidding me?"

"Prove it," Andrew said. "You take a minute to think it over. Think how badly you want to try my patience right now. I'll be back."

Andrew pushed away from the wall and slipped into the crowd. Neil watched him go, then braced himself against the wall and started down the length of it. He didn't know which way led to the door, but if he could at least find a stairwell off the dance floor he could figure something out. His survival was contingent on him getting out of this club while he still had some of his wits about him.

He finally spotted the stairs through a gap between bodies. He started up, only to be stopped as Nicky came down them. Nicky took his shoulders to push him back into the crowd, ignoring the way Neil shoved and pushed to break free. This kiss tasted worse, and Neil went numb from his mouth down.

The rest of the night was shattered colors and lights.

CHAPTER EIGHT

Neil woke up in a bed he didn't recognize in an equally unfamiliar room. He knew that disorienting feeling by name after moving so often, so it wasn't cause for immediate alarm. The weight of arms around him was one his body knew, but somehow it was confusing. There was something wrong with it that his hazy mind wasn't ready to process and he blinked hard against the headache pounding at his skull. He felt half-dead, though he couldn't for the life of him figure out why.

His first attempt at moving sent a stab of pain down his spine, so he relaxed against the sheets. The hold on him tightened a little in response to his shifting.

"Mom?" he said, but it came out slurred at best and barely intelligible.

The person behind him still understood, judging by the amused, "Not quite."

Neil knew that voice. Suddenly the events of the previous night slammed awake in his mind, flickering laser lights and music and bodies and Andrew's voice at his ear. He bolted upright but didn't make it far. The resulting pain had him collapsing against the mattress once more. Nicky caught at his hair to push his head off the side of the bed. There was a trash can there that Neil barely registered before he was throwing up into it. Nicky murmured reassurances Neil couldn't really hear.

As soon as Neil could breathe again, he twisted and shoved at Nicky as hard as he could. He was too sick and weak to push Nicky off the other side of the bed, but the boots he was still wearing would leave bruises on Nicky's arms and chest.

"Hey, hey," Nicky said, trying to deflect him. "It's fine. Ouch! Relax, will you?"

"Don't you fucking touch me," Neil said savagely.

Nicky retreated from Neil and sat on the edge of the bed instead. Neil struggled to get up, using the headboard and nightstand as support. Standing took so much out of him he had to stop and catch his breath once he made it there.

"He's awake?" someone asked from the door.

Neil snatched the alarm clock up and hurled it at the new arrival, who ducked out of the way just in time. It crashed off the doorframe. Aaron waited until it had fallen to the floor before stepping back into the doorway. Neil meant to look for another weapon, but moving so fast turned his stomach inside out. He grabbed at the trash can again and choked so hard he almost fell over.

"Where's Andrew?" Nicky asked, climbing off the bed and coming around to Neil's side.

"He and Kevin went to get us brunch."

"I don't think Neil can eat anything."

"He can watch."

Nicky laid a careful hand on Neil's shoulder. "Come on. I'll get you some water."

Neil shook him off, but his legs didn't want to carry him. Nicky let him try standing twice before looping an arm around Neil's back and steadying him. "Easy, now. I'm just going to help you to the kitchen, okay? No funny stuff, I promise."

"Like I trust you."

"Like you've got a choice," Aaron said, and left ahead of them.

Nicky helped Neil down the hall to the kitchen and set him up at the table with a glass of water. Neil's throat burned, but he refused to drink it. He settled for glaring at Nicky. Nicky looked to Aaron for help. Aaron stared back over the top of his coffee mug, unsympathetic and unhelpful. Nicky sighed and turned to Neil again.

"Can I check on your head, or are you going to bite me if I touch you?"

[140]

"What did I say last night?" Neil asked.

"Nothing to me besides an admirably creative death threat." Nicky's mouth quirked in the start of a smile but he suppressed it, maybe understanding Neil would punch him for it. "I don't know how your conversation with Andrew went, but it didn't end well. Rumor has it you paid a busboy a hundred bucks to knock you out. Way to cut our night short."

Neil didn't remember that, and the gaps in his memory left him cold all over.

"Drink up," Nicky said. "You'll need all the water you can get today. Crackers'll dehydrate you like no one's business."

Neil answered by upending his glass onto the floor.

"That's mature," Aaron said.

Neil threw the glass at him. Aaron smacked it away and let it shatter on the ground.

Nicky sighed. "Don't say I didn't warn you. You can have the shower first, okay? By the time you're out Andrew will be back and you can ask him about last night."

Nicky guided Neil to the bathroom. He started to say something else, but Neil shut the door in his face and locked it. Neil took advantage of the privacy to seethe, giving himself a full thirty seconds to silently rage over last night's stupidity. Then he balled it up and shoved it deep. Anger wasn't going to help him right now, and it wouldn't erase whatever did or didn't happen last night.

Neil checked his head in the mirror and found a sizeable lump near his left ear. He felt it out with careful fingers, then drank handfuls of water from the sink. When the buzzing in his head died a little and his throat wasn't burning quite so bad he took stock of the room. There was a pile of new clothes on the closed toilet lid. The shower was stocked, and a clean towel hung from a hook on the back of the door. A window between the mirror and the shower had white translucent glass to block the outside world.

Right now, the window was the only thing that really mattered. Nicky wanted Neil to wait for Andrew, but Neil couldn't stick around that long. There was no way he was getting in the car with them for the long ride back to Palmetto. He'd get the answers and explanations he needed, but not in unfamiliar territory with all of them against him.

In the zippered coin section of his wallet was an emergency pair of contacts. Neil ripped open the foil packets and put them on, then changed out of his club clothes and into the jeans and tee. The outfit was almost a perfect fit. Remembering how they'd figured out his size only ignited his anger further. Neil stuffed his discarded club clothes into the toilet, shoving them as deep into the water as he could and closing the lid on them. He rattled the shower curtain open, cut on the water as high as he could, and pulled the curtain closed again. The sound of the water was almost enough to hide the sound of Neil opening the window. Getting out took some serious wiggling since it wasn't quite big enough for him, but desperation was a valuable lubricant.

Lingering sickness from the drugs kept him from moving as quickly as he wanted to, but he'd traveled in far worse shape and he refused to give up. He cut through the subdivision without knowing where he was going and thumbed through his wallet to count bills. He'd taken to carrying several hundred dollars on him at a time, preparations for the worst-case scenario of not having his binder around. He had more than enough to get back to the upstate.

Following the larger streets brought him out onto a main road at last. He only had to go a few blocks before he could flag down a taxi. It took him to the nearest gas station at his request. There was a decrepit pay phone at the edge of the parking lot. Neil pushed coins into the slot and dialed Matt's number from memory. Matt answered after a couple rings with an incoherent mumble.

Neil checked his watch. It was almost ten. "Matt, it's Neil. Did I wake you?"

"Nah, I'm up," Matt said, but Neil heard the yawn in his words. "Where've you been? I didn't hear you come back last night."

"I'm in Columbia with Andrew."

"You're—what?" Matt went from half-asleep to wide awake in a heartbeat. The alarm in his voice only made Neil feel worse. "Jesus, Neil, what the hell did you do that for? Did he—" Matt aborted that and asked again, "Are you all right?"

"I'm fine," Neil lied.

He thought he sounded convincing, but maybe Matt wasn't really listening, because Matt said, "I'm going to fucking kill him." A girl's voice said something in the background, too muffled for Neil to understand. Neil guessed Matt turned the phone away from his ear to answer, because Matt's voice was quieter when he said, "He's in Columbia."

"Jesus Christ." That was definitely Dan, loud and furious.

Matt was back on the line in a heartbeat. "Seriously, are you okay?"

"I'm fine," Neil said again, "but I need a favor. I think Andrew's going to come looking for something of mine today. If I'm not there, can you keep him out of our room? I'll owe you one."

"You won't owe me anything," Matt said. "Didn't I tell you I'm good for it?"

"Thank you," Neil said. "We should be heading back soon, I think."

"You be careful, okay?" Matt said. "We'll see you in a couple hours."

Neil hung up and went inside the gas station. He stocked up on water bottles and a map, but he ran through the conversation a couple times as he walked the aisles. Matt's reaction to Neil's whereabouts was telling. Matt had been through this already; he knew what sorts of things Andrew got up to in Columbia. This

[143]

was what Matt meant when he said Andrew put him in his place last year. This was what Andrew and Abby had argued about on Neil's first day. Apparently it took the team's psychiatrist to patch Matt up after Andrew was through with him. Either Andrew listened to Abby's warning and toned Neil's party back, or Neil avoided the worst of it by getting himself knocked out.

Neil snagged a notepad and pen last and checked out. The cashier loaned him a phonebook so Neil could look up the number to a taxi service. The cab came by five minutes later and Neil took it to the nearest truck stop on Interstate 20.

There were a dozen or so big-rigs parked across the giant parking lot, most of them collected around the gas pumps. Neil was comforted by the number and sat on the sidewalk to unfold his map. He found three combinations of major roads that would get him to the northwestern region of the state and tucked his map away. He swallowed against the edges of nausea and approached the nearest trucker with a smile on his face.

"Good morning. I'm a sociology major, working on my summer project. Can I ask where you're headed?"

It took four tries before Neil found a northbound driver. The rig was taking 77, which wasn't Neil's first choice, but at least it crossed I-85 near Charlotte, North Carolina. That was the interstate Neil needed if he wanted to get back to Palmetto. Finding a truck was only half the problem. Convincing a driver to take a stranger along was the other.

He offered the driver his politest smile. "Would you be willing to give me a lift as far as Charlotte? I can pay you fifty dollars for the ride and for answering a couple questions about what it's like working this job."

"I'm not into taking on passengers," the driver said.

Neil accepted that without argument and moved on. None of the other five were going where he needed them to, so he waited off to one side as the twelve trucks were slowly replaced. When the set was complete, he tried again. This time he struck gold on the third try. Not only was the woman willing to take him, but she was going northwest on I-26. It was a faster route to 85. Neil only had to wait until the tank was full and then they were off.

Neil had hitchhiked like this before from New Mexico to Phoenix. Remembering the interview he'd made up was easy. He took notes on everything the driver said, careful to play the part of an interested student, and the drive passed relatively easily. She left him at a truck stop outside Spartanburg and pulled away with a honk of her horn.

It was easier to catch a ride from there. Neil went through the interview all over again. The driver had questions for him as well, and Neil made up his answers as he went. It took some work to convince the driver that yes, he was fine getting dropped off on the interstate, but Neil got what he wanted. The truck pulled off onto the shoulder a quarter-mile from Neil's exit. Neil paid him and climbed out onto the grass.

It was a little after noon by then. The queasiness had faded, but his head still ached. Neil took his exit on foot and walked to the nearest gas station. He bought a couple bottles of water, sat outside on the sidewalk to drink them, and bought a few more. While he waited for the pounding to die down he studied his map. It was about eleven miles to campus from here. The road was small enough he wouldn't likely catch a ride, but Neil was okay walking it. It'd be faster to run that far, but he wasn't feeling well enough to try it.

Without truckers to distract him Neil could use the walk to think. The only clear memory he had of last night was Andrew's accusation. He didn't know what else Andrew had asked him or what he'd said in response. Hopefully he'd been smart enough to lie through his teeth despite the drugs.

One thing was for sure, though. Neil couldn't afford another night out like that. If Andrew really thought Neil was a threat to Kevin, how far would he go to prove it? Neil didn't want to see what came next, but avoiding that meant compromising. He had to tell Andrew something. The truth was

[145]

out of the question, but Andrew would smell a lie a mile away. What Neil needed was something in-between that could explain everything: his money, his appearance, and his obsession with Kevin.

Neil spent the entirety of the three-hour walk sorting out a perfect half-truth. The details he was going to give up made his blood run cold, but if he could get Andrew to keep quiet about them somehow, Kevin couldn't use them to identify him.

Neil wasn't quite ready to face Andrew yet and he didn't want to deal with his teammates' curiosity over his prolonged absence, so he went to Wymack's apartment instead. By the time he arrived it was half past four. Wymack had made Neil keep the spare key, but Neil knocked on his door anyway. Wymack wrenched the door open like he wanted to take it off his hinges, but surprise washed out the fury on his face when he saw Neil.

"Where the hell have you been?" Wymack demanded, looking Neil up and down. "Andrew got back from Columbia hours ago. Matt called me to say you weren't with them."

"I took a different route."

"Yeah?" Wymack gestured at his drenched clothes and sweaty skin. "What'd you do, run here?"

"Walked," Neil said, and Wymack stared at him. Neil realized too late Wymack was being sarcastic. He couldn't take it back, so Neil traced his path in the air with a finger. "I hitchhiked to Spartanburg, then to Northlake, and I walked here from there. I know it's kind of sudden, but can I stay here for a little while?"

Wymack grabbed his elbow and hauled him inside. He slowed just long enough to slam the door behind Neil. "Are you stupid or just crazy? Do you have any idea what could have happened to you between here and there? What were you thinking?"

"I was thinking I wasn't going to ride back with them," Neil said.

[146]

"You should have called me," Wymack said. "Me or Abby or any of the upperclassmen. All you had to say was you didn't want to stay with Andrew. Any of us would have come and gotten you."

Neil stared at him, too startled to respond. Wymack threw his free hand up in exaggerated disgust and dragged Neil down the hall to the kitchen.

"Stretch out and drink some water," he said, letting go of Neil.

Neil did as he was told but watched as Wymack stormed out of the kitchen again. Wymack paced up and down the hall with angry, heavy footsteps. On his second pass he had his phone out and at his ear. He was out of sight when someone picked up on the other end, but Neil heard his furious voice loud and clear.

"You have five seconds to get your retarded psycho ass to my apartment! You even think about telling me no and I swear to god I'll throw Kevin's contract down a garbage disposal."

Neil didn't think Wymack stayed on the line long enough to get an answer, because he was off the phone when he came back a couple seconds later. He was carrying a towel and an armful of clothes, all of which he shoved at Neil.

"You're a sopping mess. Get out of my sight and clean up before I wring your neck."

Neil took everything down the hall to the bathroom and locked himself in. He kept the water tepid as he washed away the day's heat and sweat. The clothes Wymack leant him were ridiculously big on him, but at least they covered his scars. Neil bundled his dirty clothes into the wet towel and left the bathroom with them. He felt relaxed for the first time all day, but that faded at the sound of Wymack's angry voice. Neil crept down the hall toward the living room.

Andrew was standing silent in the middle of the room as Wymack went up one side of him and down the other. Judging by the impatient look on his face, Andrew was still sober. He was also facing the door, which meant he spotted Neil first.

"Have a nice stroll?" he asked, interrupting Wymack's tirade.

Neil returned his cold stare with a heated, "Fuck you."

Wymack snapped his fingers in front of Andrew's face, trying to get Andrew to look at him instead of Neil. "I don't know what the beef is between you two, but it ends here and now. Abby and I made it clear we wouldn't tolerate a repeat of last year, Andrew."

"This isn't a repeat." The edge in Andrew's voice said he'd already argued this point several times. "We only gave him crackers. You think he'd have made it back here on his own otherwise?"

"Don't 'only' me. What the fuck were you thinking?"

"What were you thinking, bringing him here?" Andrew returned.

Neil decided to cut in before Andrew shared any of his theories. "Coach, I need to talk to Andrew for a minute. Can we use your office?"

"No," Wymack said. "I don't trust you two not to kill each other, so you're staying right here until this is resolved."

That left only one option, but Neil hated losing his wild card so early in the game. He hoped Wymack couldn't speak German and switched languages to lay into Andrew. "What the hell is your problem? How can you threaten Nicky for coming onto me but condone drugging me out of my mind against my will? Why can't you just leave me alone?"

That wiped the irritation off Andrew's face. It was forever before Andrew answered in German. "That's unexpected. Did no one tell you I hate surprises?"

"What makes you think I care?"

"How many languages do you speak, runaway?"

Neil ignored that. "Tell me why you did that."

[148]

"I already did," Andrew said. "I'm still waiting for your answer."

"I answered you. I told you I'm not a mole. You're insane if you think I am."

"Then correct me."

"Give me a reason."

"Besides the obvious?" Andrew said. "If I can't get an answer from you, I'll get it wherever I can. How about I start with your parents?"

"Good luck," Neil said, feeling cold all over. "They're dead."

"Did you kill them?"

He said it so casually, like he was asking for the time, that Neil could only stare at him for a minute. It was such an unreasonable leap of logic Neil didn't understand how he even thought to ask it. Then he remembered who he was talking to and asked, "Did you kill yours?"

Andrew gave a dismissive flick of his fingers. "I don't have parents."

It was only a half-lie. The twins didn't know who their father was, and only Aaron grew up with their biological mother. Andrew was surrendered to foster care when he was just a few days old. He spent thirteen years in the system and three at juvie. It wasn't until he was released on early parole that his mother let Andrew move home. Five months later she died in a car accident. Neil doubted Andrew attended the funeral.

"I didn't kill my parents," Neil said, but he couldn't go on. Fear was an iron grip around his lungs, making it impossible to breathe. Neil trusted the story he'd patched together on his walk, but he didn't want to say it aloud. The words came out in jagged pieces and he hoped his struggle added realism to the lies. "Riko's family did."

That got Andrew's attention. Neil swallowed hard, trying to clear the tightness from his throat, and forced himself to explain.

[149]

"My father was a gopher for a group who did business with the Moriyamas. In the grand scheme of things he wasn't worth much, but he knew a lot of names and he knew how to move product. He did some business out of Edgar Allan, which is how I met Kevin and Riko. I didn't know who they were back then. I was just excited to meet kids my age. I thought we were going to be friends.

"Then my father started getting cocky, started getting stupid, and tried skimming from payments. He took Moriyama money that was meant for his boss. They found out, of course. The Moriyamas executed him and my mother before his boss could get to him. I took what he'd stolen and ran. I've been running ever since."

Andrew wasn't smiling anymore, but Neil was. He felt it as it curved across his lips and knew it was a sick, ghastly expression. He dug his fingernails into his mouth, trying to claw the look off his face, but it was frozen in place.

"I'm lucky Kevin doesn't recognize me," Neil said. "I don't know if he even remembers meeting me, but I remember him. Seeing him helps me remember my parents. He's all I have left of my real life. But if Kevin or Riko recognizes me and word makes it back to my father's boss, I know what will happen to me."

Andrew said nothing for so long Neil thought he'd blown it, but finally Andrew moved. Wymack shifted his weight, ready to intervene if things turned violent, but Andrew only came to stand right in front of Neil.

"Then why did you come here?" Andrew asked.

"Because I'm tired," Neil said, trying to sound defeated. It didn't take much effort. "I have nowhere else to go, and I'm too jealous of Kevin to stay away from him. He knows what it's like to hate every day of his life, to wake up afraid every day, but he's got you at his back telling him everything's going to be okay. He has everything, even when he's lost everything, and I'm—" Neil didn't want to say it, but the word was already there, broken and pathetic between them, "—nothing. I'll always have and be nothing."

Andrew reached up and forcibly uncurled Neil's fingers from his mouth. He pushed Neil's hand out of the way and stared Neil down with nothing between them. Neil didn't understand the look on his face. There was no censure over Neil's crooked parents or pity for their deaths, no triumph over having backed Neil into admitting so much, and no obvious skepticism for such an outlandish story. Whatever this look was, it was dark and intense enough to swallow Neil whole.

"Let me stay," Neil said quietly. "I'm not ready to give this up yet."

That strange look left Andrew's eyes. His expression cleared to stony indifference and he let go of Neil. "Keep it if you can. You and I both know it won't last long."

Neil's stomach gave a nauseating flip. He'd been lying since he'd first learned to speak. What he'd just told Andrew was fifty percent truth, the most honest thing he'd ever tell someone about his life, and Andrew took it without batting an eye. Neil didn't know how to feel about that. He should be relieved, because it meant Andrew might be done asking him questions, but it went deeper than that. He wondered for a moment if Andrew could handle the entire truth so calmly, but that was too dangerous and stupid to consider.

"I'll be gone by our match against Edgar Allan," Neil said. "I don't look now how I looked then, but I can't risk Riko's family recognizing me."

"Such an unexpected will to survive from someone who has nothing to live for. Next time we have a little heart-to-heart like this, maybe I'll ask you to justify that."

"Let's not talk like this ever again."

"Let's not," Andrew agreed.

Neil hesitated, then asked, "Are you going to tell Kevin?"

"Don't ask me stupid questions."

[151]

Relief was almost strong enough to bring him to his knees. Neil sucked in a slow, rattling breath and closed his eyes. As the day's anger and fear ebbed away he was left feeling exhausted and hollow. Maybe Andrew's night out in Columbia had been awful, and maybe he'd never wanted to say these things out loud, but having the air cleared between him and Andrew to some degree took an enormous weight off his chest. He'd convinced Andrew to back off and leave him alone. The Foxhole Court was his until their match against the Ravens. It wasn't freedom, and it wasn't safety, but it was breathing room. That was enough.

"We're leaving," Andrew said in English.

Neil opened his eyes. "Where are we going?"

"Back to the dorm," Andrew said. "Your teammates have been annoying us ever since we got back, demanding we return to Columbia and scour the streets in search of you."

"He can stay here if he wants," Wymack said. "I can call Dan to let her know he's safe."

Andrew didn't look at Wymack. "Neil wants to come with me."

A day ago, those words might have been an order or a threat, but today Neil heard only truth. He'd chosen the Foxes. He'd chosen to trust Andrew, whatever that meant and whatever consequences it brought down the road. There was no reason or need to hide behind Wymack now.

"Thanks for the shower," Neil said to Wymack. "I'll wash your clothes and bring them back on Monday."

Wymack glanced between them, obviously wondering if they'd really settled things that easily, and said, "No rush."

"Going now," Andrew said, and led Neil out.

Wymack must have called ahead anyway, because when they got back to the dorm all of the Foxes were in the hallway waiting for them. Kevin, Aaron, and Nicky were leaning against the wall near their suite door. The upperclassmen stood in a small clump in the middle of the hallway outside Dan's room.

Neil wanted to skip the questions and hide in his room, but as soon as he was close enough Dan caught his shoulders and patted him down for injuries.

"Are you okay?" Dan asked.

"I'm fine," Neil said.

"Andrew?" Kevin asked.

Andrew paused in his doorway long enough to look at Kevin. "I'm washing my hands of this. He's your problem now."

He disappeared into his room. Aaron and Nicky exchanged looks before following. Kevin was the last to leave, and not without sending Neil a searching look first. Neil watched the door close behind them, then faced the rest of his teammates. Dan still looked angry, and Matt looked wired for a fight. Seth and Allison were already heading for Neil's room, likely bored by the peaceful resolution. Renee's gaze was searching. Neil couldn't hold her stare for long.

"Coach said you hitchhiked your way back here," Dan said. "I'd yell at you for being stupid, but Coach said he handled that already."

"Lesson learned," Neil said. "Next time I'll call for a ride."

"There won't be a next time." Dan gave a heavy sigh and scrubbed her face. "Come on."

They went back to Neil's suite. Six piles of cards lay face down in the living from an interrupted game and were surrounded by a graveyard of crumpled beer cans. Allison and Seth were rummaging through the fridge when Neil passed. Renee continued to the living room to get her cards, but Dan and Matt followed Neil to the bedroom. They stopped in the doorway and watched as Neil went to his safe. Neil traced the lines of it with his fingers and tugged on the combination lock. It didn't look tampered with, but he couldn't check the contents with an audience.

"You were right," Matt said. "Andrew tried to get in."

"We didn't let him," Dan said. "He didn't make it further than the front door."

[153]

"Thank you," Neil said.

"Thank Renee," Dan said. "She doesn't take sides all that often."

"It's so much easier when she does, though," Matt said.

"Andrew seems to like her," Neil said.

"They've got an understanding," Matt said, but didn't explain. "We're between rounds in our game. You should join in. It'll help clear your head, I think. Spending too much time with Andrew's lot will rattle anyone."

"I'm probably going to crash early," Neil said. "It was a long day."

"We'll take our stuff to my room," Dan said, and they closed the door on their way out.

Neil waited until their voices faded before unlocking his safe. He found everything where it was supposed to be. As he slipped the lock into place again he realized his hand was trembling. He held up his shaky fingers where he could see them better and wondered at the equally weak flutter in his chest.

Hope was a dangerous, disquieting thing, but he thought perhaps he liked it.

CHAPTER NINE

Neil didn't see Andrew's group again until practices on Monday. He was happy to keep his distance, and they seemed to finally have lost interest in him. When they had to interact on the court they kept it short and civil. Even Kevin seemed to have forgotten his lines. His barbed remarks were gone, replaced by a heavy, unwavering stare that somehow made Neil feel even more insignificant than he had before. Neil refused to miss his condescension, but being the bug in Kevin's microscope made him jumpy.

He was still trying to sort it out when he climbed into bed that night, but he didn't have long to dwell on it. Someone pounded on the suite door, too heavy-fisted to be one of the girls. Matt was on his computer in the other room, and Neil heard his chair creak as he got up to investigate. Neil didn't hear what he or their visitor said, but he definitely heard the door bang closed against someone's unyielding body.

"Kevin, I swear to God—"

Kevin's name was enough to get Seth out of bed. The fifth-year senior threw his covers back and rolled off the side of his bed. Faced with both Seth and Matt, Kevin had no choice but to retreat, and the door slammed closed a couple seconds later. Neil stared at the bedroom door, heart hammering in his chest. Kevin wouldn't have come over here for either of them, which meant he was looking for Neil. Neil didn't know why, but he desperately hoped it didn't have to do with his conversation with Andrew. Why had he assumed Andrew would keep his story a secret? Andrew and Kevin were connected at the hip.

Sleeping after that was almost impossible, and getting up for practice the next morning was a chore. He braced himself for the worst, but Tuesday was a repeat of Monday: the same casual cold shoulder from the cousins and measuring stare from Kevin. Neil was almost relieved when Kevin caught up to him at the end of practice. He'd just cut the water off when Kevin rapped once on his shower stall door.

"The next time I come for you, you will follow me," Kevin said.

"Why?" Neil asked.

"It's time to collect what's mine," Kevin said. "Andrew isn't going to interfere anymore."

Neil didn't understand, but Kevin didn't stick around to explain.

At ten o'clock, a knock came at his dorm room door again. Neil was watching a movie with Seth and Matt, but he made sure he was the first off the couch. He wasn't surprised to find Kevin waiting on the other side. Seth swore viciously at the sight of Kevin in the doorway. The movie's sounds abruptly cut off as someone paused it, and the couch creaked as the others got up.

"What part of 'You're not welcome here' do you not understand?" Matt demanded.

Kevin ignored them and shoved an Exy ball hard against Neil's chest. "Let's go."

Neil hesitated, but he didn't have long to decide. Seth and Matt were coming up fast behind him ready for a fight. Neil put his arm out to stop them. If Seth was in front, he might have bulled past Neil to get his hands on Kevin's throat, but Matt pulled up short.

"I'll be back later," Neil said over his shoulder.

"Are you stupid?" Seth asked.

"Yeah," Neil said. "Finish the movie without me. I don't mind."

Seth huffed and stormed away, but Matt moved into the hall to watch as Kevin and Neil left. Neil didn't look back at him but followed Kevin downstairs to the back parking lot. There

[156]

were more cars now than there'd been at the start of the summer, but Neil hadn't seen any new faces around the dormitory. Whatever team was moving in was on a different floor from the Exy line and Neil wasn't in any rush to play meet-and-greet.

Andrew was waiting for them in the car. Neil was surprised even though he knew he shouldn't be. Kevin didn't go anywhere alone. It didn't matter what time of night it was; with Edgar Allan in their district Kevin wasn't going to suddenly get brave. Neil thought about the last time he'd gone to the court in the middle of the night and found Andrew watching Kevin practice. It made him wonder how many times they did this.

Andrew was in the driver's seat, arms folded across the steering wheel to make a pillow for his head. His eyes were closed and he didn't stir when Kevin opened the passenger door. Kevin leaned over and looked in at him.

"I can drive, you know," Kevin said.

"The day I let you drive my car is the day I'm dead," Andrew said. "Are you getting in or are we going back to bed?"

Kevin sighed heavily as if Andrew was being unusually difficult and climbed in. Neil got in the backseat and sat in the middle where he could see both of them. Andrew twisted the key in the ignition as he sat up and drove them to the stadium.

Kevin let them through the gates and into the locker room with his keys. Andrew waited in the foyer while Kevin and Neil changed into their court gear, watched as they gathered their racquets and some gear, and followed them to the inner ring. When Kevin and Neil went for the court door, he went up the stairs into the stands to wait on them.

Kevin bolted the court door behind them, set the balls and his racquet aside, and got Neil moving right away. They ran a couple laps along the inside of the court walls, did intervals with the court lines, and stretched out at half-court. When Kevin was satisfied, he started going through drills. They started with a simple game of catch and quickly escalated to more complicated exercises. Neil recognized only a few of them. Those he didn't know were harder to pick up and Kevin's impatience, absent the last two days of practice, put in an unfriendly reappearance.

The last drill they did was the hardest. Kevin grabbed cones from the locker room and set them each up with a line of six. The name of the game was to rebound the ball off the court wall in a way that it'd knock the cones over. It wasn't enough to have an accurate throw; Neil had to be both accurate and powerful. Neil didn't expect it to be so difficult, but he'd never needed such hairpin precision before. Rebounds were used when passing the ball to teammates across the court. Teammates were intelligent, moving targets who could react to a ball's trajectory, whereas these cones were static targets.

Neil's first time through he managed to hit a grand total of one cone. Kevin got three of his six, but he was doing it with his weaker hand, so his misses didn't make Neil feel any better.

"You have too much free time if you're coming up with drills like this," Neil said after he flunked a second round.

"This is a Raven drill," Kevin said. "No one is allowed game time until he or she can knock every cone over in whichever order the master calls. Freshmen spend weeks to months trying to earn a spot on our line."

"The master?"

"Coach Moriyama," Kevin said after a pause. Neil could hear the grimace in Kevin's response, but he didn't know if it was because Neil was making Kevin say his name or because he'd slipped up so obviously. Kevin recovered by switching his racquet to his left hand and giving it an experimental swirl. "Call them for me. Don't stop."

Neil didn't think it was a good idea for Kevin to play left-handed, even if it'd been six months since his assault, but he didn't argue. He counted the cones off in random order with only a second between the numbers. Kevin didn't wait for him to finish but moved with him, scooping balls from the ground in front of him and hurling them at the wall. All six shots landed, sending Kevin's cones toppling in the exact order Neil called.

[158]

Kevin hit the last cone with enough force to send it rolling several feet.

Between the Foxes' in-fighting this past week and Kevin's bullying all through May, Neil had almost forgotten why he liked Exy so much. He did his best at practices but these days he worked mostly to keep his teammates off his back. As Neil surveyed Kevin's damage, he finally felt inspired again. On its heels was a hungry, desperate rush.

"I want that," Neil said.

"Then start really trying." Kevin lined his cones up again and switched his racquet back to his right hand. He gave his left a small shake as he returned to his starting spot. "This is the first of eight Raven precision drills. When you master this one, we will move on. We'll meet every weeknight save Friday until you can do all of them in your sleep."

"But we've lost a month of practice already," Neil said. "Why couldn't we have started this in May?"

"Because you set Andrew off unnecessarily," Kevin said, annoyed. "He said I couldn't be alone with you and he wouldn't let me bring you here."

"And you always do what Andrew says?" Neil asked.

"He is the only reason I can stay here, so yes," Kevin said. "Now shut up and practice. We're weeks behind where you should be at this point."

They spent the next half-hour on that same drill before moving on to footwork. Kevin called it quits at twelve-thirty. Neil was disappointed to stop after just two hours, but as he helped Kevin collect their balls and cones, fatigue started to set in. He was yawning by the time he followed Kevin off the court.

Kevin went into the stands to find Andrew, so Neil took a rare first shower. He was halfway through when Kevin joined him. Neil dried off and dressed in the sticky heat of the shower room and went into the locker room to drop his uniform off. He waited there for Kevin, and then followed Kevin to the lounge to collect Andrew on their way out. Andrew said nothing to

[159]

either of them as he drove back to the dorm, and they filed up the stairs to the third floor in silence.

Neil was quiet as he went into his dorm room, but the excess care was unnecessary. Matt was at his desk, bleary-eyed and half-slouched. He perked up a bit as Neil closed the door behind him, and in the light from his monitor Neil could see the worry on Matt's face.

"You good?"

Neil realized Matt had been waiting up for him. Surprise warred with unexpected guilt in an uncomfortable twinge. "Yes. He's teaching me Raven drills."

"You're going to hate getting up in the morning," Matt said, shutting his computer down.

Neil knew he wouldn't. He'd be tired and sore, but he'd be getting up so he could go back to the court. It wasn't worth arguing about, so he murmured something unintelligible and preceded Matt into the bedroom. Matt got into bed while Neil collected his sleeping clothes, and by the time Neil finished changing, Matt was already asleep. Neil climbed up the ladder into his bunk and passed out as soon as his head hit the pillow.

It felt like only a matter of seconds before his alarm was going off to wake him up again. Neil double-checked his clock to make sure it was right, scrubbed the exhaustion out of his eyes, and went down the ladder to get ready for the day.

Maybe last night's practice was an icebreaker in Kevin's strange world, because Kevin's angry comments made a comeback this morning. They harkened more to the angry disappointment Kevin started the summer with, though, and less like the hostile insults Kevin resorted to after hearing about the district change. Neil tried to appreciate the difference and almost succeeded.

The cousins still had nothing to say to Neil, but Neil noticed Nicky watching Kevin and Neil from time to time throughout practice. Seemed he hadn't missed the thawing ice between the two. Neil waited for him to say something, but

[160]

anytime Neil looked Nicky's way, Nicky feigned to find something else suddenly fascinating. Neil let it slide, unwilling to be the first to break the silence after what Nicky had helped Andrew do to him in Columbia.

Nicky's patience lasted until Wednesday afternoon. Andrew had weekly sessions with his psychiatrist on Wednesdays. Nicky dropped him off at the medical center while the Foxes were lunching and made it back in time to change out for afternoon drills. The men were all in the changing room, checking the straps on their armor and tugging their uniforms on again, when Nicky broke.

Except when Nicky finally spoke up, it was in German, and it wasn't to Neil.

"You think he's ever going to forgive us?" Nicky asked.

"Does it matter?" Aaron said. "He's not our problem."

Neil forgot the collar he was tightening around his neck and turned to stare at them. Andrew knew he could speak German, which meant these two should know Neil could understand them. Neil wondered if they expected him to join in, if Nicky was passively inviting him to forgive or condemn them without the others listening in on it, but neither man was looking at him.

"What do you mean, he's not our problem?" Nicky asked, but Aaron didn't answer. Nicky waited but lost patience before long. "Are we really doing this all over again? You want to fight these guys all the way to graduation?"

"I want to be left alone."

"This is a team sport!"

The others had been ignoring them, likely used to the occasional German conversation, but Nicky's strident tone got their attention. Seth glanced over with an irritated scowl, but Matt flicked a curious look between the cousins. Kevin didn't look up, likely used to the occasional squabbling by now.

Nicky didn't seem to notice the attention he was getting. "You can't live like this, Aaron. I can't live like this. It's exhausting and depressing."

"Okay."

"'Okay'? Just 'okay'? This isn't okay. Jesus. Sometimes you're so much like Andrew it's horrifying."

Aaron's expression was livid. "Fuck you."

"Hey," Matt said loudly. "Break it up, you two. What the hell?"

Aaron pushed off the bench and stormed out, leaving Nicky glowering after him. Matt looked from the door to Nicky, frowning.

"Nicky?" he asked.

Nicky affected a wounded look and tilted his entire body toward Matt. "Aaron hurt my feelings! Kiss it better, Matt?"

"Faggot," Seth said, stalking out.

Matt wasn't swayed. "You guys all right?"

Nicky feigned confusion. "Of course we are. Why?"

Matt looked at Kevin, then Neil, waiting for one of them to back him up. Kevin ignored him, so Neil gave a slight shrug. Matt let it go and finished getting ready. Nicky gathered the last of his uniform and left a couple seconds later. Neil watched him go.

It wasn't an act. They wouldn't have let their argument take such a personal turn if they knew Neil was listening to every word. But that meant Andrew hadn't told them, and Neil didn't know why Andrew would keep such a secret from his own family. Maybe it slipped his mind when he medicated Saturday night, but it was a big thing to forget.

Neil didn't know what game Andrew was playing or what he expected to get in return for his silence. He kept an eye on Andrew when Andrew made it back from Betsy Dobson's office, but when he might have had the chance to ask, he let it slide. Andrew was drugged and happy; Neil didn't want him to change his mind in a burst of scatterbrained amusement.

[162]

That night Kevin was at his door again. Neil bid his disgruntled teammates goodnight and followed Kevin to the car. Andrew was smoking in the driver's seat but stubbed his cigarette out upon their arrival. He took them to the stadium, waited for them to change, and went up into the stands as they continued to the court.

When Kevin locked the court door behind them, Neil asked, "How often do you two come here?"

"Every night," Kevin said.

Neil looked over his shoulder at the stands, but he couldn't see Andrew. "Isn't he bored of this by now? He's never going to practice with you, so why does he humor you?"

"He will," Kevin said. "He just doesn't know it yet."

"I didn't take you for an optimist."

Kevin ignored that and started setting out cones for interval runs. "Let's go."

Neil pushed Andrew out of his thoughts and focused on Kevin's drills.

-

They had two weeks of practice before the ERC made an official announcement regarding the district change. The day's practice was over and the team was back at the dorm when Wymack called to warn them. Matt flipped on the TV and went to ESPN to see the segment. They'd missed seeing the news itself but were in time to see the reactions on the news show. The anchorman was gesturing wildly and talking a mile a minute. One of his guests was shaking his head in exaggerated disapproval; the other kept trying and failing to interrupt.

"Here it comes," Matt said. "They'll be all over us like white on rice. Coach's phone is going to be ringing off the hook for weeks."

"I didn't sign up to be part of a freak show," Seth said, cracking open another can of beer. "Let's just send him back north and be done with it."

"Why do you hate him?" Neil asked.

[163]

Seth looked at Matt. "Told you this kid was stupid."

"Why do you hate him so much," Neil clarified, "that you'd wish such a thing on him?"

"Because I'm sick of him getting everything he wants just because he's Kevin Day," Seth said. When Matt started to say something, Seth pointed a warning finger at him and kept going. "Do you know what fame gets you, shitface? Everything. All he has to do is ask for it, and someone will give it to him. Doesn't matter what. Doesn't matter who. The world is dying to give him anything he wants.

"When he broke his hand, his fans cried for him. They flooded our locker room with letters and flowers. The amazing Kevin Day can't play anymore, they said. Their lives were over. They'd grieve the loss forever. But tell me," Seth said, leaning forward on the couch to stare at Neil, "when's the last time anyone cried for you? Never, right? They're there for Kevin every step of the way, but where were they when we needed them?"

"So you're jealous," Neil said.

Seth made as if to throw his beer at Neil. "His life is not more important than mine just because he's more talented."

"You have to admit your attitude makes it hard for anyone to care about you," Neil said. "You and Kevin both have impossible attitudes, but he can play better. Of course they chose him."

"Look here, shortbus," Seth started, incensed.

"He has a point," Matt cut in. "This is your last year, Seth. Maybe it's time for a fresh start. Give the people someone to rally behind and you'll win them over."

"What's the point?" Seth slouched back on the couch again. "We're the laughingstock of the NCAA and Edgar Allan is going to massacre us this fall. It doesn't matter what I do. No one will ever recruit a Fox to the pros."

"Awesome attitude, Seth," Matt said. "Way to encourage the rest of us."

[164]

"I am encouraging you," Seth said. "I'm encouraging you all to stop being stupid. You're not going to get anywhere so long as you play for this team."

"You're too big of a coward to try," Matt said. "Neil and I will prove you wrong. Right, Neil?"

"I'm just here to play," Neil said. "I don't care about the future."

Matt stared at him. "You don't really believe that."

Neil shrugged. "Afraid so."

Matt looked between them. Seth raised his beer in a silent toast, somehow looking both smug and angry.

"I can't believe you two," Matt said at last. Neither man answered him. Matt looked to the ceiling for answers, then said, "I guess our dinner plans are scratched. I'm not going downtown if the press is out and about; I don't care how many campus police Chuck gave us. Let's see about ordering in and watching a movie or something. You guys sit here and wallow in self-defeat or something while I check with Dan."

Seth jeered at Matt's back as Matt left, then looked at Neil. "Maybe you're not as stupid as I thought."

"Maybe I am," Neil said, and left Seth to finish his drink.

CHAPTER TEN

Classes were scheduled to start on Thursday, August 24th, so Wednesday's practice was a bit of a convoluted mess. Neil had forgotten the Foxes were supposed to meet with the psychiatrist Betsy Dobson before the semester began. Wymack scheduled them to go in pairs throughout the morning and tried to set them up in a way that didn't leave holes in his scrimmage lines. Matt and Dan went first, then Aaron and Kevin, Seth and Allison, and Nicky and Andrew. Neil and Renee were the last to go.

When Andrew and Nicky returned to the court Wymack called Neil and Renee off. Andrew waited for them in the inner ring long enough to hand Renee his keys.

"Thank you," Renee said, smiling. "I'll take care of her."

"Kevin's not allowed to drive your car but Renee is?" Neil asked.

"It's fun telling Kevin no," Andrew said with a wicked grin.

"Andrew only lets me and Renee drive," Nicky said. His smile didn't reach his eyes as he watched Renee turn the keys over in her hand. Nicky only had nice things to say about Renee, but Neil had noticed early on that no one, Nicky included, wanted Renee and Andrew to be friends. Nicky likely sided with the upperclassmen in thinking Andrew was an awful influence on someone as sweet-tempered as Renee.

"Not Aaron?" Neil asked.

"Don't keep Bee waiting," Andrew said, and headed onto the court.

Nicky only shrugged and followed him. Neil glanced between Renee and Wymack, but neither had an answer for him. Renee only smiled warmly and said, "Shall we go?"

Neil and Renee split up in the locker room long enough to change out and freshen up. There was no point in showering when they'd be coming back to a lunch break and more drills, but neither wanted to show up at Betsy's office a sweaty mess. Neil took his armor off, toweled dry, and changed into the lighter uniform they'd need that afternoon for cardio. He beat Renee to the lounge and they left the stadium together.

After successfully avoiding being alone with Renee all summer, Neil was stuck with her for the drive across campus to Reddin Medical Center. He wanted to ask her why she and Andrew got along so well, but he didn't want to open up a conversation, so he stared hard out the window and hoped she got the hint. Somehow she did, and she filled the silence between them with the radio.

There were more cars at Reddin than Neil expected, but he knew he shouldn't be surprised. The school year was just around the corner. Fox Tower was full now and he'd seen traffic around campus as the rest of the student body moved into the other dormitories. Long practices and nights spent in his room meant he'd avoided most everyone so far, but people kept showing up at his dorm looking for Matt or Seth. Neil did his best to stay out of sight anytime someone knocked, since Wymack still hadn't released his name or face to the ERC. Neil wanted to protect his anonymity as long as he could.

Reddin was split in half, with psychiatrics down a hall out of sight and an array of doctors' offices closer to the front. Renee signed them both in at the desk and went down the hall in search of Betsy's office. Neil settled on one of the pale blue couches in the waiting room and tried not to stare at the clock. Every minute that went by wound him tenser until he thought every breath would break him open, but he couldn't make himself relax. The thought of being locked up with a psychiatrist for half an hour was too awful.

What felt like an eternity later, Renee returned with a woman on her heels. Dr. Betsy Dobson had pale brown hair to

[167]

her chin and a few extra curves. Years of smiles were etched into her face the way only genuine warmth could scar. She looked friendly, but she wasn't harmless. The brown eyes looking out at him through narrow-rimmed glasses were bright and intelligent. Neil took an instant disliking to her, borne of nerves and serious distrust of her profession.

"You must be Neil," she said. "Good morning."

Neil made himself get up and cross the room to her. She held out her hand at his approach and Neil gave it a firm shake. Renee smiled a little, maybe in encouragement, and sidled past him to find a seat. Neil resisted the urge to wipe his hand off on his pants and preceded Betsy down the hall.

There was only one door open, and Betsy's name was on a plaque beside it. Neil invited himself in and looked around. A chair and a couch faced each other with a short coffee table between them. A small potted plant was in the dead center of the table, and pillows were painstakingly arranged on both the couch and the chair. The desk in the corner was clear of everything but a hot plate and kettle. A short bookshelf was against the wall, but only the bottom three shelves had books on them. The top one was covered in glass knickknacks, but even in their clutter they looked clean, as they were all set equidistant to each other.

Betsy stepped into the doorway behind him. "My name is Betsy Dobson. You can call me whatever you like; I'll answer to just about anything from Betsy to Doc to Hey You. Shall I call you Neil, or would you prefer Mr. Josten?"

"Either one is fine," Neil said.

"Then for the time being, I will call you Neil. If you're ever offended or feel this makes our relationship too personal, just warn me and I will edit it to something more appropriate to our needs. Sound fair?" She gave him a moment, then said, "Why don't you get comfortable and I'll make us some hot cocoa."

Neil sat on the edge of the couch and said, "But it's August."

"Chocolate is good any time of the year, don't you think?" Betsy said.

"I don't like sweets," Neil said.

Betsy took a mug and container of cocoa out of one of her desk drawers. "As you know, today is a casual appointment so we can get to know one another. This isn't a formal session where I'll be analyzing everything you say for feedback and advice, so don't stress too much about it. Have you seen a counselor before?"

"No," Neil said. "I don't know why I have to be here today."

"Palmetto State made it policy a few years ago," Betsy said. "The board expects a lot from all of their students, and more from their athletic representatives. This way they're allowing you a way to vent some of the pressure and stress they're leveling on you."

"They're keeping an eye on their investment, you mean," Neil said.

"That is a way of looking at it." Betsy finished stirring her drink and brought her mug to the chair across from his. "Tell me a little about yourself, Neil."

"What do you want me to say?"

"Where are you from?"

"Millport, Arizona."

"I haven't heard of it."

"It's a small place," Neil said. "The only people who live there are either too old to move out or too young to escape. There's nothing to do except play sports or bingo. We only moved there because it's halfway between Tucson and Phoenix. My mother worked in one and my father the other."

"What do they do?"

Neil hadn't talked about his family much in Millport, but he'd arrived in Arizona already knowing who the Jostens were and what their problems were like. The answers he'd kept from

[169]

his high school classmates and coach would have to be good enough for Betsy.

"Mom is an engineer," Neil said. "Dad's halfway through CDL training."

"Will they come out to watch your first match?"

Neil affected surprise. "No. Why would they? They don't like sports."

"But Exy is obviously very important to you, and you are their child," Betsy said. "What you've accomplished here is nothing short of amazing. I wondered if they might come out to support you."

"No. They don't really—" Neil gestured as if searching for words. "We're not close like that. They made sure I got to school and got my checkups and kept my grades up, that kind of thing, but they didn't know my teachers' names or watch any of my games. It's not going to change now that I'm in college. They live their lives; I live mine. It works for us."

"Does it?"

"I said it does," Neil said. "I don't want to talk about my parents with you."

Betsy accepted that and moved on without missing a beat. "How are you getting along with your teammates?"

"I'm pretty sure the majority of them are clinically insane."

"When you say you think they are insane, do you mean you feel threatened by them?"

"I mean they have issues," Neil said. "You know more than I do. Friday's game will probably be a disaster, but I don't think anyone will be surprised."

"Are you ready for the match?"

"Yes and no," Neil said. "I know I'm not good enough to play with a Class I team, but I want to try. I watch a lot of games on TV, but I've never been in a real stadium on game night. We used a soccer field in Arizona that barely sat two thousand people. Coach said we've already sold out opening night. I want to see what the Foxhole Court looks like when it's full. I bet it's insane."

"And Friday doubles as your debut," Betsy added. "The ERC has been generous, letting David keep quiet on you this long. I can only imagine the fallout when the cat's out of the bag."

It took Neil a moment to recognize the name, because only Abby used Wymack's first name. That Betsy called him David so easily hinted at a closer relationship than he expected a psychiatrist and coach to have. Maybe it was because she spent so much time with Wymack's team, but Neil wasn't convinced. Dimly Neil remembered his first dinner in South Carolina, when Abby said she'd invited Betsy over to dinner with them. The three were friends of a sort, which didn't bode well for Neil. How much did they talk about the Foxes?

"You're friends with Coach," Neil said.

"Abby and I went to school together in Charleston and stayed in touch after graduation. I met David through her," Betsy said. "I am their friend, but I respect the sanctity of our relationship as doctor and patient. What you and I say in here is meant for us alone. They will never ask, and I will never tell. Do you believe me?"

"How can I?" Neil asked. "I just met you."

"I respect that," Betsy said. "Hopefully I can earn your trust over time."

Neil wasn't planning on seeing her ever again, no matter all his promises of a next time, so he went with a neutral, "Hopefully."

He glanced at the clock, calculated how much time was left, and swallowed a sigh. If Betsy noticed his distraction, she didn't comment on it. Instead she filled the rest of the session with idle chitchat about the season and the upcoming semester. Neil continued feeding her easy answers that wouldn't raise any flags and counted minutes in his head. When his time was finally up, he got up and preceded her from the room.

Betsy followed him down the hall but stopped in the doorway to the waiting room to clasp his hand. "It was nice to meet you."

"You, too," Neil lied.

Renee stood, bid Betsy another farewell, and went with Neil out to the car. As she unlocked the doors she looked over the roof at Neil and said, "That wasn't so bad, was it? Andrew was convinced it would be a disaster. He put money on you hating Betsy."

"Did you bet against him?"

"Yes," Renee said. "It was a private bet between the two of us."

Neil spent the summer blurring the truth with his teammates, but a half-hour talking to Betsy left him too worn out to care right now. It helped a bit that honesty in this case put Renee at a disadvantage. Andrew might be trouble, but he was easier to understand than Renee's polite smiles.

"I hope you didn't lose much," Neil said. "Why does Andrew tolerate you, anyway? You two should hate each other on principle."

"Either you think too highly of me or not highly enough of Andrew," Renee said, getting into the car. Neil slid into the passenger seat. Renee waited until they were buckled before turning the key in the ignition. "My faith keeps me and Andrew from always seeing eye-to-eye, but he and I understand each other."

There had to be more to Renee than her cross jewelry and pretty smiles if she'd qualified for a spot on Wymack's broken team, Neil knew, but he hadn't thought he'd misjudged her this badly. He mulled over everything that could be wrong with her from split personalities to clinical insanity. None of his theories sounded plausible, but it kept him busy for the ride back to the stadium.

Their return signaled the midday break for lunch, which they ate in scattered groups in the stands. They had the better

[172]

part of an hour to digest afterward and ended the day with two hours of exhausting cardio. Normal practices would have kept going until dinnertime, but with classes starting tomorrow, Wymack was willing to give them a one-time break.

Neil was the last one out of the showers and he found everyone waiting for him in the lounge. Wymack gestured for him to sit. Neil went to his usual chair and glanced around the room, wondering what was going on. None of the others looked bothered by this unexpected meeting. Andrew's group was more distracted by Andrew, who was already fast asleep. He'd been wide awake a few minutes ago, but he'd spent this week tweaking his medication schedule in preparation for the school year. His body wasn't used to it and he was crashing at odd times. Wymack worked around it when he could.

"All right, maggots," Wymack said, snapping his fingers to get all eyes on him. "School starts tomorrow, which means we're switching our practice times. Mornings are going to start at six o'clock at the gym. Afternoon practices are here at three. I've seen your schedules. I know you can get here on time, so don't any one of you be late, you hear me?"

"Yes, Coach," they said.

"This isn't our campus anymore," Wymack said. "Everyone's checked in and ready to go, which means a lot of people to contend with. Campus police doubled their numbers this summer but they can't cover everything or everyone. Be smart, be careful. If someone's looking for trouble, get help. If the press slips past and wants answers, you tell them we're not saying anything until Kathy's show on Saturday."

"Kathy?" Dan asked.

"Kathy Ferdinand." Wymack took one look at her confused face and scowled at Kevin. "Didn't you tell them?"

"There wasn't a need to," Kevin said.

"Like, morning show host Kathy Ferdinand?" Matt asked.

"That's the one," Wymack said. "We have to do some publicity at some point. It was part of our agreement with Chuck

[173]

and the ERC. Kevin chose Kathy because she agreed to wait until after our first game. Saturday morning we're heading up to Raleigh to give her an exclusive first interview."

"She must have fainted when you said yes," Matt said. "When's the last time you made an official public appearance?"

"December fourth," Kevin said.

"Why didn't you tell us earlier?" Dan asked. "I'll wake up early to watch it."

"Or you could come to the studio with us," Wymack said, ignoring the look Kevin sent him for that. "Kathy invited the entire team to the broadcast. If we show, we get front row seats. We've got to take the bus up anyway to fit all these yahoos, so there's plenty of room."

"Did you want us to sit out?" Renee asked Kevin.

"It doesn't really matter," Kevin said.

Nicky grinned and reached over Andrew to pat Kevin's shoulder. "He just knows he has to play nice for her show. He doesn't want you to see his civilized side. Can you imagine how his fans would react if they saw the real Kevin Day?"

"Do you even remember how to smile?" Matt asked. Kevin glared at him, but Matt only laughed. "Well, that's worth going for. I'm in."

"I'll buy us doughnuts for the ride," Dan said. "Renee? Neil?"

"No thank you," Neil said.

"I vetoed your choice on the matter," Wymack said. "The ERC is outing you Friday morning. I don't want you out of my sight until the initial hubbub dies down."

"I can take care of myself," Neil said.

"Watch me beam with pride. It's not your job to take care of yourself anymore. It's your job to play, and mine and Abby's job to look after you. Get your priorities straight." Wymack gave him a second to argue, then gave a satisfied nod and looked around at his team. "Questions, comments, concerns? No? Then get out of here and get some sleep. Kevin, wake that dingbat up without getting punched in the face. I don't need you starting the school year with a shiner."

"I got it." Nicky grimaced and gave Andrew a hard shake.

Their talking hadn't been enough to rouse Andrew, but Nicky's touch got Andrew up in an instant. Andrew was moving before he was fully awake, slamming his fist so hard into Nicky's chest Neil's entire body ached in sympathy pain. Nicky gave a sick wheeze as Andrew knocked the breath out of him and sagged back against the arm of the couch. Andrew twisted on his cushion to stare at Nicky. Neil hadn't expected Andrew to look guilty over his reaction, but he certainly didn't expect Andrew's blank-faced surprise, either.

"Nicky, are you dying?" Andrew asked.

"I'm good," Nicky rasped.

"We're done here," Kevin said. "Let's go."

Andrew looked around the room, taking everyone and everything in. "I missed the powwow."

"Kevin can summarize it for you later," Wymack said. "Clear out of here before I decide you're all better off doing more laps."

The locker room emptied in seconds.

—

Morning practice ended at eight the next morning so the Foxes could get to their first class on time. It was close enough Neil finally accepted Matt's offer for a lift back to the dorm room. He changed out of his morning sweats into something more appropriate for class, grabbed his messenger bag, and was out the door in time to join the small wave of athletes heading down Fox Tower's hill. Most of the others were wearing their jerseys as a first-day celebration, so the sidewalk by the crosswalk was an eyesore of orange and white. Neil's intention was to blend in as long as he could, so he opted to skip the tradition. He wouldn't have a choice tomorrow; the entire team was expected to be in colors on game day.

[175]

He made it to his English class with time to spare, so he managed to snag a desk in the back corner. The teacher didn't show until the bell rang, and then she came bouncing in with curls flying. She was a perky teaching assistant who acted like freshman composition was the greatest thing they'd ever study at Palmetto State. Neil followed along with her as she went through the syllabus and decided she was mental. Instead of midterms, they'd have reports of varying lengths due. Neil was suddenly grateful for the tutor hours he had to slot into his days. It'd made scheduling and registration a headache, but at least he could get some help with this. He was an average writer at best, and this lady made it clear average wouldn't cut it.

The only things she wanted to cover today were the syllabus and short self-introductions. As soon as that was finished, she dismissed them with a cheery farewell until the following Tuesday. From there it was off to chemistry, which was a large enough class it was held in an auditorium. Neil took a spot in the top row. It was impossible to see the board from where he was, but at least he had a wall at his back.

Unlike his English class, the chemistry professor only spent a few minutes reviewing the syllabus before starting on an overview of introductory chemistry. His voice was an unwavering monotone that could put any living creature to sleep. Neil resorted to stabbing himself with a pen every time he started drifting off. He probably should have taken last night's practices with Kevin off in preparation for today, but he didn't think Kevin would have allowed it. Neil was doomed to spend the school year exhausted.

After seventy-five mind-numbing minutes of science, Neil finally escaped back into the sunlight. The campus had come alive in his absence. The late sleepers and early risers were finally meshed on campus, which meant elbow-to-elbow people on the sidewalks between classes. More than half of the students were sporting school colors, and Neil saw a few headbands with fox ears.

[176]

The amphitheater in the middle of campus was packed with booths representing various student organizations. Volunteers were ready to hand out paraphernalia and point out buildings for lost freshmen. The clumps around the tables were buzzing with enough energy to power a small town, with most of the talk centered on either Friday's Exy or Saturday's football games. Neil got a small stack of magnets pressed into his hand as he passed. He sorted through them as he walked. There was one for every fall team with schedules printed on each. Neil kept the Exy one, tossed the rest into the trash, and buried his magnet deep in his pocket where he didn't have to look at the dates. Wymack had gotten the finalized fall schedule a few weeks ago. Palmetto State was facing Edgar Allan on Friday, October 13th. It felt close enough to choke Neil.

He detoured around students toward one of Palmetto State's three dining halls. Two were for the general student body. The third was for athletes only, justified to the general populace because of teams' training schedules and nutritional needs. All three halls were set up as buffets, but the athletes only ever had one unhealthy thing available a day whereas the regular dining halls' menus frequently boasted pizzas and a wide selection of desserts. The meal plan included in Neil's contract gave him limitless access to any of the halls, but Wymack strongly recommended he stick to his own.

The dining hall was busy when Neil arrived, though it might have just looked busy because it only sat a hundred people. He swiped his meal card at the front register, collected a tray, and tried to pack in enough food to fuel him through the end of practice at eight o'clock that night. Afterward he was free to return to the dorm, since he'd scheduled most of his classes on Monday, Wednesday, and Friday.

His room was empty when he showed up, so Neil settled at his desk with his syllabi. It was only the first day of school and he already had three assignments: a short paper, a fifty-page chapter to read, and a page of questions about said chapter. Neil

[177]

debated for a minute as to which one sounded least painful. Five minutes later he was still uninspired, so he put his head down on his desk.

He didn't realize he'd fallen asleep until a gunshot jarred him awake. Neil bolted upright so fast he sent his pile of textbooks crashing to the ground. Too late he realized the crack he'd heard wasn't a gun but the lock snapping undone on the suite door. A bemused Matt stood in the doorway.

"Hard at work already, I see," Matt said dryly.

"Something like that."

"I'd say it gets easier, but." Matt shrugged. "You should probably cut back on your late practices now that classes are in session."

"I'm fine," Neil said. He knew he'd never give up those practices. If he had to choose between class work and Exy, the answer was obvious. Neil was only here for a couple more months. He wasn't going to give up a single second of his time on the court no matter what else it cost him.

"You say that an awful lot," Matt said. "I'm starting to think you don't know what it means."

There wasn't really a good way to answer that, so Neil let it slide. Luckily Matt didn't push it but crossed the room to his computer. Neil spent the last half-hour until practice thinking about October and the Ravens.

CHAPTER ELEVEN

Thursday's excitement had nothing on Friday's. The whole school got decked out overnight with vibrant orange and white streamers. Ribbons and banners hung off every sidewalk lamp. Live student bands took over the amphitheater for short concerts and the student newspaper released that morning gave details for the afternoon parade. Cheerleaders roamed the campus in small packs, flaunting their short skirts and bright smiles and revving up school spirit wherever they could.

Traffic around campus that day was horrendous as spectators flooded in and settled down for back-to-back weekend opening home games. None of the Foxes expected to win that night, as they were opening the season against their longtime rivals Breckenridge. Until Edgar Allan made its move, Breckenridge was the largest and first-ranked school in the district. Fortunately the football team's chances for Saturday afternoon's game were much better. It would be too much of a downer if Palmetto lost both opening games.

Campus police were out in full force that day, helping direct traffic and making sure guests didn't interrupt classes. Neil hated the sight of their blue uniforms, but having them around was better than dealing with the press. He had enough problems getting along with his classmates now that he was wearing his Exy jersey. He caused a small disruption wherever he went. Neil wanted to cut class and hide at Fox Tower until game time, but athletes weren't allowed to call out without a legitimate medical excuse. Someone from the athletics committee went around all day counting heads through classroom windows, and Wymack would be the first to hear Neil was absent.

Luckily Neil's teammates had anticipated trouble. Matt was waiting for him outside his Spanish classroom to walk him to his next class. It didn't matter if the school rallied behind their Exy team or not; Neil was a secret finally let out of the bag. Anyone who followed the school's news knew the ERC had bent the rules to protect Neil's anonymity. Neil had checked the internet periodically throughout the summer to make sure it was working. As of this morning, though, his name was everywhere.

Almost as disturbing was finding out Andrew hadn't lied to Neil back in May. In almost every article that talked of Neil's pathetic experience Kevin was quoted as having high hopes for him. Kevin really had said Neil would one day be Court. It was a bold statement from a former champion, and it only added to the intrigue surrounding the Foxes' tenth player. The looks Neil kept getting made his skin crawl, but Matt kept them moving through the crowd without a problem.

After math Renee took Neil to history, neatly bypassing a group of cheerleaders before they noticed the jerseys in their midst. Allison found him after his history class. He had an open period, so she dragged him to lunch with her and Seth. Neil's nerves killed his hunger, but he obediently put food on his tray and sat with them.

It was the first time Neil had been alone with them, and it went better than he expected it to. They were in an "on" stage in their relationship, which helped. They talked mostly to each other, sparing only a few words for him, but Neil was content to watch. Seeing Seth act something other than completely hostile was fascinating, but he still didn't know what Allison saw in him. A girl with her money and connections could have had anyone and anything, but she chose to be a Fox and date Seth. Neil didn't think he would ever understand that decision.

"Well?" Allison asked, startling Neil from his thoughts. "What are you going to do about a date?"

They'd spent most of lunch talking about the Exy kickoff banquet. Every school in the southeast would put in an

[180]

appearance, including the Ravens. Neil wasn't planning on attending, but he hadn't yet figured out the logistics of skipping it.

"I'm not bringing one," Neil said.

"That's stupid," Allison said. "Even the monster's got a date."

Neil wasn't expecting that, but he could guess. "Renee?"

"She hasn't asked him yet, but it's inevitable." Allison picked her pita bread into pieces and mopped up leftover salad dressing with it. "Money's on the table as to whether or not he says yes. Pot's getting pretty big, so get your bet in fast."

The only thing the Foxes had in common besides Exy and hardship was their strange obsession with betting on the stupidest things. Neil had figured that out only two weeks into practice. A week didn't go by when there wasn't money on something or another.

Neil looked between Seth and Allison. "Are Andrew and Renee...?"

Seth looked like he might be sick. "Better not be."

Allison gave a prim shrug. "Renee promises it'll never happen. I believe her," she said, glancing at Seth like she was daring him to argue. He stabbed at his chicken and kept quiet. Allison pointed a chunk of bread at Neil. "You're running out of time to find a date. Ask Aaron to set you up with a Vixen. I'm sure Katelyn knows a pretty face or two."

The last thing Neil wanted to do was hook up with a cheerleader. He had no fond memories of Millport's high school squad. "Who is Katelyn?"

"Aaron's unofficial girlfriend. Look for her at the game tonight. It's pretty pathetic watching them moon over each other long distance." Allison checked her watch and pushed back her chair. "Have to run. Meeting my advisor." She leaned across the table to give Seth a quick kiss and carried her tray away.

Seth and Neil finished up a couple minutes later. Seth took Neil to his speech class. Dan met Neil afterward and escorted

Neil across campus to Fox Tower. She left him at the crosswalk, since she still had another class to get to before she was done for the day.

"Rest up," she said. "Tonight's going to be a long night."

Neil was too tense from the morning to follow that advice, but he made a beeline for his bed anyway.

He'd lived in several towns like Millport over the years and dealt with small-town curiosity and distrust most of his life. Somehow Palmetto State grated more against him, maybe because his jersey and place on the team demanded people pay attention to him. He couldn't fade into the background here, not with these colors and not after tonight's game. There were twenty-one thousand people enrolled at Palmetto State University. Neil wasn't playing for himself anymore; he was playing to represent them.

Friday afternoon's practice was canceled because of the game. The team was expected to be at the stadium by a quarter after six for their seven o'clock serve. Matt collected Neil from the bedroom at five-thirty for a light dinner with the upperclassmen. Dan finished first and went to check on Andrew's lot. Her expression was grim when she returned, but Matt gave her hand a reassuring squeeze.

"He'll be fine," Matt said. "He was last year."

"I thought Kevin didn't play last year," Neil said.

The upperclassmen exchanged looks. Neil looked from one face to another, trying to track their silent conversation. Seth and Allison radiated impatience and disapproval, but Renee was smiling a little. Matt grimaced and shrugged, leaving the decision to Dan. Finally Dan sighed and turned on Neil.

"There's something we haven't told you yet," Dan said. "We were going to tell you a while ago, but you and Andrew were having so many problems we figured we'd wait. We didn't know how you'd react."

"We didn't trust you to keep your mouth shut," Allison translated.

[182]

Dan made a face at her but didn't deny it. "So Andrew's technically legally required to take his medication, right?"

Neil had a feeling he knew where this conversation was going, but he didn't believe it. "Yes. It was part of his plea bargain."

"He struck a bargain of his own with Coach," Dan said. "The only reason he signed with us is because Coach agreed to let him come off his drugs for game nights. Coach ran it by us first since we're the ones out there on the court with him, but no one else can know. Not even Betsy knows he does it. She's his doctor; she'd have to put an end to it."

"How is Andrew supposed to guard our goal when he's sick?" he asked. In Columbia Andrew softened his withdrawal with alcohol and cracker dust, but he couldn't do that here. Neil still remembered how violently Andrew shook as he puked on the roadside.

"He's not sick yet," Matt said. He put his hand up at eye level. "Andrew's withdrawal is a three-stage process. Imagine you're flying high all day. Then suddenly you stop drugging. First you crash." He smacked his hand down to waist height. "That's stage one. He doesn't get sick until stage two."

"Andrew adjusts his schedule on Fridays depending on what time our serve is," Dan said. "He misses his dose a half-hour before the game starts and always plays first half. Usually he can ride stage one until halftime. Then he takes his medicine again and spends the rest of the night on the bench."

Neil guessed that was how Andrew slept all the way to Columbia. He almost made it all the way to Sweetie's before getting violently ill. "What's stage three?"

"Give him his drugs or get stabbed in the face," Matt said dryly. "It's not fun. Luckily we've only ever seen him get that far once."

"He won't get that bad tonight," Dan said. "Besides, you'll be half the court away from him. We just thought you should

[183]

have a heads-up, even if it's a couple months late. Are you going to be okay with this?"

"Is it going to jeopardize our match?" Neil asked.

"No more than anything else will," Matt said.

"Then I don't care," Neil said. "He can do what he wants."

It wasn't the complete truth, but Neil didn't know how to put his remaining reservations into words. Andrew said he hated this game, so why would he make it worse for himself by coming off his drugs for them? At least medicated he might find the matches entertaining. The only guess Neil had was that Andrew hated his medicine more than he hated Exy. That was interesting to consider, but Neil didn't have time to think about it tonight.

It didn't take long to clean up their dinner mess and they met Andrew's group in the hallway. Andrew looked on top of the world as usual, but Kevin's expression was tense. Tonight was Kevin's first season game since his injury and his debut as a right-handed Fox striker. Kevin had to shine tonight if he honestly wanted to make a comeback. How he was supposed to do that with his weaker hand and a team like the Foxes as backup, Neil didn't know.

They left the dormitory early, but traffic was so backed up they were almost late. The stadium had turned into a madhouse sometime between morning practice and now. The parking lots were crammed and security was everywhere, directing fans and watching for drunken foolery. Every gate was open and the guards manning them wielded metal detectors. A line of police cars and two ambulances kept a path clear for the athletes' cars. Two guards stood outside their door, and after a cursory check to make sure none of them were carrying anything illegal into the stadium, they were allowed into their locker room.

Wymack was in the lounge and immediately directed them to the changing room. Neil was halfway through the men's door when Kevin snagged his collar and hauled him down the hall to the back door. Kevin pulled it open and pushed Neil ahead of him through it. Neil stumbled a step, caught his balance a second later, and went to the inner court.

The Foxhole Court was the second collegiate stadium he'd been in, the first being Edgar Allan's Ravens' Nest, but he'd never been in one on a game night. It was one thing to admire the dizzyingly high seats, and another thing entirely when those seats were full. Not all of the sixty-five thousand seats were taken yet, but at least three-quarters were. The stadium rumbled with the sounds of tens of thousands of feet. The crowd's yelling and laughing were deafening, and this was before the crowd had a reason to be loud. Neil wondered what they would sound like after the Foxes scored. Maybe it'd be loud enough to crack his bones inside him.

It didn't take anyone long to notice Neil and Kevin in the inner court. When the closest section went crazy, the sound ignited a small wave up the stands. Orange Notes, the campus band, was still filing into their section, but they reacted to the excitement unquestioningly. The drumline beat out a ferocious rhythm and a couple trumpets started the school fight song. A few seconds later the students joined in, yelling the words at one another and the empty court.

"Don't waste their time tonight," Kevin said at his ear. "They came to see you play, so give them something to believe in."

"They're not here for me," Neil said. "They're here to see the famous Kevin Day."

Kevin put a hand to Neil's shoulder blade and gave him a small push. "Change out."

Neil took one last peek up at the stands before heading back to the locker room.

Wymack called them to the foyer when they had all their gear on and passed around the Breckenridge Jackals' roster. Matt took one look at the starting line-up and made a face.

"Hey, Seth. Looks like Gorilla's back."

"Shit." Seth held out his hand in a demand for the paper.

[185]

"At least they're taking us seriously from the start," Aaron said.

"Easy for defense to say." Allison took the roster from Matt and gave it to Seth.

"Gorilla?" Neil asked.

"Number 16, Hawking," Nicky said. "AKA Gorilla. Six and a half feet tall and three hundred pounds of pure douchebaggery. You'll know him when you see him, trust me. He looks like a football player that got lost on his way to the field."

"He's also dumb as a brick, so he sat out of championships last year on academic probation," Matt said. "It's kind of a yearly ritual for him."

"He's defense," Dan said, looking at Neil, "and he loves body-checks. Don't get between him and the wall, Neil. He'll break every bone in your body if you give him the chance."

"Don't worry, though," Matt said. "He'll probably be too busy killing Kevin and Seth to notice you."

"This is my reassured face," Neil said, pointing up at his blank expression.

"Are you done wasting my oxygen yet?" Wymack asked. "Let's get moving. We're on home court for warm-up. We're doing simple relay shots first, Andrew and Renee twice through each. Andrew, keep them on our side. You hit a single practice shot onto the Jackals' side of the court when they're warming up and I won't start you until second half."

Neil looked at Andrew at that. Andrew looked fine so far, but maybe they were still too far out from first serve for him to be feeling any withdrawal.

Wymack kept going. "Starters down the line: Seth, Kevin, Dan, Matt, Aaron, Andrew. I've got three subs each half, so you'll all get a swap except the goalies. Kevin, you're out if your hand so much as itches. Don't be stupid tonight."

"It's been eight months," Kevin said.

"Don't risk it your first game back," Abby said.

Kevin grimaced but gave up arguing. That was good enough for Wymack and Abby, so they sent the Foxes scrambling for their helmets and racquets. They lined up at the door in order of playing position, with Dan out of place at the front as their captain. Wymack had an earpiece in that linked him to the announcer's booth. When he heard the okay, he led his team out to the benches. Neil's helmet muffled some of the crowd's screaming, but his ears were still ringing when he followed the Foxes onto the court.

Neil knew the Fox team was the smallest in the NCAA and Breckenridge one of the largest, but he hadn't expected the difference to feel so vast. The tan-and-black Jackals seemed crowded on their half, making the Foxes look pathetic and small on theirs. Neil tried not to feel intimidated. When that failed, he put everything he had into warm-up drills instead. The twenty minutes flew by faster than he thought they would and they were shepherded off the court by the referees: the Jackals out the north door, the Foxes out the south.

The announcer's voice just barely carried over the crowd's racket, but as it got closer to game time someone thought to turn up his volume. By the time he called the team's rosters his voice was echoing off the court walls. As their names were called, the Foxes lifted their racquets in silent salute. The crowd roared in response to each one, and Orange Notes' drumline pounded away on whatever their sticks could reach.

"For the Breckenridge Jackals," the announcer said, and went through the list of players slotted to play tonight. The Jackals' names were greeted with mixed boos and polite applause from the Foxes' side, but there were large sections of Jackal fans in attendance on the north side of the stadium. Their pep band played the fight song as soon as the last name was called, but Orange Notes promptly drowned them out with Palmetto's song.

The six referees for the game opened the doors on either side of the court and entered. At their beckon, Dan and the

[187]

opposing captain joined them at half-court for an obligatory handshake and the coin toss. The head referee signaled first serve for the Jackals and home court for the Foxes. Three referees followed each captain off and arranged themselves along the wall near the court lines.

Wymack made shooing motions at his starting line. "Get out there and make them sorry they showed up tonight. I want my subs at the wall cheering them on, but if you trip up a referee I will cut you. Let's go."

Dan led her players to the door and thumped the wall when they were ready. The announcer called off the Foxes' starting line-up from offense to defense. Kevin was the first onto the court, and the entire stadium had a fit at the sight of him. It didn't matter what school the fans were here to support; Kevin was in uniform after an eight-month absence. All predictions said he'd never play again, but he carried a racquet with him to half-court like he'd always known he would return.

Seth followed Kevin on and joined him at the half-court line. Dan was the Foxes' offensive dealer and stood halfway between half-court and first-fourth. Matt and Aaron spaced themselves out on first-fourth, and Andrew was the last one in place in their goal.

Breckenridge filed on next. Nicky pointed to Gorilla as soon as the player made his entrance, but Neil didn't need any help spotting him. "Remember to thank Seth and Kevin later for getting crushed in your stead."

He might have been joking, but Neil nodded anyway. Anyone who could make Matt look delicate was not someone Neil wanted to face on the court.

Nicky looked at Neil. "Hey," he said, sounding uncharacteristically hesitant. "We haven't really had a chance to talk after... Well. I wanted to say sorry, but I kept chickening out. Are we okay?"

"I don't know yet," Neil said.

Nicky weighed that for a minute, then sighed and said, "Fair enough."

The referees slammed the doors with a resounding bang and bolted them shut. There were vents and fans along the ceiling to keep air circulating on the court. The vents would let out echoes of serves and checks, but the players would have to yell for their voices to filter out into the stadium. Neil didn't know what they were saying to each other now as they waited for the game to start, but he doubted it was pleasant seeing as how Seth was flipping off one of the Jackals' strikers. Seth turned the gesture on Kevin a couple seconds later.

"Oh Lord," Abby said at Neil's back. "They could at least pretend to get along when playing against this team."

"Not a chance!" Nicky said. "Ten bucks says they hit each other inside fifteen minutes."

"I'm not taking that," Allison said.

"You could try to be optimistic about the first game of the season," Renee said.

"Maybe you saw who we're up against," Nicky said, pointing at the opposing team. "You really think optimism is going to help us?"

"I think it can't hurt," Renee said with a smile.

Allison started to say something, but the warning buzzer drowned her out. If Neil looked up he could almost see the scoreboard where it hung over the dead center of court. A clock, the score, and shots on goal statistics were displayed on all four sides, as were screens for replays and close-ups. Right now the board would be counting down the last minute to game start, but Neil didn't strain to see. He didn't want to take his eyes off the court. He pressed his gloved hands to the wall and leaned forward, trying to see all of it at once. His heart pounded in his chest, sending shuddery heat through every inch of his body. He held his breath waiting for first serve.

The buzzer went off again, and the game began. Breckenridge's dealer flicked the ball into the air and slammed it

[189]

with his racquet. The distinctive crack had Jackals and Foxes breaking formation and rushing forward to find their marks and places on the court. The nerves Neil felt earlier evaporated under the wild weight of the crowd's enthusiasm. Their screams jarred against his skin and the stamping of a hundred thousand feet beat in time to his pulse. Two bodies crashed on the court as the game started rough from the get-go. There was a roar of approval from the rafters.

The ball hit the wall in front of the subs and went careening away. Dan caught it before it went far and threw it to Seth. Her momentum sent her into the wall further up and the Jackal dealer slammed into her a second later. The wall shuddered under their weight. Dan practically threw him aside to get back into the game, and the subs pounded on the wall in support.

Neil raked his gaze along the court, past the Jackal striker that was struggling with Aaron. Aaron and Matt were pushing the Jackal strikers up the court away from goal, but they didn't want to leave too much empty space between them and Andrew. Andrew stood alone on the white line marking the goalkeeper's territory, watching the game unfold in front of him. He spun his racquet in a circle, mocking the Jackals' efforts with that carefree stance.

The ball hit the wall further down the court, and Neil turned his attention back to it. Dan was the first to it again, and she sent it high over Seth's head. Seth and Gorilla raced each other up the court to catch the ball on the rebound. Seth caught it but couldn't hold it for long. He carried it only half a step before Gorilla took a swipe at his racquet. It didn't look like much of a strike, but it sent Seth's racquet flying. Gorilla caught the ball as it bounced off the ground and turned to heave it all the way down the court. It hit the wall a few inches to the right of the home court goal. Andrew watched it bounce away.

One of the Jackal strikers got around Matt and ran for it. Andrew stopped spinning his stick and shifted, readying himself just in time. The striker took a fast shot on goal and Andrew beat it forcefully away, sending it right back down the middle of the court. The Jackal dealer tried to catch it, but it was going faster than he anticipated and it bounced out of the net of his racquet. Dan stole it from him. He bowled her over in response, and the ball went rolling away. Dan beat her stick against the ground in anger as she scrambled back to her feet to chase him. The Jackal dealer already had the ball and was running toward home court.

"Atta girl," Abby said. "You've got him."

Dan couldn't catch up to him in time to stop him from passing the ball, but she didn't slow. She slammed into the dealer hard enough to send them both sprawling. Jackal fans roared in outrage, demanding a card for that trick, but the referees didn't move. Body-checks were only legal when played by or against players who were carrying the ball, but allowances were made for hits that happened in the first two seconds after the ball left a player's net. Officials knew sometimes athletes were simply going too fast to stop in time. It allowed a loophole for spiteful collisions like Dan's, but that only made the game more fun for the fans.

Aaron was small enough he could get duck under his striker's arm. He intercepted the ball in an impossible move and kept spinning back to face home court. He passed the ball to Andrew without slowing and was back on his feet a heartbeat later. Andrew hit the ball with an underhand swing to clear it out of home court. The ball bounced off the ceiling and fell back into the fray.

"Move it, Foxes!" Wymack roared.

"Let's go, Foxes, let's go!" the Vixens called out further down.

The crowd picked it up and echoed the chant back to the cheerleaders. The other subs joined in, but Neil was numbed into silence by the speed and skill of the game.

He'd watched his teammates fall apart to in-fighting all summer long, but now he finally saw them as a whole. As much

[191]

as the Foxes disliked each other at times, they disliked their opponents more. They were still too fractured to be truly great, but they were good enough to give him chills. Neil finally understood how the Foxes made it to third place last fall and scored a spot in championships.

Unfortunately, Breckenridge was better. Twelve minutes into the game they finally broke the Foxes' defense line. A Jackal striker caught the ball and carried it right into Aaron. Aaron was bulled over, giving the striker a straight path to the goal, and all of the Jackals crushed forward inside the first-fourth line. The striker got dangerously close to goal before taking a shot. Andrew snapped it right back at him, bouncing it off his helmet. The Jackal dealer caught the ball next, and Dan was a second too slow to stop him from aiming for the goal. Andrew deflected that shot as well, but the Jackals were pressed too close for him to clear the ball. He aimed high, but Gorilla was close enough and tall enough to snag it from the air.

"Get it out of there!" Wymack yelled at the wall.

Gorilla knocked aside two Foxes like they were nothing and ran for the goal. Matt threw himself into Gorilla like his life depended on it, taking them both out. Matt's unguarded striker caught the ball and fired, and the goal flared up red behind Andrew. Breckenridge's fans went crazy as the buzzer sounded first point. Wymack swore viciously and turned in an angry circle, looking for but not finding something to vent his anger on.

"Nice try, Foxes!" Renee called, clapping.

The Jackals pounded each other's backs in congratulations as they ran back down the court. Gorilla was the last to go where he and Matt were still picking themselves off the ground, and he stopped by the goal to say something to Andrew. Whatever it was, Andrew didn't seem impressed. He stood his racquet in front of him, folded his arms across the net, and perched his chin on his arms. Gorilla waved a hand at him in dismissal and jogged across court. Dan swung past Matt to give him a quick pat-down.

They almost made it to their starting spots without incident, but then Kevin's defenseman shoved him on his way by. Kevin shoved him back almost hard enough to knock him over. The Jackal backliner spun around to say something, and Seth gestured expansively as he joined in. Kevin ignored the Jackal to say something to Seth, and Seth answered by throwing a punch at him.

"I win," Nicky said. "It's only thirteen minutes."

"No one took your bet," Abby said, sounding weary as she watched Kevin and Seth fight.

"Don't you bet on these retards," Wymack said.

Dan caught up with the two and shoved them roughly apart. She stuck her finger in Seth's face as she chewed him out, then did the same to Kevin. Kevin and Seth finally spread out on half-court to take their spots. The referees by the doors waited to see if they needed to intervene, then decided Dan had handled it appropriately and let it go.

The game started up again with another Breckenridge serve, but the Foxes were fired up and angry from losing the first point. Kevin seemed to take that personally, and he played with a vengeance. As soon as Dan got him the ball, he laid his backliner mark flat and flew up the court unguarded for a perfect point on goal. The goal went red and the crowd surged to its feet at the Foxes' back. Neil couldn't hear his own triumphant yell over the sound of the excited students. Orange Notes blared the fight song and students screamed the words like a battle cry.

The fight song wasn't half-over before Kevin and his mark were brawling. It took Matt, Dan, and three Jackals to tear them apart. By the time they put a safe distance between the two the referees were there. The yellow card went to the Jackal for throwing the first punch, and the crowd cheered. Overhead on the screens a cartoon jackal got brained by an oversized hammer. The Jackal fans booed, but their anger was drowned out by the home crowd.

When the teams were set up in starting spot, the referees left. Dan served to get the game moving.

They were twenty minutes in when Gorilla crushed Seth up against the wall. Fans roared with hatred and excitement as Gorilla raced after the ball unguarded. Neil expected Seth to go after him, but Seth scrabbled ineffectually at the wall for a second and then crumpled to the ground.

"David," Abby said, but Wymack was already running down the wall to stand opposite Seth. One of the referees crouched beside him and gestured through the wall at Seth. Wymack hit the wall to get Seth's attention. Seth painstakingly pushed himself onto his hands and knees. Neil looked from him to the game in helpless frustration. Until Seth signaled the referees to call him out, the game was still going, which meant Kevin suddenly had two backliners riding him.

It didn't take Dan long to notice Kevin's predicament. She spun in a circle, wasting precious seconds and losing track of the ball to find her missing striker. Halfway across the court from her, Kevin got sandwiched between the Jackal backliners. He lost the ball and his racquet but somehow kept his feet.

"Call it, Seth!" Nicky yelled, kicking the wall.

Seth finally lifted his racquet, alerting the referees he was unable to continue the period. An alarm went off to stop the game. Matt had just caught the ball, so he passed it to Andrew for safekeeping. The crowd went silent to watch as Seth struggled to his feet. He stumbled sideways into the wall and leaned heavily against it, waiting to get his balance back before trying to walk. Dan ran to help him, and Allison kept pace with him on the outside of the court. Abby hurried ahead of her to the door.

Wymack smacked Neil's shoulder. "Move it."

A flicker of nerves turned Neil's stomach cold. Now that he'd seen the teams in action, it proved what he'd said all along:

[194]

he wasn't ready to play with a team like this. He didn't have much of a choice, though, so he grabbed his racquet and ran after Allison to the court door.

"Get some!" Nicky called after him.

Allison took Seth from Dan at the doorway and held him still long enough for Abby to get his helmet off. Allison helped Seth over to the bench, and Dan gestured to Neil to step through the door onto the court. Overhead the announcer called out the swap: "Going on for Seth Gordon is freshman Neil Josten, number ten, of Millport, Arizona."

Neil wondered if casket lids sounded like court doors slamming shut.

"Ready?" Dan asked.

"Ready to try," Neil said.

"Let's do this," she said, clacking sticks with him.

They jogged across the court together. By the time Seth finally called out, both teams were up inside first-fourth again. Dan took a spot by her mark. Because Neil was a mid-play substitute, his starting spot was up against the home court wall.

"Is it true?" the Jackal dealer called over to him. "Coach says you're a one-year rookie."

"Are you kidding me?" a girl demanded, and Neil stared in surprise. The backliner Kevin had been fighting with all game was a woman. "A national champion and an amateur? South Carolina's gotten even crazier than usual."

"An amateur and a cripple, you mean," the dealer said.

Andrew slammed his racquet against the goal, making several athletes jump and drawing more than a few wary looks his way. Neil couldn't see Andrew's expression from where he was standing, but he hoped Andrew was faking a smile. Their opponents would announce Andrew's sobriety in a heartbeat if it got him out of the Foxes' goal. Neil waited, expecting the worst, but Andrew only took two steps back into his goalkeeper's territory and waited. A buzzer sounded overhead when everyone was settled and still. Andrew lifted the ball in his gloved hand.

[195]

"Hey, Pinocchio," he said without looking at Neil. The cheer in his voice was too mocking to be real, but Neil doubted anyone but the Foxes noticed. "Time to run. This one's for you."

Andrew bounced the ball off the ground and swung with everything he had. Neil didn't wait to see him hit it. He threw himself away from the wall and flew down the court as fast as he could, vanishing past the backliners and strikers who were just starting to move. Kevin's mark cut across the court toward him, meaning to cut him off, but Neil was faster than she expected and he led her all the way down the court.

The ball hit the far wall and came soaring back. Neil jumped to catch it before it could go over his head. His mark was there when he landed and he bounced away from her, counting steps instinctively as he swung his racquet out of her reach. Her racquet just barely missed his fingers as she took a swing at him. He could only carry the ball ten steps and had already used six. He knew he couldn't get around her in four, so he twisted and passed the ball back to Dan. His mark collided with him a second later and he went skidding, arm out and stick dragging along the ground for balance.

Dan passed the ball to Kevin. Gorilla was massive, but his size slowed him down. Kevin got around him and caught the ball, then twisted and threw the ball further up court to buy the strikers breathing room. Gorilla smacked Kevin's racquet out of his hands in retaliation. Kevin swore and gave his arms a violent shake. The Jackal goalie left goal to smack the ball back down the court at them. Matt intercepted it and aimed high, wanting it to hit the ceiling and come down near the strikers again. Kevin caught it but only had two steps to aim and shoot it before Gorilla crashed into him. Kevin hit the ground so hard he rolled.

The goalie deflected the ball to Gorilla. Gorilla threw it at home court wall again, and the Jackal backliners chased after it to force Neil and Kevin back down the court. They were dragged all the way to first-fourth. Neil decided he hated their "everyone gang up on the goalie" strategy. It was frustrating watching them hammer Andrew like this, especially from this far back. He couldn't get into the fray if there was a chance the Foxes could shake the ball loose. He could only watch as the Jackals steamrolled the Foxes. Three shots later they scored.

"You can't win against us," the female backliner said to Neil. "You guys suck."

"I'd rather be a Fox than a Jack̲___ ___ ̶n by hurting your opponents," Neil said. "You're a ___ ___ ̶ullies."

She shoved against him chest-t___ ___ ̶t again. I dare you."

Neil wasn't impressed by her attitude. He gave her a bored look and pressed one finger hard against her shoulder. "Get out of my face. You already got carded once. Start another fight and you'll be out the rest of the game."

"Leverett!" the dealer yelled in warning. "Back off!"

She curled her lip at Neil in scorn, took two exaggerated steps back, then spun on her heel and stormed off to her starting spot. The Jackals served as soon as everyone was ready. Neil couldn't go far before he caught up with Leverett again. She shoved him with her shoulder as she forced him back toward half-court. Across the court Kevin gained possession of the ball, but he lost it a second later as Gorilla knocked his stick away. Neil didn't know if Gorilla really was hitting his racquet that hard every time or if Kevin was just afraid to hold on when the reverberations would go all the way up his hands to his elbows. He wasn't sure which answer he hoped it was. He didn't want Kevin injured, but the Foxes couldn't afford for Kevin to bring his psychological damage onto the court for a game.

Matt stole the ball from his striker and passed it to Aaron. Aaron's only clear shot was to Andrew. It bought him a couple seconds to get ahead of his striker mark, and Andrew hit the ball to rebound off the wall in front of Aaron. Aaron caught it and threw it with everything he had.

"Neil!"

Neil was already moving, following the arc of Aaron's racquet and realizing the pass was meant for him. Leverett swiped at his racquet, trying to ruin his catch, and Neil grit his teeth at the twinge in his wrists. He brought his stick around to beat hers out of the way. It cost him the precious second he needed to snag the ball, and he almost overextended his arm to catch it. Leverett rammed into him, trying to knock him over, but Neil hugged his racquet close, protecting the ball between his body and his net. Leverett snapped his racquet again to pop the ball free. Neil took another step back to brace himself, gave her a chance to catch the ball, and shoulder-slammed her hard enough to knock her to her ass. He snagged the fallen ball and bolted with it.

"Fucking whore!" she yelled after him.

Neil carried the ball ten steps and threw it to Kevin. Kevin caught it, only to get his racquet smashed away again. Gorilla pounded past him after the ball. Kevin pressed his left hand to his gut and twisted in search of Matt.

"Get him off of me!"

Matt didn't answer, but he heard. The next time both teams were up inside the first-fourth line, Matt dropped his striker and went after Gorilla. Matt tossed his racquet aside to free up his hands and took one powerful swing, punching Gorilla right under his chest armor. Gorilla slumped forward a bit under the blow and the buzzer called a foul. Gorilla needed only a second to get his breath back and then went after Matt. Matt backpedaled away from his giant hands, putting as many people between him and Gorilla as he could. Gorilla shoved his teammates out of the way as he chased Matt across the court.

As soon as Matt passed the goal, Andrew stepped into Gorilla's path. He looked ridiculously small as he watched Gorilla bear down on him, but he stood his ground and waited with his racquet at his side. Gorilla jerked a beefy hand at him in a demand to move, but Andrew stayed silent and still. Neil held his breath, waiting for Gorilla to move Andrew with force.

[198]

Andrew might be psychotic, but he was also half Gorilla's size. One perfect punch from Gorilla would crush his skull.

Luckily the referees got there before things could escalate. Matt accepted his yellow card without argument and flashed Kevin a thumbs-up. Through the open court doors Neil could hear the crowd jeering and cheering the short fight. Matt jogged off the court to let Nicky on and was greeted by the home crowd like a returning champion. Gorilla left the court through the Jackals' side a couple seconds later. Neil saw him limping through the wall.

"Matt can hit," Neil said.

Dan smiled. "His mother's a professional boxer. She taught him a couple tricks. Now what...?" Neil followed her distraction to the court door where Wymack still waited. It was almost time for Allison to come on for Dan, but Wymack had both Seth and Allison with him. Wymack gestured between them, leaving the choice to Dan. It only took Dan a second to catch on and she whipped around, looking for Kevin.

Kevin was standing with Andrew inside the goal line, left hand out so Andrew could tug at his outer glove. Andrew undid the straps and peeled it off, then hooked it under his arm so he could take off Kevin's arm guard. He left Kevin's under-glove on, but unhooked the loop from Kevin's middle finger so he could slide the black cloth to Kevin's wrist. Kevin flexed his fingers slowly, staring at his scars, then turned his hand over and flexed his fingers again.

"Kevin!" Dan said.

Kevin and Andrew looked her way and followed her pointing finger to the door. Neil couldn't hear what Andrew said, but Kevin shook his head. Andrew pushed Kevin's glove and armor against his chest and took a step back, and Kevin turned toward the court door. Dan squeezed his shoulder on his way by. As soon as Kevin was out of earshot she muttered something vicious under her breath and sent Gorilla a dirty look through the court wall.

The crowd outside greeted Kevin's arrival with the same enthusiasm they'd shown Matt. He'd only played half an hour, but for now it was good enough just to have him on the court.

"Line up for a foul shot," Dan said as Seth took Kevin's place on the court.

The referees left and locked them in. Foxes and Jackals moved out of the way to let Gorilla's replacement have a clear shot on goal. A buzzer gave the backliner the go-ahead. He took a couple extra seconds to weigh his options, then fired at the corner of Andrew's goal. Andrew slammed the ball all the way down to the far court wall.

Neil ran down the court as fast as he could, wanting more than ever for the Foxes to win this game. He knew they couldn't, but the way the Jackals were playing was infuriating. Gorilla really had been trying to hurt Kevin's hand his first day back on the court, which was unbelievably cruel. Neil hoped Matt had bruised some ribs with that punch.

He snagged the ball from the air as it came flying his way. He ran for the goal, making five steps before Leverett was right on his tail. He fired a shot at the goal that the goalkeeper just barely deflected. Seth dodged around his new backliner mark to catch the ball, but he didn't have a clear shot. He threw the ball back to Neil instead.

Leverett moved as if to intercept it, but Neil didn't let her. He slammed his stick into hers almost hard enough to send both their racquets flying. She cursed as she lost her grip, and then there was nothing to stop Neil from getting to the goal. He caught the ball and carried it all ten steps, calculating angles and the goalkeeper's body language as he ran. His last step was a half-step that helped tilt him forward and he put everything behind his throw.

The goal lit up red as Neil's ball hit home. The buzzer went off overhead, and Neil wheeled around for half-court as his teammates cheered.

Leverett stepped in front of him. "You got lucky."

[200]

"You're getting slow," Neil said.

She moved as if to hit him but stopped before taking the swing, maybe thinking about her yellow card. Neil pushed her roughly out of the way and kept going. She spat obscenities at his back that he ignored. He was more interested in Seth, who'd crossed the court to give his shoulder a violent clap. Neil clacked racquets with him as they split up for their spots on the half-court line. Dan whooped behind Neil.

"Let's do that again, Foxes!"

Neil didn't score again until he came on during the second half. Two points weren't enough to earn his place on the line, but it made him feel better about standing on their court. It was almost enough to ease the sting of their eventual loss to Breckenridge at seven points to nine. The season had just begun, after all, and Neil had until October to improve.

CHAPTER TWELVE

When Neil's alarm went off at one the following morning, it took a minute of groggy staring before he remembered why he was getting up. He stuffed his alarm clock under his pillow, wished Kevin and Wymack both an early death, and dragged himself to the edge of his bed. Matt's alarm sounded when Neil was halfway down the ladder. Seth grumbled something rude across the room when Matt didn't immediately turn it off. Matt's pillow muffled whatever he said in response but his tone was unfriendly.

Neil stopped at the bottom of the ladder to scrub sleep out of his eyes. Matt finally found his alarm and silenced it. Seth huffed, noisily rolled over, and started snoring again right away. Matt glowered blearily across the room at him before looking at Neil.

Matt looked as miserable as Neil felt. Wymack warned them last night they'd have an early start today, but there was no way the Foxes could start the season without a small party. Andrew's group predictably sat out of it, but Neil and his roommates had ended up hanging out in the girls' room. The upperclassmen put away most of a bottle of vodka even without Neil and Renee helping them. At the time they all thought it would be worth it. After getting less than an hour of sleep, Neil wasn't so sure.

Someone pounded on their suite door. Neil went down the hall to answer it. The hall light was brighter than Neil expected. Neil rubbed his eyes again, both to get the spots out of them and so he wouldn't have to look at Wymack. It should be impossible for Wymack to look so awake at this hour, but there he was looking completely refreshed.

"Stop yawning and get moving," Wymack said, clapping his hands in Neil's face. "We're on a schedule. I want everyone on the bus in five."

Neil shut the door in his face and went to get dressed.

He was still dead tired when he left his room a minute later, but his mind was waking up to survival mode. Renee gave him a tired smile and half-wave in greeting. Dan stumbled over to Matt, looped her arms around his neck, and fell asleep against him almost immediately. Andrew's group was the last to show. Neil took one look at the wrist braces Kevin was wearing and instantly felt more awake.

Wymack pointed at Kevin. "How the hell did they wake you up?"

"They didn't let me sleep." Kevin sent Andrew a sour look, but Andrew ignored him.

"Smart," Wymack said, and waved them toward the stairs. "Let's go."

Abby was out back by the team bus. It was Neil's first time seeing the bus, since it was usually locked in a gated compound to prevent vandalism. It was painted to match the stadium, orange trim and paw prints against a white background. On the inside, instead of the traditional two rows, the bus had only one. The cushions were big enough to comfortably seat two athletes or let one curl up and nap. In his tired state Neil thought it was the greatest bus ever invented.

Andrew led his group all the way to the back. Abby took the first row. Matt and Dan went in behind her, and Renee sat alone behind them. Neil left an empty row between Renee and himself. He leaned against the window and stared at the seatback ahead of him as Wymack got settled in the driver's seat. He heard the engine cut on, saw the dorm disappear in his peripheral vision, and then tilted over to sprawl on the cushion. He was asleep before they reached the highway.

It was almost six when they reached Raleigh, North Carolina. Wymack stopped at the next fast food joint he passed.

[203]

Abby and Renee went inside to buy the team's breakfast and coffee. As soon as they left, Wymack stood in the aisle to face his team.

"All right," he said, then promptly forgot what he was saying when he got a good look at the back of the bus. "Damn it all to hell. Hemmick! You were supposed to wake them up ten miles ago."

"I don't want to die," Nicky said.

Dan tried to pass her laugh off as a cough. Wymack wasn't fooled, and the look he shot her as he stomped to the back of the bus was annoyed. Dan was undeterred and grinned at Renee. Curious, Neil half-turned in his seat to watch. Wymack went all the way to the last row, pulled his wallet out of his back pocket, and threw it at Andrew. Judging by the resounding thud, Andrew woke up as violently as always.

Wymack put his hand out in a demand. "Give it back."

Leather creaked as Andrew moved. Andrew sat up a couple seconds later with Wymack's wallet in hand. Wymack stuffed it into his pocket once more and went up a row to Kevin. He planted his shoe against whatever part of Kevin was closest and started pushing him.

"Up," he said over and over, getting louder each time until he was almost shouting. "Get your ass up and moving!"

Kevin's hand darted into view as he tried to shove Wymack away. Wymack grabbed his elbow and hauled Kevin out of his chair into the aisle. Before Kevin could fall over Wymack pushed him back, dropping him heavily onto his cushion. Kevin slumped against the back of his chair immediately, looking for all intents and purposes like he'd nod right back off. Wymack smacked the back of his head to wake him up.

"I hate you," Kevin said with feeling.

"Breaking news: I don't care. This was your brilliant idea."

Andrew leaned to one side to rest against his window and looked out at the parking lot. "Are we here?"

"Close enough," Wymack said. "You know what to do."

[204]

Andrew didn't answer, but Wymack didn't push it. He was distracted by Kevin, who was already drifting off again. Wymack gave his shoulder a rough shake. Kevin slept through it, so finally Wymack dragged him out of his chair and sent him on laps up and down the length of the bus. Neil watched him pass. Kevin was walking, but his eyes were barely open.

"Morning, sunshine," Matt said with exaggerated cheer.

"Fuck you," Kevin said.

Dan yawned into her hand. "Glad to see you're still a morning person."

"Fuck you too."

Kevin turned at the driver's seat and headed to the back of the bus. He tried to sit down again, but Wymack turned him around with a hand on his shoulder. Kevin got the hint and kept making laps. Walking kept him awake but just barely. He looked half-asleep every time he passed Neil's seat.

"Kevin," Andrew said, moving for the first time since he'd slumped against the window.

Kevin was only halfway through his lap, but he pivoted at the sound of his name and went back. Wymack moved out of the way so Kevin could get to Andrew's seat. Kevin dug Andrew's medicine out of his pocket and handed the bottle over. He and Wymack watched as Andrew tipped a pill into his hand and swallowed it dry. Neil half-expected Andrew to give the bottle back, but Andrew shifted in his chair as he stuffed it in his own pocket.

Odd, Neil thought, that Kevin would have Andrew's medicine at all. Kevin had it at Sweetie's, too. Neil wanted to ask why Kevin held onto it, but he didn't think either of them would explain.

Abby and Renee were back a minute later with bags of food and trays of drinks. The Foxes munched on sausage biscuits and Dan's promised doughnuts. The coffee helped wake them up, as did the reminder they were about to meet one of the

[205]

highest-rated talk show hosts in the nation. Dan, Matt, and Renee buzzed with excitement as the bus got on the road again.

It was fifteen more minutes to the two-storey building that housed Kathy Ferdinand's daily show. Wymack parked by the security gate and got out to talk to the guard. Neil watched out the window as he and the guard checked IDs and paperwork. Wymack was back on a couple minutes later with a parking tag and a pile of guest badges. The gate squealed as it opened and Wymack drove them to the employee parking lot.

Wymack was the first off. He stood to one side of the door and handed out badges as the Foxes passed. Abby followed them out and locked the bus doors behind her. They were halfway to the building when Kathy herself came into the parking lot to greet them. She looked more awake than even Wymack did. Neil hoped it was just her makeup, because that couldn't be possible or natural.

"Kevin," Kathy said, reaching for him. "It's been so long. I'm so glad you could make it today."

"It's good to see you again," Kevin said, and smiled as he took her hand.

Behind Kathy's back, Dan feigned swooning into Matt's arms. Neil understood the mockery. In the four long months he'd known Kevin, he'd seen Kevin smile only once or twice before. Kevin's smile was a brittle and bitter thing. In Neil's files he had pictures of Kevin smiling alongside Riko, but most of those shots were taken after games when the pair looked more triumphant and condescending than anything. This smile was something else; this was Kevin's public face. It was meant for interviewers and fans who were better off not knowing the arrogant, ruthless side of a world-class champion. Kevin looked every inch a charming celebrity. Neil found it horribly disorienting.

Kathy turned her smile on the rest of the team. The morning sunshine glinted off perfect teeth only money could buy. "You were amazing last night. Kevin, you have the magic

[206]

touch. This team has been doing so much better since you transferred."

"They were already on their way up," Kevin said. It was the first positive thing Neil had ever heard Kevin say about the Foxes. Usually Kevin only cared about their shortcomings. He listened for the lie in Kevin's tone, but Kevin was too good an actor to show Kathy his real feelings about his team. "They deserve their Class I status. This year will prove it."

"Brilliant," Kathy said, distracted. She'd just spotted Neil. The look in her eyes was hungry. "Neil Josten, good morning. I suppose you've already heard the good news? As of eleven o'clock last night, your name is the third-highest search string for NCAA Exy strikers. That puts you right after Riko and Kevin. How does it feel?"

Neil's stomach bottomed out. "I didn't need to know that."

"Did you talk to him?" Kathy asked Kevin.

"I didn't think we needed to talk about it," Kevin said.

"About what?" Neil asked.

"I want you on my show this morning," Kathy said.

Neil had to have misheard her. He stared blankly at her, waiting for the punch line.

"Everyone wants to know who you are," Kathy said, spreading her hands in a grand gesture. "You're a mystery addition to the Fox line, a rookie out of a tiny town in Arizona. Coach Hernandez says you picked Exy up in a year by reading a guidebook and showing up to practice. Kevin says you're going to sign with the US Court after graduation. Such ambitions and dreams from such a humble beginning, don't you think? It's time for your debut."

"No," Neil said. It was her turn to stare at him. Neil shook his head. "No. I'm not interested."

Her smile twitched a little. She reached out as if to pat his shoulder, but Neil backed out of her reach. Abby gestured at him, silently warning him to watch his manners. Neil ignored her.

[207]

"Don't be shy," Kathy said. "If you can play in front of sixty-five thousand fans in a game ESPN2 picked up and broadcast live, you can sit on my stage for ten minutes. This is the easy part. I'm just going to ask a couple questions about why you started playing and where you hope to go from here, that sort of thing. It's all written down so you can think on your responses before you step onto the stage. Your fans deserve answers from you."

"I don't have fans, and they don't want my answers," Neil said.

"Be smart, Neil." She spoke with the air of one who'd seen far more of the world than a simple teenager had. Neil wanted to hit her for it. "You can't spend this season running from the press when you're playing with Kevin Day."

"I said no."

Impatience finally worked its way into her expression. "You're not looking at the big picture. This year can make the world for you. If you want to get anywhere, you need our help. Everything has fallen so perfectly into place for you. Don't let it collapse so early in the game or you'll regret it the rest of your life. Kevin, you understand, don't you?"

"He'll do it," Kevin said.

"It's not your decision," Neil said in venomous French. He didn't realize what he'd done wrong until he felt Wymack's piercing stare. Andrew's lot knew Neil spoke French. Neil could explain it to the upperclassmen later and they wouldn't think twice about it. But Wymack, like Andrew, had also heard Neil speak fluent German. Neil ground his teeth and refused to return Wymack's look. "I'm not going on stage with you."

Kevin's smile never faltered, but his French response was cold. "You are being an idiot."

"I can't be on TV."

"You already were," Kevin said. "You will do this today, or you and I are finished. I will wash my hands of you on the court and you can struggle your way through mediocrity alone. You

[208]

can return your court keys to Coach when we get back to campus. You won't need them anymore."

It was like getting punched in the chest. "That isn't fair."

"Did you or did you not promise me you would try?"

"But this isn't—I don't want—"

"Did you or didn't you?"

Neil thought he'd choke on every argument and protest he didn't say. He was sure his breakfast would come back up in another second. The thought of getting on stage and letting a camera get a good look at him was nauseating, but not as frightening as Kevin cutting him off. Neil only had until mid-October to play with the Foxes, and then he'd lose Exy forever. Every time he saw a calendar he died a little on the inside. He couldn't give it up any earlier than the Raven game. He wouldn't survive.

Kevin nodded to Kathy and switched back to English. "It's settled."

Kathy's smile returned immediately. "Brilliant."

She motioned for them to follow and led the way toward the building. Kevin caught Neil's shoulder and pushed him after her. Neil twisted out of his grip and swatted at Kevin's hand. Kevin made a second grab at him, but Matt reached over Neil and shoved Kevin back. Abby hissed at them to behave, but Kevin and Matt were too busy glaring at each other to notice.

With Kevin pushed back a step, Andrew was now in Neil's line of sight. Andrew tipped his head to one side as he considered Neil, and Neil made the mistake of looking at him.

Apparently Andrew's drugs were already kicking in, because Andrew's smile was bright and mocking. "You're so stupid."

Andrew was right, so Neil didn't waste his breath defending himself. He turned and started after Kathy.

Dan caught up with him in a couple strides. "Neil? You don't have to do this, you know."

Neil only shook his head, too angry to speak.

Kathy handed them off to a couple aides. One man read a list of rules regarding appropriate studio behavior. The Foxes went one way to find their seats, and Neil and Kevin were led another way. They went down a hall and around a corner to a dressing room. Their escort took a couple quick measurements of their bodies and disappeared.

Neil's temper only worsened when he realized the dressing room was a one-room place with nowhere to hide from Kevin. One whole wall was a vanity lined with mirrors and lights. Six stools were pulled up against the counter. An empty clothes rack stood in the middle of the room. Neil folded his arms over his chest, trying to squeeze himself hard enough to drive his scars under his skin.

The aide returned to drop off clothes, promised the makeup artists would be by in ten minutes, and left again. Kevin's smile disappeared the second the door closed. He thumbed through the hangers and tossed an outfit at Neil. Neil let it land on the ground at his feet. Kevin pointed at it.

"Get changed," he said. When Neil made no move to obey, Kevin said, "I'm more worried about you making a disaster of this appearance than I am about your scars. Get over yourself."

Neil glared until Kevin started to change, then grabbed his clothes and turned his back on Kevin. He pulled his new shirt on over the one he was already wearing and wrestled the bottom layer out from underneath. It took a bit of work, but he managed to keep most of his skin hidden. Changing out his pants was easier, since most of the damage was on his upper half. Neil smoothed his shirt down obsessively, and then carried his discarded clothes to the counter. He stood as far away from Kevin as he could.

"Stop acting like a child," Kevin said.

"I shouldn't be doing this."

"Yes, you should, and you are going to make a good impression somehow." Kevin checked his reflection and tugged gently on his shirt sleeves. After a moment's consideration he undid his braces and set them aside. "Follow Kathy's leads, but don't let her dominate. This show is about us, not her. She is the enabler, not the star."

"Smile and lie," Neil said to his reflection.

"There is no reason to lie," Kevin said. "She's only going to talk about Exy."

"No reason to lie," Neil echoed. "Says you, who just lied to her face about how much the Foxes are worth, who told the ERC—" Neil faltered, unable to say the words. He tipped his head forward and pressed his forehead to the mirror. He counted his breaths to keep from panicking, but his gut was trembling so hard it ached. He clenched his hands around the corner of the counter and willed himself to stillness.

"Who told the ERC what?" Kevin asked.

Neil closed his eyes. "Why did you tell the ERC I would make Court?"

"Because when you stop being impossible and do what I tell you to, you will."

Andrew hadn't lied. The articles hadn't lied. Despite Kevin's angry words and rude impatience, Kevin believed in Neil's potential. Kevin wanted to train Neil. He wanted to play with Neil, and he wanted to shape Neil into the star he'd once been. Kevin would never forgive Neil for vanishing on him without warning this fall, and Neil hated that. As complicated as Neil's obsession with Kevin was, one truth was undeniable: he didn't want Kevin to hate him.

"So what are you going to tell Kathy?" Kevin asked.

"That I hate you," Neil muttered.

"You don't."

"How would you know?"

"Because if you did, Andrew would not let you anywhere near me," Kevin said.

Neil opened his eyes and turned his head to look at Kevin. "Right. I almost forgot about your guard dog. How did you win him over, anyway?"

"When you know what someone wants, it's easy to manipulate them. Case in point," Kevin said, gesturing from Neil to the room they were standing in.

"I was under the impression Andrew wants nothing."

Kevin didn't bother to explain. They waited in silence until the makeup artists arrived. Kevin let them in when they knocked. He was all smiles and polite charm as the artists set to work. When the two were ready, they were escorted to a lounge to wait. A widescreen TV showed the stage, which was currently empty. Neil checked the clock on the wall and saw they were ten minutes out. He passed time looking at the questions laid out for him. Most of them were basic, the same sorts of questions his teammates had asked him at the beginning of summer.

An aide came to collect Kevin when it was almost time for the show to start. Neil watched him leave, then looked back at the TV. At seven on the dot the show's opening music started and Kathy waltzed onto the stage to applause. She stopped in the center to bow and wave at her morning crowd.

"Ladies and gentlemen, good morning! I know it's a little early for most of us to be awake on a Saturday morning, but we've got a fantastic show in store for you today. Our musical guests are the four extremely talented men from the up-and-coming Hobgoblin's Thunder." She paused for the resulting cheers. "But let's start the morning with last night and the start of the NCAA Exy season!"

This drew even louder cheers. Kathy beamed as she slowly paced the front of her stage. "How many of you had a chance to go to a game last night? Oh, wow! How many, like me, watched the game from the comfort of your own home?" She raised her hand and laughed at whatever response she got from the crowd. "Some of you are probably already taking bets on the season's rankings and spring contenders. Right? This year has potential to be the greatest college season we've seen yet. Think of all the changes, all the amazing possibilities. We're going to talk a little about that today, but to do that, I'm going to need a couple special guests.

"It's been a year since you saw him here last and nearly nine months since his last public appearance. I present to you our first guest of the day: former starting striker for the US Court, the Baltimore Wildcats, and the Edgar Allan Ravens, current starting striker for the Palmetto State University Foxes, Kevin Day!"

She almost didn't make it through her introduction. At "nine months" the bigger Exy fans in the crowd caught on, and halfway through his titles the entire audience was cheering. The camera followed Kevin as he stepped out of the wings onto the stage. With the studio's expensive clothes on and his smile in place, Kevin looked every inch the adored idol Kathy was selling him as. He took her hand as he reached half-stage, leaned in to kiss her cheek, and turned with her to face the crowd. Kathy threw her hands up, a million-watt smile on her face, and Kevin waved hello to the audience.

It was an endless minute before the crowd calmed down, and by then Kathy had retreated behind her desk. There were two couches on stage with her, one to either side of her desk. Kevin sat on the one to her right, half-turned so he could see both Kathy and the audience. Kathy leaned over her desk to smile at Kevin, looking impossibly pleased with herself. Neil guessed she was already imagining her ratings.

"Kevin, Kevin, Kevin," Kathy said, shaking her head in time to his name. "I still can't believe I talked you into this. I hope you'll forgive me when I say it's surreal to see you back here alone! I still think of you as one half of a whole."

"At least I have room to stretch out now," Kevin said, neatly avoiding a real answer. "I might have to do so in a minute. I can't believe you expect us to be awake and presentable after last night's games."

She laughed and lifted her hands. "I suppose you're right. But you clean up nice, as always."

[213]

Someone in the audience cheered in approval, and Kevin laughed. "Thank you."

Kathy poured them both water and set a glass down on the edge of her desk where he could reach it. "So let's talk about last night. First, what it means, that the NCAA season started and you're wearing orange. Please don't take offense to this, as I mean no slight against your new team, but why did you transfer to Palmetto State? I understand you came as an assistant coach, but once you knew you could play again, why sign with the Foxes? I'm sure you had choices. Why would you go from the top of the ladder to the bottom?"

"Coach Wymack was friends with my mother. As I'm sure you know, she taught him how to play. Even after she died and Coach Moriyama took me in, Coach Wymack kept in touch with me." Kevin studied his left hand with a removed look on his face. "Last December I thought I would never play again. I was a wreck. Coach Wymack was the only one I could think of turning to, and he didn't disappoint me. He and his team took me in without hesitation. I enjoy working with them."

Kathy reached across the desk and clasped his left hand. Kevin forced his gaze up from his scars to her face and smiled. Kathy smiled back at him and said, "I admit I expected you to return to Edgar Allan this fall. Regardless of where you are, it's amazing to see you back in action. You deserve a round of applause for that."

The audience was happy to oblige.

Kathy squeezed Kevin's hand and let go. "Kind of unfortunate that your first game back was against Breckenridge, isn't it? You took three points last night, fifth-year senior Seth Gordon bagged two, and your newest teammate scored two. Let's talk about Neil Josten for a moment, shall we?"

"Of course."

"You really know how to upset things around here, don't you?" Kathy said. "What were you thinking, recruiting someone as fresh as Neil?"

[214]

"Neil is exactly what the Foxes need right now," Kevin said. "His inexperience is inconsequential. We went through a hundred files looking for a striker sub for this year, but Neil is the only one we approached after Janie. We knew as soon as we saw him we needed to sign him. We're just lucky we got there before anyone else did."

"You went to great lengths to get him, I hear," Kathy said. "Refusing to even give the ERC his name, is that right?"

"Our primary concern was keeping Neil safe," Kevin said. "Spring was very difficult for Palmetto State. Announcing him as ours would put a target sign on his back. The ERC was initially hesitant to fly blind on him, but they eventually sided with us."

"You didn't think the ERC could keep his secret?"

Kevin didn't answer that immediately, likely figuring out the most tactful way to respond. "Let me put it this way: 'Three can keep a secret if two of them are dead'. I mean no offense by that, but let's be honest. Sixteen people are assigned to the ERC and one of them is the coach of a fiercely competitive team. Even gossip shared in confidence can get out and destroy a man's life."

It was a lesson Kevin learned the hard way, Neil knew. ERC chatter led to Riko and Kevin's violent fallout.

"So much work and effort for a single player," Kathy said. "I can't wait to see what you make of him."

The lounge door opened and an aide leaned in to motion at Neil. "One minute. It's time to move."

Neil got up and followed the aide down the hall to the wings of the stage. A woman waiting for them had a radio linked to Kathy's ear bud. She looked Neil over, checking his appearance, and sent Kathy an okay.

"Why don't we all take another look at him?" Kathy said. "Let's see the man who replaced Riko Moriyama at Kevin's side. Introducing Neil Josten, the newest Palmetto Fox!"

[215]

Neil clenched his teeth, then forcibly relaxed his expression. The audience clapped in anticipation and Dan cheered his name. Neil buried his reservations deep and crossed the stage to Kathy's desk. She stood up to shake his hand, then motioned at the cushion beside Kevin. They sat at the same time. Kathy poured him water, and Kevin passed the glass to Neil.

"Isn't this an interesting picture?" Kathy asked the audience. "Kevin is paired again."

She propped her chin on her hand and leaned over her desk to smile at Neil. "I'm not exaggerating much when I say you're the talk of the nation, Neil. You're the amateur who caught a national champion's eye. This kind of thing should only happen in fairy tales, don't you think? How does it feel?"

"Undeserved," Neil said. "I gave Millport everything I had because I knew it was going to be my only chance. Kevin was the last person I expected to see in Arizona."

"Lucky for us he found you," Kathy said. "You have a natural talent for the game. It's a pity you started so late. Imagine where you'd be today if you'd started a couple years ago. Maybe you would have been snatched up by Edgar Allan or USC, if Kevin's right about your potential. Why did you wait so long?"

Neil thought of his little league team and lied through his teeth. "I was never really interested in team sports before. I only tried out at Millport because I was new in town and thought it'd help me get to know people. I didn't mean for things to turn out this way."

"If it bothers you, I'll take your spot," Kathy said with a wink. "I don't mind cozying up to Kevin."

"Would you really come between two strikers?" Kevin asked.

"Is it possible?" Kathy asked. "It's no secret there was hostility between you and the Foxes' strikers last year. Last

[216]

night made it obvious there are still problems to work through with Seth. That doesn't seem to be the case with you two."

Neil slid Kevin a sideways look, but Kevin didn't bother correcting her. "Seth graduates in May, so there is less a chance or need to rehabilitate his style to mine. Neil, on the other hand, is just starting out. We have all the time in the world."

Kathy pounced on that wording immediately. "That implies you see this as a permanent gig. Do you really have no plans to return to Edgar Allan? Does it depend on how well you adjust to playing right-handed this season, or do you intend to graduate from Palmetto State regardless?"

Kevin's pause rang too loudly in Neil's ears. "I would like to stay as long as Coach Wymack will have me."

Neil flicked Kevin another look, not liking that vague response.

"Ahh, the Ravens must be sad to hear that," Kathy said. "I imagine Riko misses you."

"We will see each other again this fall."

"Indeed you will. They're in your district now," Kathy said. "Why the major change?"

"I don't presume to understand Coach Moriyama's motivations."

"You mean they didn't tell you?" Kathy's surprise looked genuine.

"We are all very busy. It is difficult to keep in touch."

"Well then." Kathy recovered with a bright smile. "Have I got a treat for you!"

Music blared from the speakers, a dark melody with heavy drums. The crowd jumped to its feet and started chanting in unison: "King! King! King!" Neil looked out at them, recognizing the music but unable to place it, refusing to believe what the crowd was saying. He spotted the Foxes easily, as they were the only unmoving bodies in the crowd. They sat blank-faced with shock. Neil looked back at Kevin's pale face.

[217]

Movement in Neil's peripheral vision brought his attention back to the wings of the stage. The man who stepped onto the stage wore the same outfit Kevin did, save his version was black from head to toe. When he reached for Kathy's hand, his sleeve billowed around his arm like the wings of his school's raven mascot. The number one tattooed on his left cheekbone told everyone in the audience who'd just walked onto Kathy's stage.

It had been nine months since Riko Moriyama and Kevin Day stood in the same room together, nine months since Riko destroyed Kevin's hand, and now they were reunited on live television. The audience cheered their hearts out, delighted by Kathy's surprise, but they weren't quite loud enough to drown out Kevin's soft voice at Neil's side.

The words sounded like a desperate prayer.

CHAPTER THIRTEEN

The self-proclaimed King of Exy kissed Kathy's cheek in greeting. Whatever Riko and Kathy said to each other was lost in the audience's racket, but Kathy was beaming when she leaned back. Riko took the last few steps to Kevin's couch alone and stood over him. He was smiling, but neither Kevin nor Neil was stupid enough to think he was happy. The only look in his eyes was murder.

Any animosity Neil felt toward Kevin for forcing him onto this show evaporated. He couldn't be angry when Riko was here, not when Riko was to Kevin what Neil's father was to him. Petty anger had nothing on this full-fledged terror.

Only after the crowd quieted down did Riko speak. "Kevin. It's been so long."

There was a scuffle and crash in the audience. Neil didn't want to take his eyes off Riko, but it was instinctive to look. Renee was sitting sideways in Andrew's lap, one foot braced against the ground to keep him from shoving her off. She had a hand over his mouth as they both stared up at the stage. Matt had one of Andrew's wrists in both hands. Wymack had the other. The looks on the Foxes' faces ranged from horror to fury.

Riko moved, and Neil forgot about his team in favor of staring Riko down. Riko ignored him completely and held his hand out to Kevin in invitation. Kevin stared at it for a couple seconds, then slipped a hand into Riko's and let Riko pull him to his feet. The crowd applauded as Riko embraced Kevin, apparently oblivious to how slowly Kevin returned the hug.

Riko let go and held Kevin at arm's length. "I think you've shrunk since I last saw you. Don't they feed you down here? I always heard southern food is heavy."

[219]

"I run it off on the court, I guess."

"What a miracle."

There was an edge in his voice, but Kathy smiled and gestured between them. "It truly is a miracle. Take a good look, everyone. Your golden pair is back, but for the first time ever, they're rivals. Riko, Kevin, we thank you from the bottoms of our hearts for tolerating our incessant fanaticism."

She motioned for them to sit. Riko backed away from Kevin to sit on the other couch. Kevin sank back onto his cushion, but he was paying more attention to Riko than where he was going. He ended up with his thigh pressed against Neil's, hard enough Neil could feel him trembling.

Kathy looked at Riko. "From what I've just heard from Kevin, it sounds like neither of you have spoken in a while. Is that right?"

"It is," Riko said. "You sound surprised."

"Well, yes," Kathy said. "I didn't think it possible for you two to grow apart."

"A year ago it would have been impossible," Riko said, "but you have to understand how emotionally crushing December was. The injury was Kevin's to bear, but we all suffered for it. Some of us couldn't handle the reality of what that accident meant, myself included. Kevin and I grew up at Evermore. We built our lives around that team and our pair work. I couldn't believe we'd lost it. I couldn't accept that our dreams had collapsed. Neither could he, so we withdrew from each other."

"But for nine months?"

She looked at Kevin, so he answered, but his voice had lost its easy edge for something duller. "Perhaps it was inevitable. We made Exy the center of our lives, Kathy. We showed you our best, but we didn't show you what it cost us. Juggling three teams, university classes, and public pressure was wearing us down, but we refused to admit it. We didn't want to believe we had limits."

[220]

Kathy nodded. "I can't even imagine that stress and pressure. I suppose it had to put a strain on your friendship."

"We are human sometimes," Riko said, "and therefore we can't help but have our differences, hmm, Kevin?"

"No family is perfect," Kevin agreed quietly.

Kathy nodded sympathetically. "Can I just say it was terrifying when you two disappeared? The last we heard, you two had gone skiing to celebrate the end of the semester, and then no one saw either of you in public for a month. I feared the worst, but I didn't realize what the worst really was until Coach Wymack made his announcement."

"The worst was having everything and losing it," Riko said. "We signed with Court last year, which meant we had only one dream left to achieve: to play together with Court at the summer Olympics. We knew it was coming, that it was just a matter of time, that a lifetime's worth of effort and sacrifice was about to pay off. Then Kevin broke his hand."

"Everything changed," Kevin said, so low no one would hear him if not for the microphone he was wearing. "We weren't ready to acknowledge that. It was easier to just walk away. Unwise," he allowed, glancing at Riko, "but easier."

"Heartbreaking," Kathy said sadly. Kevin looked at his water and said nothing. Kathy finally got a clue that the conversation was going the wrong way. She turned on Riko again, giving Kevin time to pull himself back together. "But look at him now. Isn't it amazing how far he's come this year?"

"I'm not sure it is," Riko said, "but I'm saying that as his brother, as his best friend. You saw him last night, Kathy. I'm worried his wishful thinking and obsession will lead him to injure himself again. Can he recover a second time, emotionally or mentally?"

His tone was concerned, but Neil could practically feel his knife twisting deeper in Kevin's chest. Everything Riko was saying was meant to hurt Kevin, and it was working. It wasn't

[221]

Neil's turn to talk, but he'd heard enough. His temper couldn't stomach any more of Riko's cruelty.

"I thought friends were supposed to cheer each other on," he said before Kathy could answer Riko. "Believing in him now is the least you could do after completely abandoning him last winter."

A couple people in the audience booed at that. Matt and Dan whooped to balance it out.

"Ah, forgive my bad manners," Kathy said to Neil. "I didn't forget you over there, I just got distracted. Let's get the pair of you introduced, though I'm not sure either one of you needs an introduction by now. Riko, Neil. Neil, Riko. Kevin's past and present, or should I say past and future?"

Riko finally looked at Neil. "To address that accusation of yours: mine and Kevin's relationship is unique, and I do not expect you to understand it. Do not impress on us your petty ideas of friendship."

"Was unique," Neil said, and emphasized again, "Was. I'm pretty sure your relationship died when he couldn't keep up with your team anymore."

"Kevin chose to leave Edgar Allan," Riko said. "We mourned his absence but were glad to hear he found a coaching position."

"But you're not happy that he's playing again," Neil said. "Isn't that why you transferred to our district? You don't think Kevin should be on the court again, so you'll cut him off at the pass. You'll destroy his chance of making a comeback and make him watch as your team succeeds yet again. You're rubbing his face in everything he's lost, and from where I'm sitting, it looks like you're enjoying it."

"I will ask you only once to tone down that animosity."

"I can't," Neil said. "I have a bit of an attitude problem."

Riko's smile was all ice. "A bit?"

Kathy intervened before things could get nasty. "Neil does bring up a valid point I'd like to discuss. This district change is an unprecedented move. For it to be Edgar Allan makes it more surprising. Neither your coach nor the Exy Rules and Regulations Committee has given a satisfactory reason, but I don't think Neil's far off in thinking you transferred because of Kevin."

"Kevin plays only a small role in our decision," Riko said, "and not for the reasons this child claims. It was not a decision made lightly on our part and we've taken an unfair bit of criticism for it. The north says we are transferring to keep our ranking secure, as if they ever had a chance of unseating us, and the south cries unfair at having to contend with us. We are the nation's best team, after all, and the southeastern district is... Well, it's subpar, to be polite. To be honest, its teams are dreadful. We hope our transfer changes that. We're here to inspire the south."

"You want to do for the south what Kevin is doing for the Foxes," Kathy concluded.

"Yes, but it will be much easier if Kevin plays along," Riko said.

"How so?"

"Kevin cannot and will not play for us again. He knows this; this is why he did not return to us this spring. Our affection for him doesn't forgive his new inadequacies on the court, and he respects the Ravens too much to drag us down. That doesn't mean Evermore isn't his home. His work with the Foxes this spring proved we can find a place for him on our staff. We'd like him to return to us as one of our coaches."

"Sounds like a difficult choice, Kevin," Kathy said. "I have to admit both ideas fascinate me. As much as I love watching the Foxes improve, it breaks my heart to see you away from Edgar Allan."

"You wouldn't honestly have him go back, would you?" Neil asked. "I can't believe it."

"This has nothing to do with you," Riko said.

[223]

"Stop being so selfish," Neil said, and Kathy gaped at him. Kevin pinched Neil's arm in warning, but Neil shrugged him off. "If Kevin's dream has always been to be the best on the court, what right do you have to take it away from him? Why would you ask him to settle for less? The Foxes are giving him a chance to play whereas you'd relegate him to the sidelines. He has no reason to transfer back."

"Palmetto State is a waste of his talents."

"Not as much as Edgar Allan was," Neil said. Someone in the audience laughed, entertained by Kathy's mouthy guest. "Your team's ranked first? Congratulations and big deal. Maintaining a top position is far easier than starting over from the gutters. Kevin is doing that right now. He's facing entirely new schools and learning to play with his less dominant hand. When he masters it, and he will, he'll be better than you could ever have made him.

"Do you know why?" Neil asked, but he didn't let Riko answer. "It's not just his natural talent. It's because he's with us. There are only ten Foxes this year. That's one sub for every position. Think about it. Last night we played Breckenridge. They have twenty-seven people on their roster. They can burn through players as fast as they want because they have a pile of replacements. We don't have that luxury. We have to hold our ground on our own."

"You didn't hold your ground," Riko said over the Foxes' applause. "You lost. Your school is the laughingstock of the NCAA. You're a team with no concept of teamwork."

"Lucky for you," Neil said. "If we were a unified front you wouldn't have a chance against us."

"You cannot last and your unfounded arrogance is offensive to everyone who actually earned a spot in Class I. Everyone knows the only reason Palmetto qualified for this division is because of your coach."

"Funny, I'm pretty sure that's how Edgar Allan qualified."

"We've earned our prestige a thousand times over. You've earned nothing but pity and scorn, neither of which should be tolerated in a sport. Someone as inexperienced as you are has no right to have an opinion on the matter."

"All the same, I'll give you one more," Neil said. "I don't think you're telling Kevin to sit out because of his health. I think you know this season is going to be a disaster for your reputation. You and Kevin have always played in each other's shadows. You've always been a pair. Now you have to face each other on the court as rivals for the first time, and people are finally going to know which one of you is better. They're going to know how premature this was." Neil gestured at his face, meaning Riko and Kevin's tattoos. "I think you're scared."

Riko's smile could have frozen hell. "I am not scared of Kevin. I know him."

"You're going to eat those words," Neil said. "You're going to choke on them."

"That sounds like a challenge," Kathy cut in with a quick look between them. "You've got seven weeks until your match and I, for one, am already counting down the seconds. There's so much to look forward to this year, but one question can't wait: orange or black, Kevin? What color is your future?"

Kevin clenched his hand around Neil's arm, cutting off circulation all the way to Neil's fingertips. "I already said it," Kevin said without looking at Riko. "I would like to stay at Palmetto as long as they're willing to have me."

The Foxes cheered at that. The rest of the audience was quick to join in. The tension between the strikers had seeped into the crowd, and it broke now in an uncontrollable wave. Kathy didn't even try to calm it but pointed at the cameras. Neil barely heard her announce the end of the Exy segment and the cut to commercials. A light at the foot of the stage went dark, indicating they were off the air. Kathy covered the microphone on her shirt collar and looked at her guests.

[225]

"You boys made my day," she said with her biggest smile yet. The three got to their feet and Kathy shook their hands. "Keep the clothes. There're refreshments in back and we've got seats up front so you can watch the rest of the show."

"Thank you," Kevin said.

Neil had no intention of hanging out here any longer. He looked out at the crowd. Wymack sliced a hand across his throat and jerked his thumb over his shoulder. Neil hoped he was right in translating it as "Let's get the hell out of here." He reached past Kevin to put his water on Kathy's desk. Kevin didn't look like he was moving anytime soon, so Neil put his body between Riko's and Kevin's and pushed Kevin toward the wings.

Riko followed them off the stage and behaved until they were in the hallway. The aides who'd been waiting in the wings rushed past them to check on Kathy and adjust settings during the commercial break. Neil thought maybe one would linger long enough to distract Riko, but maybe the time crunch was more important than autographs right now.

Neil hated having Riko at his back, but Riko moved just as Neil turned to face him. Riko caught Neil by his shoulders and threw him up against the wall. Neil went rigid as they stared each other down, trapped more by the death in Riko's eyes than the fingers leaving bruises on his shoulders. Riko had the same stare his father did: he looked at Neil and saw only flesh that knew how to bleed.

"I do not approve, Kevin," Riko said. "You should get rid of him as soon as possible."

"You saw our game last night," Kevin said quietly. "He has potential."

"Potential." Riko slammed Neil against the wall again and whirled on Kevin. Kevin stared back at him, white-faced and tense. "You said that goalkeeper had potential and then wrote him off as useless when I offered him to you. You'll get bored of this one just as quickly. Believe me."

[226]

Kevin pressed his lips into a hard line and looked away. Riko made a disgusted noise low in his throat. He said something in a language Neil didn't understand. Neil guessed it was Japanese. Whatever it was, it sounded furious. Kevin flinched and offered a weak response. Riko stabbed a finger at him in angry accusation and rattled away, getting louder and more incensed by the second. Neil watched Kevin wilt beneath the weight of his brother's—no, owner's—fury and kissed his survival instincts goodbye. He grabbed Riko's shirt and hauled him back.

"Leave him alone."

A black look twisted Riko's expression into something ugly and unrecognizable. He reached for Neil, but Kevin caught his arm to stop him. Riko slammed his elbow back into Kevin's face without missing a beat. Neil retreated as fast as he could, but there was only so far he could go before he would end up on stage again. He'd just started tripping over wires when Andrew appeared in front of him.

"Riko," Andrew said, spreading his arms as if he intended to hug Riko hello. "It's been a while."

Riko jerked back a bit in surprise, started to school his expression into something more civil, and gave up when he realized who had joined them.

"We were just talking about you," Riko said.

"With your fists, it seems," Andrew said. "Don't touch my things, Riko. I don't share."

He reached back without looking and pushed at Neil's shoulder. Neil took the hint and skirted around Andrew and Riko. He half-expected Riko to stop them, but all of Riko's attention was on Andrew. Neil grabbed Kevin's arm and hauled him down the hall, looking for the exit. They were almost there when the team caught up with them. Abby jogged the last couple steps to Kevin and crushed him in a fierce embrace. Kevin held onto her for dear life while the team hovered nearby.

Wymack looked at Neil. "Are you seriously retarded or something? You would have been safer back at Palmetto after all."

"Leave him alone, David," Abby said, muffled against Kevin's shoulder.

"When I said Abby and I would look out for you, I didn't mean you should pick a fight with Riko on national television," Wymack said. "Should I have spelled that out beforehand?"

"Probably," Neil said.

"It's fine, Coach," Andrew said, catching up to them. He touched Neil's back on his way by, fingers light enough to give Neil goose bumps, but didn't slow on his way to Kevin's side. He pressed a hand to Abby's arm in a silent demand for her to back off. "Kevin, we're going. Right now, okay?"

Kevin let go of Abby, and Andrew pushed him out the door into the parking lot.

"Coach says stupid, but I say you have balls of steel. I didn't think you had it in you," Matt said, looking Neil over as if wondering what he'd missed this summer. "I thought you were the quiet type."

"If Neil was quiet, Andrew wouldn't have brought him to Columbia," Renee said.

"True," Matt agreed.

When Neil looked between them, Renee smiled and said, "Andrew's welcome parties are his way of sizing up and eliminating threats. Not everyone gets invited."

"You went," Neil said, not believing it but knowing somehow he was right.

"The three of us were," Renee said, gesturing at Matt and Dan. "No one else was until you."

"Let's go," Wymack said. "I am going to drop you off at the dorm and spend the rest of the day drinking. Damage control can wait until tomorrow."

[228]

They caught up with Andrew's group at the bus. Wymack unlocked the door to let them on, and he got them on the road as fast as he could.

Neil spent the ride staring out the window and trying to figure out the consequences of what he'd done. Neil knew harmless conversation with his teammates was better than his dire thoughts, but he wasn't in the mood. He was too tense to play nice with them. Luckily Renee got the hint after a couple attempts and left him alone.

They were almost halfway back when Andrew had to take his medicine again. Abby went to the back of the bus to make sure he really swallowed it. Neil half-expected Andrew to fight it after what had happened at Kathy's show, but Andrew was surprisingly compliant.

They stopped only to get gas and made good time back to campus. Neil was so relieved to see Palmetto State again it was almost painful. Wymack let the bus idle out back of Fox Tower and watched his team climb out. He said nothing until Andrew approached, then put a hand in Andrew's path.

"Be smart."

Andrew flapped a hand at Wymack. "I know, I know."

Neil didn't know if Wymack actually trusted Andrew, but Wymack nodded and dropped his hand. Andrew took the stairs down and didn't slow on his way to the dorm. Wymack didn't leave until they were all inside. They took the stairs to the third floor, and Dan stopped outside Andrew's room.

"Hey," Dan said as Andrew unlocked his door. "Let's have lunch together as a team. We don't have to talk about this morning if you don't want to."

Andrew pretended to think about it. "No."

He opened the door and stepped out of the way to send Kevin a pointed look. Kevin started into the room.

"Don't worry, Kevin," Dan said. "We'll figure this out together."

Kevin glanced back at her, but he didn't get to answer. Andrew put his hand to Kevin's back and shoved him into the bedroom. Dan scowled at Andrew as Aaron and Nicky followed Kevin inside. Andrew smiled and slammed the door in her face.

"Asshole," Matt said.

"They're upset," Renee said. "They couldn't help him today."

"They didn't have to," Matt said. "Neil did it for them."

They went to the men's suite and found Seth and Allison tangled together on the couch. They were watching a movie, dressed but just barely. Neither seemed embarrassed about being walked in on. The upperclassmen didn't bat an eye, as if this was a normal sight around these parts, but Neil averted his eyes from the pair. The most Allison did to cover up was to put one of the couch pillows on her lap over her pink thong.

"He's looking fancy," she said, pointing at Neil.

"Surprise guest on Kathy's show," Dan said. "Kathy wanted the exclusive and Kevin wanted the publicity. Did it record all right?"

"I haven't checked it yet. We were busy."

"You think?" Matt asked.

Dan elbowed him. "Pause that, would you? We have to talk. Something went wrong this morning."

"We're Foxes. Something is always going wrong," Seth said, but he fished the remote out from under a cushion and turned the TV off.

Dan got right to the point. "Riko was on the show."

Seth stared at her for a second before bursting into raucous laughter. Allison smothered him with her pillow and said, "On the show like how?"

"Kathy sat him down seven feet from Kevin and asked why they split up."

Seth pushed the pillow out of the way. "I should have gone. Did he freak? I bet he freaked."

"Seth, shut up," Dan said. "It isn't funny."

[230]

"He held it together after Neil told Riko off," Matt said. "Kid's got a serious mouth on him. He made Riko look like a stupid asshole who sells out friends on a daily basis. You really should borrow the tape from us later and watch it."

Seth looked dubious. Allison arched an eyebrow at Neil and asked, "What'd the monster think?"

"He was drugged to high heaven," Dan said. "Abby made sure he dosed up on the way back, but I recommend avoiding him the rest of the weekend."

"What else is new?" Seth said.

Renee let the silence settle between them for a minute. When it seemed the serious part of the conversation was over, she said, "Is anyone else interested in lunch? I'm starving."

They ordered a couple pizzas to be delivered to the room. Allison and Seth dressed while they waited, and then Neil took over the bedroom to change out of Kathy's clothes. He buried them at the bottom of the dresser beneath his more practical outfits and tugged on worn jeans and an oversized tee. He and his teammates wasted a few hours with food and a movie. Afterward talk turned to the season, but the upperclassmen seemed as happy to talk about the Ravens as Neil was to think about them. Allison tolerated the moping for only a minute before distracting them with talk of the banquet.

"We should go shopping tomorrow," Allison said. "I'm going to need time to find the perfect dress. You," she pointed between Matt and Seth, "are in charge of getting Neil something real to wear. I've seen everything he owns. I don't trust him to choose something appropriate."

"I could just not go," Neil said.

"You have to go," Dan said. "It's a team event."

There was a knock at the door. Dan was closest, so she got up to answer it. Nicky was waiting in the hallway, smiling but visibly tense.

"How bad is it?" Dan asked.

[231]

Nicky winced. "Does your armcandy there know how to install a window?"

Matt looked over his shoulder at the bedroom window. "I can try, but I'm not going anywhere near him tonight."

"Tomorrow's cool, too," Nicky said. "Just, you know, preferably before Coach comes around to check on Kevin again. There's three hundred bucks in it for you if it's fixed before noon."

"You get Andrew out of the room and I'll see what I can do."

"Awesome." Nicky looked at Neil. "Andrew wants to see you."

Neil looked at the clock and did the math. If Andrew took his midday dose on time, he should be popping another pill any minute now. Neil wondered if he'd really take it and idly hoped he would. If withdrawal didn't upset Andrew enough, being able to finally react to this morning's events without drugs in his veins would make him downright murderous. Neil wouldn't want to be Kevin tonight.

He got up and followed Nicky down the hall to Andrew's suite. He hadn't been in their room since he'd come to yell at them for breaking into his things, and they were pretty good about keeping their door shut, so it was weird to step inside again. He spotted Kevin first, curled up on one of the oversized beanbag chairs facing away from the door. Aaron was washing dishes in the kitchen and didn't look up as they went by. Nicky pointed down the hall and went to sit with Kevin. Neil went alone into the dark bedroom and closed the door behind him.

The cousins had pushed two of their dressers against the wall under the window. Andrew sat on top of them, leaning forward so he could fold his arms across his knees. Neil smelled blood and looked past Andrew at the window. Andrew had taken the screen off in the main room so he could smoke, but this window still had one. It was probably all that saved his hand when he punched a hole in the glass.

Andrew wasn't looking at him but at the bloody hand dangling between his knees. He flexed his fingers occasionally as if checking the extent of the damage he'd wrought.

"You could have destroyed your hand with a stunt like that," Neil said.

Andrew laughed. "Oh my, where would I be then?"

"Off the team," Neil said. "Where would Kevin be then?"

Andrew didn't answer. Neil crossed the room to stand in front of him. Andrew didn't look up, but he smiled wide enough to show Neil his teeth.

"Oh, Neil, as unpredictable as he is unreal," Andrew said. "The last time we spoke you were afraid Riko would notice you. Either you lied to me or you changed your mind. I do hope it's the latter, because I hate being lied to."

"I didn't change my mind," Neil said, "but I didn't have a choice."

"There is always a choice."

"I had to say something."

"And what a thing to say! You took a swing at Riko on live TV. He's not going to take that sitting down, you know. How's that target on your back feel?"

"Familiar," Neil said.

Andrew sat up and slumped back against the screen. Neil glanced down at Andrew's hand as it slid into Andrew's lap, but he couldn't see the actual cuts past Andrew's drying, smeared blood.

"Give him a couple days and he'll know everything about you," Andrew said. When Neil looked him in the eye again, Andrew smiled. "Money greases the wheels of the world easier than blood does, and Riko has access to both. He'll look for a way to get back at you, and it won't take him long to see how cold your trail is. How long do you think it'll take someone with his connections to figure out the truth?"

Neil was lightheaded with nausea. "Shut up."

"What will you do when he finds out? Run?"

[233]

"You know I will."

"I know," Andrew agreed. "I can see it. You've got that look in your eye that says you know where every exit to this dormitory is."

Neil turned away, but Andrew was faster. He rocked forward and grabbed Neil's collar, dragging him to a halt before he could leave. He left sticky blood on the back of Neil's neck from his messy fingers. Neil reached back and tried to pry him off, but Andrew refused to let go.

"Hey, Neil. Neil, listen. Running won't save you this time."

"Let go of me."

"Don't you understand? Running was only an option when no one was looking. You knew that back in June. It's why you wanted to leave before October. You could have left before Riko knew you existed. You should have left before you insulted him in front of all of his adoring fans. Now you can't go. Riko wants to know who defied him, and he'll get his answers. You can't outrun your past anymore."

"I have to try," Neil said.

Andrew hummed a little in mock disapproval. "Have to nothing. There you go again, thinking there's only one choice. I thought you didn't want to leave."

"I don't want to," Neil said.

"What would it take to make you stay?"

The question was so unexpected Neil had to turn back. "What?"

Andrew laughed quietly at his shock and leaned forward. "Name it and it's yours. It doesn't matter what it is so long as you stand your ground here with us."

"I can't."

"You can. You have everything you need to survive. You're just too afraid to see it."

"I don't understand."

Andrew sighed as if Neil was being difficult on purpose. "Riko will find out the truth, but he can't tell his brother. For starters, Riko and Ichirou aren't allowed to associate with each other, seeing how they belong to separate branches. More importantly, Coach Moriyama won't let him. This year is about Kevin and Riko, see? He won't want news about you getting out and distracting people from their showdown. They're free to make your life a living hell and they'll try to use the truth against you, but they can't sell you out yet.

"Use that time to narrow the angles they can get at you. Kevin wants to make you a star, so let him. Take what he is giving you and make it your shield. It's hard to kill a man when everyone's eyes are on him. Make them love you, make them hate you, I don't care. Just make them look at you. You have one year to figure it out," Andrew said, putting a finger in Neil's face. "For one year, I'll stand between you and the Moriyamas if you stand at Kevin's side. Next year your life is your problem again, understand?"

"Why?" Neil asked. "Why would you help me?"

"Ask me later," Andrew said. He tapped bloody fingers to his mouth and grinned at Neil around them. "It's better if this isn't in the way, don't you think? You'll get your answers in Columbia. Oh, but no one told you yet, did they? You're coming out with us tonight."

"Never again."

"Shh, Neil, shh," Andrew said. "If you want to stay, you'll come with us at nine. If you're stupid enough to run, pack up and leave before then. That's three hours, almost, for you to make up your mind. Aren't I generous?"

"That's not enough time."

"I doubt you're a stranger to snap judgments when it comes to saving your skin. You gave your game to Kevin. Give your back to me."

Andrew dug his medicine out of his pocket and shook a pill onto the dresser. He snapped the lid on, tossed the bottle to the corner of the room, and plucked the pill up with his bloody fingers. He held it up where he could see it, turning it this way

[235]

and that like he'd never seen it before, and finally pushed it between his lips. He dropped his hand to his lap as he swallowed and bared his teeth at Neil in a fierce grin.

"Tick tock, says the clock. Get out of my room."

Neil left as fast as he could, but he only made it as far as the hallway. As soon as he shut the door behind him, his legs locked, and he grabbed desperately at the wall. A spike of panic wrenched his stomach into his throat. He dug the side of his hand into his mouth so hard he tasted blood.

Was he supposed to honestly think some rabid goalkeeper could protect him?

His thoughts went unbidden to the confrontation in Kathy's studio. Andrew showed up in time to protect Neil. He should have gone straight for Kevin, since Kevin appeared to be the center of his strange world, but he'd put himself between Riko and Neil instead. Andrew knew exactly who the Moriyamas were and he knew hints of what Neil was involved in, but he thought he could stand between them just the same.

Neil shoved away from the wall and went to the stairwell. He was running before he reached the ground floor, and he slammed the front door open so hard it banged on its hinges. Louder than that crash was his heartbeat thundering in his ears.

What if he could stay? What if a psychotic teenager really was enough? What if Andrew was right that the Foxes' infamy could protect his identity?

Neil should know better than to believe such dangerous promises, but Andrew's words haunted him every step of the way.

CHAPTER FOURTEEN

The dormitory was uncharacteristically busy when Neil made it back at nine. The football game had ended about the same time he'd run away, and now some of the after-party crowds were slowly drifting back. People yelled to each other up and down the hall, and loud music blasted through open doors here and there. Neil wound his way through the chaos toward the Foxes' rooms. They were the only three closed doors this side of the stairwell.

He stopped in front of Andrew's door but couldn't make himself knock. His hand was shaking when he looked at it, so he balled it into a fist. He'd almost gotten up the nerve to move when the door opened without warning.

"Oh, he made it," Andrew said. "That's interesting."

He pressed two fingers to Neil's throat, checking his pulse. When Neil tried to bat him away, Andrew caught his wrist with his free hand. His smile was small and fierce as he leaned forward into Neil's space.

"Remember this feeling. This is the moment you stop being the rabbit."

Neil was too startled to answer, but Andrew didn't wait. He slid past Neil, using the weight of his body and his grip on Neil's wrist to pull Neil with him out of the way of the door. He let go in the middle of the hallway and slipped his hands in his pockets to wait.

Nicky was the next out of the room. When he saw Neil his grin lit up his entire face. Aaron looked skeptical when he followed, but he glanced at Andrew and said nothing. Kevin's expression was the hardest to read as he stepped out and closed the door behind him. Neil looked from Kevin to Andrew, who was still watching him like he was waiting for something.

Movement two doors down gave Neil a reason to look away from Andrew again. Five strangers were knocking on his suite door. Seth stepped out to greet them, slapping backs and high-fiving as he moved into their ranks. Allison wasn't far behind them. She pressed against Seth's back and slid her hands down his sides to his pants. Neil watched as she systematically dug through all of his pockets. She came back with just a lighter and a crumpled stick of gum.

Seth sent her an annoyed look over his shoulder. "I'm not stupid."

She kissed him to shut him up and put his lighter back where she'd found it. The gum she tossed behind her as worthless. She almost hit Matt with it as Matt and Dan stepped into the suite doorway. When Matt turned to avoid it, he spotted Neil. The relief on his face was unexpected.

"Neil, you made it," he said, loud enough even Allison and Seth turned to see. Neil looked from one face to the other, wondering what he'd missed. "Seth and Allison are going bar-hopping downtown, so the rest of us are prepping a movie marathon. Any requests or recommendations?"

"You're leaving campus?" Nicky asked Allison. "Are you serious?"

Allison scowled at him and wound her arms tighter around Seth. "It's none of your business."

Matt glanced at Allison, expression tight, but kept talking to Neil. "Renee should be back with drinks any second. She said she'd get something nonalcoholic for the two of you."

"Oh, what a waste," Andrew said. "I'm buying Neil's drinks tonight."

It took them a couple seconds to catch on. When they did, Dan lurched out of the doorway with a hard, "You're joking."

Andrew laughed at her outrage. "You wish I was."

[238]

"The last time he went out with you he hitchhiked his way back," Dan said. Seth's friends looked from her to Andrew with blatant interest, but Dan didn't seem to notice the attention. She stabbed a finger at Andrew and said, "He is not going out with you again. He'll probably wind up dead this time."

"Jesus, Dan," Nicky said. "When you say things like that it makes me think you don't trust us."

"No one trusts you," Matt said. "What are you playing at?"

"It's not really any of your business," Aaron said.

"I said he's not going," Dan said. "Neil, don't let him push you around."

Andrew nudged Neil with his elbow and said in German, "Hey, Neil. Isn't that amazing? Isn't that touching? Look how they weep over you. Ah, such misplaced concern. Tell them you can take care of yourself."

Andrew was daring him to cross a line, to give up a little more of the lie that was Neil Josten. It went against everything Neil knew to give in, but he'd chosen this path. He'd chosen Andrew. He buried his fear as deep as he could and answered in German.

"They're not stupid enough to think it's only a drink."

"Oh shit," Nicky said, switching languages in a heartbeat. "Since when do you speak German? Andrew, you knew about this? Why didn't you tell us?"

"Boring," Andrew said. "Figure things out for yourself once in a while."

Nicky waggled a hand at Aaron. "Quick. Have we said anything totally incriminating these past few months?"

"Aside from your endless inappropriate comments about what you'd like to do to him, I don't think so. Looks like you've managed to completely embarrass yourself in both languages." Aaron looked at Neil. "When were you going to tell us?"

"I wasn't," Neil said. "After everything I've put up with from you this year I figured I didn't owe you any favors."

[239]

Aaron shrugged and let it slide. Nicky rubbed at his face and muttered under his breath. Down the hall the upperclassmen stared at them in disbelief. Matt was the first to get his tongue back, but the best he came up with was, "I thought you spoke French. That was French this morning, right? At Kathy's?"

"I'll see you tomorrow," Neil said in English.

"We're going," Andrew said, and went down the hall with Kevin on his heels.

"Neil, this isn't a good idea," Dan said.

"I know," Neil said, and turned after Kevin and Andrew. Aaron and Nicky fell in behind him. They went down the stairs as a small procession, a line of black with Neil the sore thumb in the middle. He ended up in the same seat as last time, tucked between the brothers in back. He'd just buckled when Nicky reached back and dropped a bag in his lap. Neil poked it open and saw dark cloth inside.

The last time they went to Columbia it was a quiet ride. This time it couldn't be, since Andrew still had a bit over an hour's worth of energy from his medicine. Nicky and Andrew talked the whole way there, Nicky bouncing topics from movies to music and Andrew cheerfully arguing with almost everything he said. They were almost to Columbia before Andrew's answers started slowing down. Nicky started dominating more of the conversation, and Andrew's silences stretched a little longer.

Sweetie's was just as busy tonight as it had been on their first visit, but they were lucky enough to show up when a car was pulling out. Nicky stole the spot with a triumphant pump of his fist and the five headed inside together. There were two groups ahead of them waiting for a table. Kevin gave their name to the hostess. Andrew looked at Neil.

"We need a number for crackers. Are you in or out?"

"Do I really have a choice this time?" Neil asked.

"From now on you do," Andrew said.

[240]

Neil didn't believe him, but he shook his head. Andrew pointed at Neil's bag and walked off to the salad bar to collect cracker packets. Neil looked for a bathroom sign, but Nicky tapped him on the shoulder and led the way. Neil followed him into the bathroom and dumped the bag out on the counter.

"This is new," Neil said.

"It'd be tacky to wear the same thing twice, wouldn't it?" Nicky asked.

"Don't buy me things."

"Sure, next time Andrew says to outfit you, I'll just tell him no. I can see that going over marvelously." Nicky rolled his eyes.

"Then let me pay you back."

"How to say this?" Nicky thought it over for a second, then gave up on tact. "You could obviously use the money more than he could right now. Let Andrew give you things if he wants to. He's not normally the gifting type, so it's kind of fun."

"I have my own money," Neil said. "I don't need handouts."

"Really?" Nicky asked, sending Neil's clothes a meaningful look.

Neil stared at him. He knew Andrew hadn't told the others about his fluency in German, but he hadn't realized Andrew kept quiet about his money, too. That meant Andrew had kept all of Neil's secrets save one: the truth about his eyes. According to Nicky it hadn't been much of a secret. But Andrew had found Neil's money before their truce in Wymack's living room. He hadn't had a reason to protect Neil then, so why had he stayed quiet?

"Really," Neil said at last. "I saved some up before I moved here."

"Good," Nicky said. "Then we should go shopping tomorrow and buy you new clothes. Coach is pretty mad we haven't done it yet. He's as sick as we are of seeing you in the same things over and over."

"There's nothing wrong with my clothes."

[241]

"That's what you think. Now that you're ours, we've got to take care of you. First order of business is fixing your miserable wardrobe." Nicky's grin faded a bit at the look on Neil's face. "Okay, no. What's with the blank stare? You do know what you're doing out with us tonight, right? Andrew squeezed some sort of explanation into his usual crazy nonsense?"

"Sort of," Neil said. "He said he'd have answers for me later."

"You've got to be kidding me." Nicky looked pained. "This means Andrew is keeping you, same as he kept Kevin. It means you're part of the family now."

"I don't believe in family."

"Who does these days?"

It was a strange thing for Nicky to say considering he had cousins on the team. Judging by his heavy sigh, Nicky had no problems interpreting Neil's expression. Nicky made air quotes with his fingers. As soon as he spoke Neil knew whose words he was echoing, but Neil doubted Andrew sounded so tired when he first said it: "Being related doesn't make us family."

Nicky stuffed his hands in his pockets and turned a pensive look on his reflection. "I know why Andrew feels that way, and I understand why he and Aaron can't stand each other, but I'm not willing to give up on them yet. I want to fix this and show them they're wrong."

"Do they hate each other?" Neil asked, surprised.

He searched his memories for signs of trouble between the twins and came back with nothing. It was that nothingness that now stood out in his thoughts. Andrew and Aaron didn't fight, but they didn't really interact either. He'd only seen them speak to each other a couple times. He'd never even seen them sit side by side; someone always sat or stood between them. Aaron wasn't even allowed to drive Andrew's car.

"I wouldn't say they hate each other, but they've got some pretty serious issues. Wouldn't you if you were them?" Nicky asked. "Family means something different with us because it has

[242]

to. It's not about blood. It's not even about who we like. It's about who Andrew's willing to protect."

Neil's stomach twisted with another chilly what-if. "And he's including me because of this morning?"

"Partly," Nicky said. "But partly because you're the reason Kevin's going to stay with our team. Andrew's got Kevin's back, but you've got Kevin's attention. You're as freakishly obsessed with Exy as he is. That makes you invaluable to Andrew."

Neil weighed that in silence, then finally gathered his clothes and turned to a stall. Nicky touched his shoulder before he could step away from the sink.

"Look, I know we screwed up last time. Please believe me when I say Andrew was just looking out for the rest of us. He didn't want to take any chances. But things are different now. You're one of us, which means we'll never push you further than you're willing to go. Okay?"

"I guess we'll see." Neil locked himself in the stall and changed.

Nicky's stare was appreciative when Neil returned, but for once he kept his mouth shut. Neil started for the door, then doubled back to the sink. He pulled out his contacts and flicked them into the trash. When he looked up at the mirror, bright blue eyes stared back. Neil couldn't be himself, but maybe he could be the Neil he'd given Andrew in Wymack's living room.

The others were already seated by the time they made it out of the bathroom. A waitress finished jotting down their orders and stepped out of the way to let Neil and Nicky sit. Nicky went first, graciously leaving the outside seat for Neil.

Aaron arched an eyebrow at Nicky. "Drown in the toilet?"

"Even quickies take time, you know," Nicky said.

"Don't make me sick."

"You know, if you'd get around to popping Katelyn one, you wouldn't be so anal." Nicky ducked when Aaron threw a wadded-up napkin at him. "It's true. You are bringing her to the banquet, aren't you?"

[243]

"I haven't asked her yet."

"I think Andrew should ask her and see if she can tell the difference."

Andrew's smile was slow. "Okay."

"You aren't funny," Aaron said to Nicky. "Shut up."

They ate in silence when their ice cream showed up. The money Aaron left on the table was too much for just dessert, so Neil assumed they'd gotten their drugs.

The line outside Eden's Twilight was half the size as it was last time. Nicky blamed it on South Carolina's blue laws. Apparently alcohol sales were prohibited on Sunday, which meant the bars had to stop serving it at midnight Saturday. The group only had an hour and a half to drink, but Nicky promised there was a stash at "the house".

"But whose house is it?" Neil asked.

"Technically it's mine, but I consider it ours." Nicky waved to include the entire group in that. "I left Germany so I could be Aaron and Andrew's guardian, did you know? It was me or my super religious parents, and I figured I had a better chance of surviving Andrew. I bought that house so we'd have a place to stay. Dad cosigned it, but Erik helped fund it. I use my monthly stipend to make payments on the mortgage."

"If you have a house, why did you stay with Abby this summer?"

"Because Andrew didn't feel like driving Kevin back and forth to the upstate for practice every day," Nicky said.

He pulled up to the curb outside Eden's Twilight long enough to collect a VIP parking pass. The others went inside while he went down the street to the garage. It was easier to get a table tonight thanks to the shortened hours, but the club was still more crowded than Neil was comfortable with. Andrew left Aaron and Kevin to guard their seats and brought Neil with him to get their drinks. Roland the bartender was on duty again. Judging by the look on his face, he remembered Neil and couldn't believe he'd returned.

[244]

"He said no," Andrew said. "Keep them clean."

Neil was half-sure this was just a show, but Roland passed him an empty cup and a sealed can of soda. Neil checked the glass for residue as soon as Roland went to mix the others' drinks.

"Paranoid," Andrew said.

"If you're such a control freak you shouldn't be drinking either."

"I know what my limits are," Andrew said. "I'm not going to test them."

"And dust?"

"Too much crazy in this system for dust to make a difference, I guess. We got into dust for Aaron's sake. He needed something safe to get on when he was coming off everything his mother gave him."

Andrew gestured between their faces. "Do you remember this game? We're doing the honesty thing again, at least until I grow bored of it. In a moment you're going to be perfectly honest with me and tell me what I have to do to keep you here."

"Here's some honesty," Neil said. "I don't like you, and I don't trust you."

"It's mutual," Andrew said. "That doesn't change anything."

"Nicky says you're only keeping me here because of Kevin," Neil said. "What happens if Kevin gets bored of me?"

"Keep his interest," Andrew said, and it wasn't really a suggestion.

Neil gazed at him in silence, wondering how stupid and desperate he must be to put his trust in someone like Andrew. "Can you protect me from my past?"

"Your father's boss," Andrew guessed.

The truth burned Neil's tongue, sharp and sour like fresh blood. He swallowed it and said, "Yes. Word got around that the Moriyamas didn't trust his people anymore, and his business never really recovered. He's been after me ever since. He was arrested on some small charges a while back but he won't be in

[245]

jail forever. You said the Moriyamas can't touch me this year because of Kevin, but he won't stop. If he finds me, he'll kill me."

"What a mess." Andrew sounded unsympathetic. "Easy enough to take care of, though."

A group of people shouldered their way up to the bar counter at Neil's back, pushing him into Andrew. Andrew didn't budge beneath his weight. He was something solid to lean against, something violent and fierce and unmoving. Neil couldn't remember what it felt like to have someone hold him up. It was terrifying and liberating all at once. His life was out of his control now; he was giving it to Andrew and hoping Andrew would keep it safe.

Roland returned with a tray of drinks. Andrew took it and motioned for Neil to go ahead of him and lifted the tray over his head. He'd just finished unloading drinks onto their tabletop when Nicky showed up.

Neil thought he'd seen them drink fast last time. It had nothing on tonight when they were racing the clock to midnight. He nursed his soda and watched them get trashed. They broke out the dust earlier this time, and Aaron and Nicky vanished to the dance floor shortly afterwards. Andrew collected empty cups and took the tray back to the bar.

It was the first time Neil and Kevin had been alone since the broadcast. Despite everything that happened that day, they had nothing to say to each other. They stared in opposite directions and sat in awkward silence the entire half-hour Andrew was gone. Neil was starting to think Andrew had gotten lost on his way back from the bar when Andrew finally returned with a load of drinks. He almost said something about it, but let it go in favor of watching them drink.

Last call for drinks went up at ten 'til midnight. Aaron and Nicky came back for a final round. Kevin had to climb up Andrew's side to get to his feet after downing thirteen drinks in an hour and a half. Neil thought it a miracle he stayed standing.

Andrew helped Kevin out, so Neil kept Nicky from wheeling off the sidewalk into the road. Neil offered to drive, but Andrew ignored him and got into the driver's seat.

Neil didn't remember leaving the club last time, so he paid attention to the drive this time. The house was seven minutes away, off the interstate a short ways and in a small neighborhood. Andrew was pulling into the driveway when Aaron's phone rang. Aaron fumbled through his pockets looking for it, but it took him four rings to find it. He flipped it open, stared blearily at the screen, and made a face.

"Coach," he said, and answered. "Do you know what time it is? What? Wait, what? You're lying. I don't believe you!"

Aaron jerked the phone away from his ear and shoved it at Andrew. Andrew took time to light a cigarette before taking it. He cradled the phone between his ear and shoulder as he put his pack of cigarettes away.

"What do you want?" he asked, and listened as Wymack explained all over again. "Overdosed like how?"

"Again?" Nicky said incredulously. "That stupid bastard."

"Never again," Andrew said over his shoulder. "He's dead."

There was a second of absolute silence before Nicky moved. He grabbed Andrew's shoulder and gave him a violent shake. "No. What?"

Andrew shrugged him off and spoke into the phone. "No, not a good idea. I'll call you when we're back in town."

Nicky slumped forward in his chair and groaned low in his throat. "Shit, shit. No way."

"Who overdosed?" Neil asked.

"Seth." Andrew hung up and tapped the phone against his thigh. "Someone found him face-down in the bathroom at Bacchus where he drowned in his own puke. It's exactly how I warned him he was going to clock out, not that he ever listened to me."

Neil was hearing things. "Seth overdosed?"

"Keep up with the conversation," Andrew said.

[247]

"I thought he was on something, but I never saw him using," Neil said.

"He cleared most of it out of his system years ago," Andrew said. "Only thing he's on these days is antidepressants. Curious."

"I might be sick," Nicky said miserably.

Neil looked at him, surprised by how hard Nicky and Aaron were taking it. He wondered if he was supposed to feel something besides shock, but a mental check came back clean. He'd grown up around death. It was nothing to him now but ice in his system and a reminder to keep moving. Seth should have been an exception, since Neil had been living with him for months, but Neil had never liked him.

"Are we going back?" Neil asked.

"When they're all drunk and cracker high and I'm off my meds? I'll be back in jail before you can say 'threat to society'. We'll wait until morning."

Andrew got out of the car, but no one else moved.

"What about the line-up?" Kevin asked.

Nicky winced. "Kevin, the man is dead. Like, permanently."

"It's not a major loss," Kevin said.

Nicky got out of the car and paced the driveway with his hands linked behind his neck. Neil looked from Aaron to Kevin, and then slid out Nicky's open door. Andrew was fiddling with his key chain on the front porch when Neil caught up with him. Andrew finished whatever he was doing, transferred the key chain to one hand, and pointed his cigarette at Neil's face.

"That's interesting," he said. "That apathy doesn't bode well for your sanity."

"I don't understand suicide," Neil said. "Staying alive has always been so important I can't imagine actively trying to die."

"He wasn't," Andrew said, like Neil was being stupid. He unlocked the door but didn't bother with the lights when he went in. Neil followed him into the dark hallway and left the door

[248]

open behind him for the others. "He wanted a way out for a little while, a few hours where he didn't have to think or feel. Problem was he picked an out that's easy to die on. That's his fault."

"Is that why you drink?" Neil asked. "You don't want to feel?"

Andrew turned to face him. Neil wasn't expecting it and almost ran into him. Andrew dug his fingertip into the hollow of Neil's throat in warning. This close Neil could smell the alcohol and cigarettes on him. It made him think of his mother burning to ashes on the beach. He reached out without thinking and took Andrew's cigarette away. For some reason Andrew let him keep it.

"I don't feel for anyone or anything," Andrew said. "Don't forget that."

"So Kevin's just a hobby for you?"

"Seth didn't kill himself. He couldn't have."

"What do you mean?"

"Seth only takes his pills when he and Allison are on the outs," Andrew said. "When they're together she's enough to hold him up. She went with him tonight, so she would have made sure he left his pills at home. She knows he likes chasing them with drinks."

Neil remembered watching her dig through Seth's pockets. "She checked him. I saw her."

"So did I," Andrew said.

"If he didn't have his pills on him, how did he overdose?"

"Not by choice," Andrew said. "My theory says Riko won this round."

Neil stared at him. "You don't really think Riko did this."

"I think the timing's too convenient for it to be an accident," Andrew said. "Riko broke Kevin's hand for being better. He crossed districts because Kevin picked up a racquet and got back on the court. What do you think he's willing to do to you for calling him useless on national TV?

[249]

"You said our greatest strength is in our small size. How strong do you feel now that you've been bumped to our starting line? You think you and Kevin are ready to carry us to championships?"

"And you called me paranoid," Neil said quietly.

"They were supposed to stay on campus tonight," Andrew said. "Renee stopped by after you left and asked how soon we could expect Riko to respond. Kevin said we would hear back tonight. Pity you didn't see the busybodies panic when they realized you weren't at the dorm anymore. I told them you'd be back at nine, so they built their plans around you."

Neil remembered how relieved Matt looked to see him in the hallway. More than that, he remembered Nicky's incredulity that Allison and Seth were leaving. Nicky rarely paid attention to the two and he shouldn't have cared that they were socializing. He reacted because they were deviating from the plan.

"I don't believe you," Neil said.

"I can't prove it, but I know I'm right."

"If you are, then what?" Neil asked. "I'm willing to gamble with my life. I won't gamble with theirs. They don't deserve that."

"You don't have to," Andrew said. "I do, and I say the odds are good. The Foxes are famous for having terrible seasons, but even bad luck only goes so far. One death is a believable tragedy. Two brings us below the bare minimum number of requisite players to compete. Coach Moriyama wants Kevin and Riko to face off on court, so Riko can't risk disqualifying us."

Neil said nothing. Andrew hooked his fingers in the collar of Neil's shirt and tugged just enough for Neil to feel it. "I know what I'm doing. I knew what I was agreeing to when I took Kevin's side. I knew what it could cost us and how far I'd have to go. Understand? You aren't going anywhere. You're staying here."

Andrew didn't let go until Neil nodded, and then he reached for Neil's hand. He took his cigarette back, put it between his lips, and pressed a warm key into Neil's empty palm. Neil lifted his hand to look at it. The hardware logo engraved in it meant it was a copy. To what, Neil didn't know, but it only took him a moment to figure it out. Andrew used this key to unlock the front door and then took it off the ring on the porch. Now he was giving it to Neil.

"Get some sleep," Andrew said. "We're going home tomorrow. We'll figure this out then."

Andrew went around Neil to the front door. He had no sympathy or comfort for his family as they grieved Seth's unexpected death, but he would keep watch on them from the doorway until they were okay again. It was harder than it should have been for Neil to look away from him, but he finally set off down the hall. He passed the den, then backtracked and curled up in one of the recliners.

Despite Andrew's promises and confidence, chances were good Neil was going to leave Palmetto State in a casket before spring. Neil thought he would be okay with it. He would spend his last few months as Neil Josten, starting striker for the Palmetto State Foxes. He'd be Kevin's protégé, a teenager with a bright future, and his death would be a tragedy. It sounded a lot better than dying scared and alone halfway around the world.

Neil looked down at the key in his hand. "Home," he whispered, needing to hear it aloud. It was a foreign concept to him, an impossible dream. It was frightening and wonderful all at once, and it set his heart racing so fast he thought it'd drum out of his chest. "Welcome home, Neil."

[251]

This series will continue in
THE RAVEN KING

Acknowledgements

To the lovelies at Courting Madness who refused to give up on the Foxes even when I might have: your support has meant the world to me. I hope you enjoy the final result as much as I've loved writing it. To KM, Amy, Z, Jamie C, and Miika: thank you for editing this with me. This would be an unintelligible wreck without your patience and insight.
Cover art designed by my younger sister.

THE PALMETTO STATE FOXES

Danielle Leigh Wilds, #1, Offensive Dealer
Kevin Day, #2, Striker
Andrew Joseph Minyard, #3, Goalkeeper
Matthew Donovan Boyd, #4, Backliner
Aaron Michael Minyard, #5, Backliner
Bryan Seth Gordon, #6, Striker
Allison Jamaica Reynolds, #7, Defensive Dealer
Nicholas Esteban Hemmick, #8, Backliner
Natalie Renee Walker, #9, Goalkeeper
Neil Josten, #10, Striker

David Vincent Wymack
Abigail Marie Winfield
Betsy Jo Dobson

For more information on the Foxes and Exy, visit the author online at courtingmadness.blogspot.com.